Where All Roads Meet

Where All Roads Meet

Marie O'Connor

POOLBEG

Published 2025 Poolbeg Press Ltd

123 Grange Hill, Baldoyle, Dublin 13, Ireland

E-mail: poolbeg@poolbeg.com.

www.poolbeg.com

1

A catalogue record for this book is available from the British Library.

ISBN 978-178199-664-5

About the Author

Having worked as a digital editor in television and as a window dresser for a leading high-street retailer, being creative on a daily basis has been a regular part of Marie O'Connor's life. It is hardly surprising that her debut novel, *Whispers on Main Street*, was such a roller coaster of a read. Marie possesses a joie de vivre and sense of adventure which is reflected in her writing.

Having grown up in the countryside in the West of Ireland, she spent several years living in Dublin but is presently living and working in Galway City.

Acknowledgments

I would like to give a huge thank-you to the team at Poolbeg Press for their guidance and input, especially Paula Campbell, Publisher, for managing the process from start to finish without a hitch, and also to Gaye Shortland, Editor, for reining in my ramblings, turning me in the right direction and helping me to polish the story until it sparkled.

I would like to thank my family and friends for their ongoing unconditional support and getting as excited about everything as much as I did!

Finally, I would like to give a heartfelt appreciation to the people I don't know who read my last book *Whispers on Main Street*. It's scary putting yourself out there with your debut but your feedback was so positive and nurturing it gave me a great boost to put pen to paper again, so please, don't ever underestimate the power of a few kind words.

Dedication

Dedicated to Michelle, Stephen and Emily. My No.1 fans!

PART 1

Chapter 1

Longings

June 1963

♫ Calico Jack, is back! ♫

"You're listening to Calico Jack 96.3FM. It's just gone one o'clock. No stuffy news bulletins here, only the issues that matter to us. I hope you're enjoying this beautiful June afternoon and you're making the best of the fine weather! Here is Jimmie Davis with the ever popular 'You Are My Sunshine'..."

———————————

Bangharda Caitlín Kennedy sat down on a bench in the town park of Ballantur on a lazy Friday afternoon. She couldn't stop yawning. It's not that she had done much – it was because she had done so little that she was lethargic. She kicked off her heavy shoes and wriggled her toes within her restrictive nylon tights. A cloudless sky gave strength to the sun so she put her head back, closed her eyes and absorbed the heat. Her cap fell off but she didn't care.

While this Guardian of the Peace continued to take advantage of her undemanding job, ironically she was oblivious to a crime being committed right under her nose.

Local businessman, Nate Wheatley, was driving through the town in his purple truck to begin his rounds on the other side of Ballantur, selling groceries at the homesteads of his loyal rural customers. The back door of his vehicle had become problematic lately and today was no different. The seal around the doorframe was becoming detached and it frequently caused the doors to make a very annoying rattle. Knowing he wouldn't be able to tolerate this racket, he pulled in on the main street to remedy this before going any further.

However, a much more serious event had commenced just before his arrival. An individual had frantically banged on the door of the post office which was closed for lunch. Mrs. Russell, the postmistress, responded immediately, thinking that it must be an emergency and that someone was in distress. When she opened the door, a man wearing a scarf cowboy-style to hide his face under a peaked cap forced his way in and demanded that she "*hand over the money*". Mrs. Russell had literally frozen in fear, so he raised a metal bar, which he had been concealing at his side, in the air.

"*Now!*" he snarled.

Mrs. Russell walked slowly backwards towards her counter, nearly falling over the bin on her way. She tried her best to control her fear. Friday was pension day so she had a sizable amount of cash on the premises. She went in behind her glass partition and hesitated about doing what he asked but didn't know what else to do either.

"*Come on, hurry up!*"

Mrs. Russell just stood and blinked at him. The impatient robber raised his weapon and struck it hard against one of the partitions of glass,

4

smashing it into pieces. Mrs. Russell covered her face with her hands to shield herself from the flying glass.

"*I said, give me the fucking money!*" he shouted at her.

With no other choice, she started to shove the cash into a cloth money bag as quickly as she could.

Outside, Nate heard the noise of the glass shattering. His bad feeling and good nature collided but without hesitation he ran towards the post office to see what had happened. The door was slightly ajar and he slid in. Immediately he saw a robbery was in progress. The robber grabbed the bag from the postmistress before he lunged at Nate, ready to strike him. But his medium build was no match for Nate's stronger one and Nate was able to tackle him to the floor. However, the robber struggled free and, being apparently younger and lighter on his feet, made a run for it with the money in hand. Moments later he made his getaway on a motorbike, with the bag full of pensioners' dreams.

Nate made Mrs. Russell a strong cup of very sugary tea while the gardaí, including Bangharda Caitlín Kennedy who was now back on the beat, set about gathering the minimal information that Mrs. Russell and Nate had to offer. Other than the facts that the robber was of average build, average height, wore a brown leather jacket and had his face covered, there was little to go on apart from the fact he made his getaway on a motorbike. The worst thing about a one-horse town, according to Sergeant Lamb, who was in charge of Ballantur's Garda Station, was that "it was straight in and straight out".

The next day Caitlín was sitting at her desk, procrastinating over the required paperwork for an impending car rally coming to Ballantur, when Sergeant Lamb called her into his office.

"How are you getting on, Kennedy?"

"Good, sir, although John Malone won't move his trailer of hay off the side of the road and it's very narrow there at the bend going down to his yard."

She could tell he was not listening and instead was focused on a letter he was reading.

"Sorry," he said. "The biggest show in this country will be President Kennedy's visit to Ireland in a couple of weeks. Any relation?"

"No," said Caitlín with a laugh. "Although my father is doing our family tree at the moment, just in case he missed a branch."

"Well, you're certainly going to get a lot closer to him than your father. Headquarters are deploying six hundred gardaí from around the country to provide unprecedented security for the first ever visit of an American President to Galway, in cooperation with the White House's Secret Service. What do you think of that? I have been instructed to spare one or two of you for the Galway leg of his visit so I'm going to nominate yourself and Garda Seán Tully."

Caitlín was surprised and thrilled. "Great! I'd be delighted to represent our station."

"Good. There will be a pre-visit training course which you both will be required to attend at the army barracks in Galway City. That's all the information I have as of now. I'll come back to you with dates and times when they are to hand and I'll pull yourself and Tully back on the same roster for now."

"Thank you, sir."

After leaving his office she closed the door and gave a quiet squeal of delight. Thank God! Something with a bit of excitement to look forward to at last!

Chapter 2

Answers on a postcard

Babs Wheatley was married to Nate. Babs was another resident of the town who didn't realise how her day was going to be flipped on its head when she got up that morning. A surprise was about to be sprung on her.

Babs felt blessed that lately she had learned to drive. Her husband Nate had brought her a cream Volkswagen Beetle and she loved it for all the independence it brought her, especially not having to depend on others for a lift to and from work. Having a job was another thing she was grateful for and both brought a sense of pride.

Babs was on her day off from waitressing part-time in the Humbert Hotel in Castlebar. Outside, Cody their dog made his usual daily attack on the postman who dropped some correspondence through the letterbox of her home. Babs heard the flutter of it falling on her vinyl tiled floor and went to pick it up.

Back in the kitchen, she saw that the first letter was clearly labelled as the ESB bill so that was quickly cast aside. The second was a notification about renewing their television licence so that didn't get much attention either.

The third was a postcard from Sicily.

Puzzled, she turned it over and read the very short message: *'You have always been part of my life. Soon you will be all of it and I have so much to share. R, XX'*

Babs grabbed the back of the kitchen chair before slumping down on it.

What the hell? No. It can't be. Could it? Now? she asked herself, trying to make sense of it. The only possible sender she could think of was Rosario Fratelli. He who had broken her heart all those years ago. He who had been sent back to Naples to help his uncle, or was it Sicily? She couldn't remember. But she'd never forgotten him.

She had met him in her native town of Westport. His family, who were originally from Naples, had set up a successful chip shop there. He was very handsome and all the girls were mad about him but he only had eyes for Babs. They started courting, fell in love and talked about planning their life together. Then one day out of the blue Rosario didn't show up when they had arranged to meet. A few days after that, still not hearing from him, she had plucked up the courage to ask his formidable mother where he was but she was told very abruptly that he had been sent back home to help his uncle run his olive farm. Babs enquired if he was coming back. If he had left a letter or a note for her? Or perhaps an address so she could write to him? But Mrs. Fratelli was not partial to sharing anymore information. Babs remembered thinking that maybe Mrs. Fratelli's heart was broken as much as her own.

It took Babs a long time to get over Rosario. Brylcreemed hair and bad teeth didn't prove to be very attractive when presented to her at dances in the aftermath. But eventually, over time, her feelings for Rosario withered away and, as the years went by, she felt foolish about how serious she was in her first flush of love.

Staring at the postcard in her hand, she continued to fuss over it. Was it him? How did he know where she lived? Did that mean he was coming to Ireland? For a visit? Or to reclaim their relationship and sweep her back to Italy with him? What would she tell Nate? No, she wouldn't tell him anything at all. There was nothing to tell him ... yet. She hid the postcard in a book called *The Feminine Mystique* and left it on her bedside table, knowing that Nate wouldn't go near it.

Caitlín was delighted when she had saved up enough to buy a car. She promptly fell in love with a black split-screen 1954 Morris Minor with a convertible blood-red roof. She loved getting out on the open road and the trip home to see her family in Ennis was a pleasure these days, compared to the arduous journey by bus or train she had been forced to take in the past, but today she groaned as she clambered out of it when she arrived at work. She had a slight hamstring injury from camogie-training the evening before and it had left a tight uncomfortable feeling.

Caitlín had been delighted when she heard that Ballantur had a camogie club and signed up straight away. The twenty-two-year-old Clare woman had clashed the ash from a young age, even playing hurling with the boys when they needed the numbers, but played camogie competitively throughout her school years. She hadn't been picked for the Ballantur team yet. Surely the coach had to recognise her skills? She was adaptable to any position and, being a fast runner, capable of covering a lot of ground. She hated that he picked his players out of loyalty rather than performance. In addition to doing a bit of jogging in her spare time, at least it maintained her fitness levels so in meantime all she could do was wait.

Her sporting analysis was interrupted by the telephone ringing. She limped across the room to answer it.

"Hello? Ballantur Garda Station. Oh hello, Cassie...A robbery at your shop? ... Are you okay? ... Are the robbers gone?... We'll be straight there."

"What's up?" asked Sergeant Lamb, swinging his head around the door of his office.

"Cassie Quirke. She said her shop has just been robbed."

"Right, come on!" he said and went to grab his cap off his desk.

But Caitlín had already taken off, hobbling at speed as best she could.

"Oh, it's you," remarked Cassie disappointedly as Caitlín came in her shop door.

"Are you alright, Cassie?"

"I'm fine," replied the stalwart proprietor.

Cassie was a single lady in her late fifties and had worked in the family grocery shop all her life. She continued to run it mostly on her own since her parents passed away. It was her vocation and she only closed the shop on Christmas Day, St. Stephen's Day or to go to Mass, which also was the only time she removed her cross over apron. Her services came at a price, though, as one could not enter or leave her shop without bartering the currency of news and gossip which she lived for. Her opinions were often blunt and this resulted in a lot of people preferring to do their shopping across the street where one was not subject to the additional cost of her nosiness.

"You said this happened just now during lunchtime?" asked Caitlín.

"Yes, I was flat out busy with customers on their break. But the robbers are long gone. No fear of your lot catching them, that's for sure.

This town is gone to hell. No law or order at all. First, the robbery at the post office and now this – what's next?"

Caitlín ignored her typical derogatory remark. "How did they make their getaway? Car? Motorbike? On foot?

"I don't know. Well, it wasn't a motorbike because I would have heard it."

"Did they get away with much money?"

"They didn't get away with any money. It wasn't the shop that was robbed, it was my house upstairs."

"What did they take?"

"A jewellery set of a 12-carat-gold Celtic pendant and matching earrings. It was a family heirloom, belonging to my grandmother. '*With Love*' was engraved on the back of the pendant."

"And did they come in through the shop and up the stairs?"

"No. They came in the back door."

"A forced entry?"

"Well, no, not exactly, "Cassie replied, not wanting to own up to the fact it wasn't.

"I need to take a look at the back door and then upstairs," said Caitlín, turning towards the back of the shop and raising her eyes to heaven.

She examined the open back door and scanned the kitchen. All appeared to be organised chaos, like most domestic settings. Nothing appeared to be ransacked or disturbed here. The only thing Caitlín found unsettling was a bottle of milk left out on the table that had not been put back in the fridge. Slowly she walked up the threadbare carpeted stairs.

Cassie's bedroom bore all the evidence of a robbery. Wardrobe doors were left open, hat boxes tossed on the floor, blankcts, sheets and pillows strewn around and the mattress misaligned where it had been lifted. Messy drawers were left pulled out with the garments in heaps inside.

Caitlín took some notes before returning to the shop floor where Sergeant Lamb was talking to Cassie.

"Ah, thank you so much, Sergeant Lamb, for coming down so quick. Is there any more information you need?"

"I have a few more questions," Caitlín piped up. "What was the jewellery kept in?"

"Its original black-velvet box with a royal-blue satin lining."

"Do you leave sums of cash on the premises?"

"I'm not that stupid. I go up to the bank every day at three o'clock and lodge my takings. You could set your watch by me."

"Actually, that is a bit stupid," said Caitlín.

"I beg your pardon?" Cassie looked affronted.

"What I mean is, with all due respect, going to the bank every day at the same time could make you a target. You should vary your time and your route."

"Oh, you mean walk up the right-hand side of the main street instead of the left?" Cassie said sarcastically. "You don't need to worry about me. I pity the fool who would try and relieve me of my profits. You just concentrate on getting my jewellery back, miss. Now, Sergeant, do you want to come through for a cuppa?"

Caitlín left the shop and walked back to the station. She didn't feel one bit sorry for the old windbag. She would do the paperwork on the theft and put it on the Garda Siochána circulatory forum. Other than that, she was not inclined to be that bothered about it.

Unfortunately, the same heedless attitude did not apply to Babs Wheatley who could not get that postcard out of her head. She had to try and do something to see if it really came from Rosario. So she decided that the next day she was off she would drive to Westport and see if she could find out anything. She still went there occasionally to see her family and friends but it was a long time since she had been to the Italian chipper where Rosario used to work alongside his mother. That would be a good place to start.

Later that week a garda from Castlebar rang the station in Ballantur. The burglary at Cassie Quirke's shop had turned up nothing –until now. Caitlín took the call and was tipped off that jewellery was being peddled with a dubious point of sale at the market in Castlebar and there was a possibility that, if a sale had not been achieved, then perhaps the same merchandise might be on offer again the next Monday. Caitlín brought this to the attention of Sergeant Lamb. Monday was meant to be her day off but she couldn't think of a better way to spend it than going undercover. This was her idea though and not the sergeant's. He reminded her of her junior position and that she had no experience in undercover work. But her enthusiasm was no match for his reluctance and, due to the fact that he hadn't any better ideas, he agreed to let her do it. Besides, if it stopped Cassie Quirke chewing the ear off him every day about her missing jewellery then it was a win-win for everyone.

The added bonus for Caitlín was that if it was her day off then it meant that Garda Seán Tully would be working, so she didn't have to wait for Sergeant Lamb to rejig the roster to see him.

Their reunion did not go as smoothly as she hoped. They were more like a bickering old couple than love's young dream.

The aging Garda car was giving some trouble of late and on this particular morning it appeared to be giving up the ghost altogether.

"It's no use, Tully, it won't start," said Caitlín.

"Give her a chance, she's never let us down yet," said Tully calmly. "The starter is going, that's all. Were you not meant to take her up to the garage last week?"

"I was on nights. I thought you were meant to take it," replied Caitlín. "And I don't know why you refer to it as a 'she'. It always lets you down when you need it most. Sounds like a 'he' to me."

On the next attempt the engine turned over.

"*Whoa-oh!* Do you hear that, Caitlín? Not a bother on her. It's definitely a 'she' – see how long it took her to get ready!"

This made Caitlín laugh. "Go on, will you, or the traders will be gone by the time we get there."

They arrived at the bustling market around mid-morning. As arranged, Garda Tully kept himself at a safe distance. Caitlín started to saunter around. She looked like any other twenty-two-year-old woman. Her slender frame looked well in a brown, speckled, tweed miniskirt with seam pockets, a tight purple knitted jumper with the lapels of a crisp white blouse pulled out neatly at the collar and long brown boots. Taking no chances, she had scooped her mid-length, straight brown hair up under a black silk turban she'd borrowed from her housemate's eclectic wardrobe and wore large dangly earrings, a look far removed from her more subdued personal style. To conceal her identity even further, she wore her cat-eye sunglasses to hide her ice-blue eyes. She had a small cross-over bag but, unlike the other browsers, the only thing that was in it was a pair of handcuffs.

The market was no different to the usual. Cattle, poultry and pigs were in pens, while stalls of cakes and fresh bread made her hungry with their tantalising scents wafting through the air. Moving on, she stood at the bric-a-brac and then moved on to the flower stand. At least the fragrant flowers masked the pungent smell coming from the fish stall beside it. She continued to stroll between the stands before idly stopping at the jewellery stall. Carefully looking at all the jewellery on display, to her disappointment all of it was silver with a lot of topaz stones used as the centre pieces.

The vendor dutifully asked Caitlín if there was anything she was looking for in particular.

"There is actually," Caitlín began, using her rehearsed plea. "It's my grandmother's seventieth birthday and I would like to get her a nice piece of jewellery. I love your stuff but I think silver might be bit too modern for her, if you know what I mean." She hardly knew what she meant herself. "I think she would prefer something in gold but if I have to go to a jeweller's it might be outside my budget."

She paused, waiting to evaluate his reaction to this.

"I have no gold, I'm afraid. Why don't you convince her that silver is all the fashion now? Look, I have these lovely silver long-chained pendants. I'm sure she'd love one of them and I could do you a good price for it."

Caitlín was disappointed that the vendor didn't try to offer her anything other than what he had on display. She could tell he was genuinely trying to make a sale in his own best interests. She kindly declined his offer and walked away.

Trying her best to look casual, she pulled a packet of cigarettes out of her pocket. While resting on one propped leg, with her back against a wall, she tried to figure out what to do next.

Within a minute she was approached by a young woman who was roughly dressed and appeared a bit edgy. She asked Caitlín if she could spare a cigarette. Caitlín had a hunch and gladly offered one.

"Heard you're looking for a nice piece of jewellery?" the girl said.

"Oh? Where did you hear that?"

Ignoring the question, her new friend continued. "I have a beautiful piece here. A twelve-carat gold chain and matching earrings, in a Celtic design."

"Can I see it?"

The girl looked around. She balanced the smoking cigarette between her lips and squinted through the rising smoke. She took a battered black-velvet box from her inside pocket and opened it.

"Oh, that's lovely! Twelve-carat, you say?"

"Yes."

"Where did you get it?"

"Do you want it or not?"

"I don't know. How much do you want for it?"

"Thirty pounds for the whole set."

"Oh, that's dear. Is it vintage? Where did it come from?" Caitlín was ninety-nine percent certain this was the set stolen from Cassie. Then she turned over the pendant and saw the '*With Love*' engraving on the back. Okay, one hundred percent.

The seller snapped the box shut.

"Fifteen pounds," offered Caitlín. "Will I get a receipt?"

"You're wasting my time. It's thirty pounds or nothing."

Caitlín rummaged through her pockets, pulled out some notes and handed her thirty pounds.

The seller handed her the box and walked off in a hurry.

"*Excuse me!*" Caitlín called after her.

The girl stopped and looked back.

Caitlín walked up to her and flashed her Garda badge with a smile. "But *you* haven't wasted *my* time."

The girl took off running with Caitlín after her. It wasn't hard to nab her because the stalls and the crowd left little room to get away. Nevertheless, the girl resisted arrest and a tussle ensued, causing them to crash across the fish stall and flatten it.

Caitlín read the accused her rights and, of course, once she had pulled her up on her feet, Tully arrived.

"You got the catch of the day there, Kennedy! Would you mind getting in the boot on the way home? You smell like a dead whale!"

"Great help you are."

The thief was brought to Castlebar Garda Station and was identified as Mary Joyce who had a string of previous convictions. Caitlín would have to give evidence when Miss Joyce appeared before the District Judge in a few weeks' time but for now she was happy at how her first undercover operation had gone.

Now, if only Babs Wheatley could predict that she would get a positive result out of her own fishing expedition, it would have gone a long way to stop her stomach rotating like a washing machine. She drove into Westport town and parked underneath the octagon monument. She hadn't told her family she was coming over – she would visit them another day. She hadn't told Nate either.

It was years since she had been to the Fratellis' eatery and the chipper now had a café adjoined to it, which Babs entered. She took a seat in one of red-leather booths and looked around. It had white utility tiles on the walls with photographs of black-and-white cityscapes. It reminded her more of an American diner than an Italian café but obviously that was the look they were going for.

It was only half past twelve but the smell of salty chips was making her mouth water. A waiter came to her table.

"Hello, what can I get you?"

"Fish and chips, please," she replied without even looking at the menu. She noticed that his name badge said '*Lucca*'. She took him to be about thirty years of age and he had a definite look of an Italian about him, with his black hair, brown eyes and sallow skin.

"It's fresh cod in batter, is that okay?"

"Oh, that sounds delicious. Can I have a Coca Cola too? Your café is lovely. I haven't been here in years. When did you open it?"

"About five years ago – a rival chipper opened up across the street, so we had to do something to beat the competition," he said with a laugh.

"Good idea. I remember coming into the takeaway side. Mrs. Fratelli ran it then.

"Yes, *mia nonna* – my grandmother. Sadly she died before the café opened."

That didn't make Babs feel in any way remorseful. "And Rosario? I remember him working here too – is he still around?"

"God, that's a long time ago!" The waiter laughed. "No. He went back to Italy years ago."

"Lucky him. He was probably dying to get back to the nice weather. What part did he go to?"

"Sicily. My grand-uncle ran an olive farm there and he went back to help him."

"An olive farm! Oh, how lovely for him! But I thought your family came from Naples?"

"Nonna was originally from Sicily and used to take Rosario and his siblings on holidays there to make sure they knew of their ancestry. That was before they came to Ireland, of course."

"Wasn't that lovely! Does he still keep in touch?"

The jovial waiter chuckled again. "Rosario knows more about what goes on in Ireland than we do!"

"Isn't that something! Does he come back often to visit?"

Suddenly the door of the chipper burst open and a raucous group of hungry schoolboys barged in.

"Sorry, I have to go, duty calls. I'll put in your order. *Buon appetito!*"

Damn it, thought Babs. If I had one more minute I could have found out if Rosario has plans to come to Ireland soon. Well, at least I know he's still alive and lives in Sicily ... where the postcard came from.

Babs felt her stomach tighten. If he knew so much about what goes on in Ireland, he probably heard or read somewhere about what happened to herself and Nate when the murder occurred in Ballantur two years before. Oh, the shame! After a few minutes of being transfixed on that thought, a plate of fish and chips was placed on her table by an older waitress who visibly was no relation to the Fratellis so Babs did not engage with her. Besides, the smell beneath her nose had wooed her senses. She knew she would be cooking dinner that evening for herself and Nate but these chips looked so good she was not going to leave them behind, not even the burnt one.

While Caitlín and Tully drove back to the station after their covert operation, they continued to catch up. They hadn't had an opportunity for a good chat for a long time. Both of them were very excited about the upcoming training in advance of the arrival of President John F.

Kennedy and had talked about it on the way to Castlebar. Now, once they got the trivial details about work out of the way and the compulsory complaining about the boss voiced, they concentrated on the important stuff: socialising. They exchanged stories about local rendezvous but, with the venues being a bit on the scarce side, there wasn't much to report. The only club in town was the Pink Flamingo, locally known as 'The Fla'.

"Yeah, but I like the Fla," said Tully, disagreeing with Caitlín's disdain for it.

"You like it because you always have a swarm of women around you."

"Is there not always a swarm of men around you?"

"More like a swerve, if you ask me. It's different for a woman. Girls love the fact that you're a garda. They think you're a great catch and your job is probably like something out of an Agatha Christie crime novel. In my case it's more of a turn-off. A lot of men are intimidated by a woman having a more powerful job than them and they don't like a woman being the main breadwinner either."

"That's daftness. I'd have no problem with the woman bringing home more bacon than me."

"Maybe I should try an older man."

"Older! Sure they're worse," Tully said, laughing. "Since when were you into older men?"

"Seriously, Tully, they treat women better."

"*Ha ha!*" Tully laughed even more now. "That's bullshit. Older men put that theory out because it's the only way to attract a younger woman."

"No, it's true. Young men don't mature as quickly as young women, so that's why some girls are attracted to older men," said Caitlín.

"Where do you read that rubbish? What's your rush anyway? I thought you were avoiding marriage like the plague. Sure you'll have to give up your job once you get married. That's the rule."

"I know," said Caitlín with a sigh. "Women are damned if they do and damned if they don't."

"You should start a petition or something to get the law changed."

"There isn't a cat's chance in hell that's going to change anytime soon."

"Pity – it might encourage more good-looking women to join the force."

"God help me!" said Caitlín, rubbing her forehead. "Now who's being immature? Here, will you get a move on! I'm hungry! Does this banger go any faster? Oh yes, I remember the car does, but you don't. You drive like an old man."

"I better be careful so, or you'll be all over me."

Caitlín burst out laughing. She always enjoyed Tully's company and she was looking forward to seeing more of him at the training – or at the Fla.

In another part of the world an old suitcase was flung on the bed and hastily packed. Somebody was going travelling.

Chapter 3

The need for speed

Caitlín was running errands for the station. She was on her way back from Castlebar Courthouse and now had to go to the post office for stamps and to get provisions for the canteen. She parked on the main street of Ballantur and set out for the post office. The weather had continued to be very pleasant so she was taking all the time in the world to enjoy the fresh air. June was her favourite month. She loved how the bright sunshine encouraged all the flora and fauna to show their shy faces to the world. Bountiful blooms sprang out from pots and window boxes, despite their urban restrictions. Her rosy observations were jolted though when suddenly around the corner came a man wearing a brown-leather jacket who bumped right into her.

During their entanglement she breathed in the whiff of the real leather hide. She loved that smell. Without making eye contact, the man apologised and went on his way.

Caitlín continued on and spotted Pa and Elsie Leonard walking up the main street towards her. She hadn't seen them in a while and had heard on the grapevine that Elsie had been diagnosed with dementia.

"Good afternoon!" Caitlín greeted them.

"Good afternoon, Garda Kennedy," said Pa.

"I was just thinking to myself that I hadn't seen you two in ages."

"You haven't been up for visit for a long time, Caitlín," said Elsie. "Why don't you call to the house some evening?"

At least she hasn't forgotten my name yet, thought Caitlín. "I know, I'm sorry. I promise I'll come up and visit you soon. When are those two lovely grandchildren of yours coming to stay with you again?"

"We'll have them again in a few days, don't you worry."

"How is their mother keeping?" Caitlín wasn't sure if it was appropriate to ask about her welfare but then again she felt it might be insensitive if she didn't.

"Grace is only middling at the moment," said Elsie. "The treatments are getting more frequent. It's definitely taking its toll on the poor thing. Hopefully the next course they give her will bring her some relief and comfort. Please God she'll be able to come and stay with the kids this time."

Caitlín noticed that Pa was happy to let Elsie lead the conversation, as if observing how well she was engaging with Caitlín. Today, obviously, she was having a good day. All her senses appeared to be normal.

Then Caitlín saw Cassie Quirke crossing the street, on her way to the bank to make her daily lodgement. She also noticed the man who had bumped into her minutes before. He was now walking gingerly behind Cassie.

Caitlín got a bad feeling.

It happened in a few seconds. The man grabbed the suede satchel Cassie had squeezed tight under her arm. But Cassie fought back and held on to the bag as tightly as she could. Aggravated, the thug punched her in the face and she fell heavily to the ground, loosening her grip. The robber absconded with the bag.

*"Oh my God, look! I bet that's the same guy that robbed the post office!"*cried Caitlín, as she ran to Cassie's aid.

"Are you alright?" Caitlín asked, as she helped Cassie to sit up.

Too stunned to do anything else, Cassie nodded, her nose pumping blood.

Caitlín turned to Pa and Elsie who had followed her. She told Pa to raise the alarm while she pursued the robber.

He was now jumping into a car.

She ran back to hers but grunted in frustration when it wouldn't start. *"Come on, come on!"* she shouted while turning the key with one hand and banging the steering wheel with the other. It was no use. There wasn't a spark of life coming from it.

She got out, furious that this thug was getting away for a second time. Suddenly a man started shouting at her but she didn't know where the voice was coming from. Then she saw someone waving a crutch at her through an open car window. She ran towards a dark-green car parked outside the butcher's shop with the driver's door wide open. She peered inside. The key was left in the ignition.

"Here, you can use my car – quick, get in!" insisted a man sitting in the passenger seat, in an English accent.

Caitlín saw that his left leg was in plaster of Paris. His hands were resting on his crutches."Do you own this vehicle, sir? Where's the driver?"

"I do and don't worry about the driver. Do you want to catch your thief or not?"

"Yes, but you'll have to vacate the car."

"I can't get out – it would take me ages," protested the portly middle-aged man.

"Well, I can't take you with me. It's too dangerous!"

"Don't worry about me. Hurry up, will you, you're wasting time!"

Caitlín got in, turned the key and accelerated. A car screeched to a halt to allow their sudden exit, causing its driver to curse at the pair of them.

Caitlín put the foot down and ripped through the gears as quickly as she could. She could see the robber's car away ahead. He was driving a blue Hillman Minx – she didn't even know what kind of a car she was driving herself, other than it smelled new. She was focused on catching her target who was travelling on the main road in the direction of Castlebar.

As luck would have it, the robber got stuck behind a van and she was soon just two cars behind him. Despite the stretch of road being as straight as an arrow, due to oncoming traffic he was unable to overtake the van. She could see him weaving in and out over the white line, trying to seize an opportunity to make his getaway.

"Don't be stupid, man," Caitlín muttered, watching his hazardous manoeuvres.

The car in front of Caitlín indicated a right-hand turn. This brought her car to an abrupt halt while it turned slowly onto another road.

"*Come on, turn!*" she shouted at the driver.

Once he did, she was only one car away from the thief but that car was driving slowly, allowing a widening gap, and she couldn't overtake it because of the oncoming traffic.

"This suspect may have already robbed the post office in Ballantur," she told her passenger, "and just now he assaulted and robbed a local businesswoman who was about to do a cash lodgement at the bank."

"I know, I saw it happen while my wife was in the butcher's."

"Won't she be worried about you and your car disappearing?"

"I think that would be her dream come true. *Look!* A chance for you to overtake!"

An opportunity had opened up for Caitlín in the oncoming traffic which was too late for the robber to avail of. She put the foot down and successfully overtook the car in front of her. Now she was on her target's tail. She was beginning to realise the car she was driving had form. The slightest touch on the pedal resulted in a lot of power.

Suddenly, the robber in front of her looked back.

Is it not enough to use his rear-view mirror, thought Caitlín.

He did it again.

"*Frig it!*" cursed Caitlín. "I should've taken off my Garda cap. Now he knows we're following him. If I'd taken it off he wouldn't have been any the wiser."

The road turned into a series of bends and, when the robber realised he was never going to be able to overtake the van in front of him, he suddenly turned off to the left.

Caitlín swung to the left and followed.

The robber drove faster now, giving Caitlín no option but to do the same. They abruptly came to a humpback bridge over the River Silt. Up the hill they drove with such a speed that Caitlín's car ascended into the air for a second before bouncing back down.

"*Woo-whoo!*" she hollered. The adrenalin had certainly kicked in.

She glanced across at her passenger. He was forcing himself back into his seat and holding onto the overhead handle for dear life.

"Oh my God, I'm sorry," she said. "Do you want me to stop? Do you want to get out?"

"Are you crazy?" he asked incredulously. "This is the most thrilling ride I've had in years!"

Caitlín didn't know where or when this chase would end, but she didn't want to give up yet. Where was her back-up when she needed it?

Realistically, she knew that the station wouldn't even know where she was at this stage.

The robber did not let up on the gas and he continued to drive at a robust speed even when navigating dangerous bends. This alarmed Caitlín. If another vehicle came in the other direction, even at a snail's pace, it was curtains for that driver and the robber. She was aware that she needed to be responsible and carry out a duty of care to other road users, her passenger and the robber. Reluctantly, she slowed down to encourage the robber to do the same before someone got seriously injured, or worse. Except the robber didn't have a moral conscience like she did. It made no difference, he just kept speeding on.

"What are you doing? You're letting him get away!" protested her passenger, raising his hands in the air.

"He's going to kill himself, us, or someone else if I don't and pursuing him could make me answerable for that. I have no choice. I could be the cause of a fatal accident."

"*Nonsense!* You're so close. His old banger and terrible driving are no match for this car, or you. Listen, I know this road, trust me. Shortly there will be a slip road to join the main road again and if he knows that you won't see him for dust. We have a better chance of taking him on here."

"No, I can't!"

"Now come on, I'll help you," rallied the passenger with more determination than Caitlín was currently feeling.

But her instincts told her to trust him, though she didn't know him from Adam, so she put her foot down again.

"There's a series of bad bends and dips coming up but we can handle them."

"*Oh, God!*" Caitlín groaned.

Coming into the first bad bend, her passenger guided her.

"Okay, sharp left coming up. Brake, drop your gear into second. That's it. Now accelerate as fast as you can then up into third. Look, a good straight ahead, so flat out now, stick her into fourth ... anticipate the dip ... crest coming up ... another wild left bend. Drop her back into third and lie on her head."

"*What? Lie on what?*" yelled Caitlín, panicked. She was sweating with concentration and dying to wipe her brow but afraid to take her vice-gripping hands off the steering wheel.

"Put your weight on the wheel to keep your curve tight. Try not to use your brakes. This is where we will make up the speed he's losing. Now a sharp right with a steep little hill. Drop her into second and once you are on the top straight into third and foot down ... yes, that's it ... flat out now, Garda, and into fourth!"

"How do you know all this stuff?" asked Caitlín.

"Not the best time to get acquainted, but I used to be a rally driver."

"Well, I wish you were at the wheel right now and not me!"

"Listen to me, you're doing fine."

Whatever he was telling her, it was working. Soon they were right behind the robber again.

"We have him – but what do we now?" she asked.

"Wish for an ample bit of road where we can overtake him and cut him off."

"On this whip of a road? Not a chance!" She was annoyed, knowing that wasn't an option.

The robber drove on but he mustn't have known where he was going because, just before the advantageous slip road, he took another sudden left turn onto a laneway that wasn't tarred. The grass was peacefully growing up through the middle of it.

"Oh my God! This isn't even a road, it's a boreen!" cried Caitlín who was wondering if they would fit. She could hear the scrawny overgrown blackthorn branches scraping the sides of their wider car.

"Looks like a dead end to me," said her passenger. "That's all the better! He'll be forced to stop."

The robber kept driving down the incline until the path ran out and ended without warning at the slipway of the river. He jammed on the brakes but the wet organic surface provided no grip for the worn tyres of his car and he skidded spectacularly into the middle of the river with a splash, causing his car to stall immediately.

Caitlín's slower approach enabled her to bring her car under control and she stopped with ease. Pulling the handbrake, she jumped out. The recent fine weather and low rainfall meant the water level in the river was low. Still persevering, the robber clambered out of his car and, with the bag of cash in his hand, stumbled across the river to the brink on the other side.

You have got to kidding me, thought Caitlín. Will this guy ever give up? She waded into the river but slipped and fell into the water. Despite the sunshine the water was cold. She recoiled and gasped, pulling herself back up. The riverbed underfoot was as slippery as a swarm of eels. The rocks and stones were masked in algae and moss but she eventually made it over to the other side. The robber had made some leeway up through the long green meadow ahead but now it was Caitlín's turn to show form. The robber was no match for Caitlín's fitness. It was like a lion and a gazelle. She didn't have to but, once upon him, she rugby-tackled him to the ground just for the hell of it. She cautioned him and quickly snapped on a pair of handcuffs.

He didn't resist.

She pulled him to his feet and snatched up the bag of cash. Then she dragged him back across the river.

Her passenger had got out of the car and was leaning heavily on his crutches.

"Are you alright?" he asked.

"I'm fine, you can get back in the car," said Caitlín who was out of breath and starting to feel the effects of the cold water.

"I thought after driving through hell I was going to lose you by drowning," her passenger said with some concern.

"Hell or high water, this one wasn't going to get away." She smiled as she guided the robber into the back seat of their car.

At an undemanding pace they drove back to the station.

"You're a determined little thing, aren't you? The gardaí are lucky to have someone like you on their side. You're one of those new *banghardas*. Did you get training to drive like that in Garda School?"

"Sir, I'll have to ask you to refrain from discussing what you have just witnessed in the presence of the assailant for operational reasons," responded Caitlín in a professional tone.

"Yes, of course," he replied, winking back at her and tapping his nose. She was surprised he was taking all of this in such good spirits.

When they arrived at the Garda Station, Sergeant Lamb ran out to meet them.

"Kennedy, where the hell did you go? Pa and Elsie Leonard said you jumped into an unmarked car and took off after the robber."

"I pursued the robber and to say he took us on the scenic route is a bit of an understatement."

"We sent a car after you but didn't know which way you went!"

"We turned off outside the town and went cross-country at speed for a while but I caught up with him in the end and retrieved Cassie's money," she said, hauling her catch out of the back seat and pulling him into the station.

"I can't argue with that, but I will have to speak to you separately about the unorthodox method you used," the sergeant said through gritted teeth, before smiling theatrically at her passenger who was now pulling himself out of the car too.

As Sergeant Lamb went to his aid, a woman came running out of the Garda station and clasped her arms around the incapacitated man.

"Oh thank God, Wesley! I could see through the shop window this crazy policewoman jumping in and stealing our car. With you trapped inside with your broken leg!" She had an English accent like her husband.

"She didn't steal it. I'm fine, dear. It's alright," he said, patting her on the back, to calm her down.

She pulled back. "*It most certainly is not!* This is outrageous. I have never seen or heard the like of it before. Something terrible could have happened to you, for god's sake! She abducted you and you are not even able to walk."

"She didn't, I'm fine," he repeated again.

"Yeah? Well, what about your lovely new car? Look at it! It's covered in mud. Good heavens! Are those scratches on it too? Where did she take you, the Amazon jungle?"

"It's not as bad as it looks, honestly, dear. They'll fix that at the garage and it'll be good as new again."

"But it *is* new!" Exasperated, she turned dramatically on Sergeant Lamb. "You idiots have a lot to answer for. I am going to report this. My husband could have died. That renegade of yours kidnapped him, subjected him to God knows what, not to mention the damage to our car. There will be consequences and compensation for this. This is completely out of order."

"*Shh, shh*, that's enough now, dear. The bangharda was very brave and determined to catch the robber. He was terrorising this town."

Caitlín came back out, oblivious to the tirade of abuse just expressed.

She walked over to the passenger. "I don't even know your name," she said. "I'm Garda Caitlín Kennedy."

"It's Wesley, Wesley Pollard. And the pleasure is all mine," he said, shaking her hand.

"Without your help today, sir, we never would have caught that guy."

"*You!* Stop talking to my husband. You won't get away with this. I am going to report you to the authorities!"

With that, Mrs. Pollard shoved her poor husband into the car, showing no tenderness for him at all. She then got in, banged her own door so hard she didn't seem to have much compassion for the car either, and then skidded out of the drive.

"What a beauty! The car, I mean," said Sergeant Lamb, setting the record straight. "A Jaguar MK2, I think."

"I was driving so fast I didn't take much notice, to be honest," said Caitlín, chuckling.

Then she saw that Lamb was glaring at her.

"Kennedy, get in my office now!" he said angrily.

In the confines of his tatty office with the door closed, he proceeded to eat the face off her, describing how her inconsiderate actions could have put the life of Mr. Pollard, herself, the robber and various other road users at risk and have the potential to end her career with the upmost finality and absolutely no chance of any reprieve. He pointed out that confiscating a citizen's private vehicle was only an option in life-and-death situations, preferably with no one else sitting in it, and the only other time was on movie sets. He asked her how she could have been so stupid. He pointed out that her actions did result in catching the perpetrator, but at what cost? If she left people dead on the side of the road, would it still have been worth it?

"You didn't see how angry Mrs. Pollard was, although I'm sure you heard her," he continued. "She said she's going to report you and, if she does, well, there is very little I can do to vindicate you, Kennedy. Your maverick behaviour broke a lot of rules and protocol and I can't condone that."

"That's not fair!" Caitlín burst out. "Wesley Pollard *told* me to use his car. I told him to get out for his own safety but he refused. He gave me great advice during the pursuit – I don't think he had a problem with it at all!"

"*It's not him I'm worried about!*" shouted Sergeant Lamb.

Caitlín subsided. "Oh, do you really think his wife will report me?"

"I don't know," he replied, shrugging. "Ultimately, it will be up to Mr. Pollard to see if he wants to press charges against you. He was the one compromised, not her. Go home, Kennedy."

As Caitlín was leaving the station, Garda Tully was pulling in.

"Hey, where the hell did you go? I've been driving around looking for you. What happened? Gosh, you're shaking!"

Caitlín didn't know if she was trembling from her wet clothes and delayed shock accumulating from the hazardous car chase, or from the dressing-down she had just got from Sergeant Lamb, compounded by the realisation of how much trouble she could be in.

"Come on, our shift is over," said Tully. "I'll take you home."

Back home, she changed as quickly as she could and persuaded Tully to go to Slattery's pub with her. She didn't want to have to retell the whole story to her housemate, Shelly. Only Tully could understand.

Over a brandy or two, Caitlín regaled him with the sequence of events.

"Fair play to you, you're a real Graham Hill. You weren't afraid to give it wellie!"

"You should have seen the car, Seán – it was something else! So much power, a real thrill. I never drove anything like that before. I swear I must have left maggots after me on the seat I sweating so much! It's a far cry from my nine-year-old Morris Minor."She laughed at herself but the light relief was short-lived as she instantly started worrying again. She lit a much-craved cigarette.

"This is all Cassie Quirke's fault. I told her not to be going up to the bank at the same time everyday to lodge her money. She was a sitting duck. Did she ever think of that? There were only a few lousy pounds in the bag and look at all the trouble it caused."

"Forget about Cassie Quirke. Look, Sergeant Lamb is right. It will be up to Mr. Pollard to decide if he wants to take any kind of action against you and the Force and, by the sound of things, he didn't seem to think the experience was as bad as Mrs. Pollard thinks it was, and she wasn't even there. So don't beat yourself up about it yet.Now give the bar a kick, it's your round."

Caitlín's housemate, Shelly, also gave her the benefit of the doubt when Caitlín told her about her controversial apprehension of the robber, which was no surprise as Shelly always saw the glass as half full. Shelly was the new receptionist at Doctor Quinlan's surgery and, while they both knew all about the code of confidentially, they used to have a great laugh all the same about the misdemeanours of their respective clients. It was great to have another girl of her age to hang out with but Caitlín was envious of all the great nights out Shelly seemed to have. All the weekend shifts Caitlín had to work clipped her dancing wings. The only red flag about socialising with Shelly was Garda Seán Tully. Caitlín knew that Shelly liked him. Shelly knew that Caitlín liked him. They didn't go there.

Chapter 4

The Reunion

The next day Babs Wheatley tied on her plastic apron and stood at her kitchen sink. The window was open, letting in a cool summer breeze. She had scraped back her long blonde wavy hair into a bun and was scrubbing the hell out of the collar of her white cotton work blouse with a nailbrush and carbolic soap. She loved working in the Humbert Hotel in Castlebar and, of late, she had started to envisage working as a receptionist there. She had already spoken to the manager who indicated that it was definitely something that he would consider. He said that she had fitted in well and quickly, she had a pleasant demeanour and was equally cordial with the guests and her fellow staff. Also, she knew the hotel inside out by now and, being a local, there was nothing about the surrounding areas and the attractions they offered that she could not recommend to both domestic and international tourists. He said all of these characteristics combined would stand to her if a vacancy arose. In fact, he said, with the busy holiday season about to launch he could see no reason why he couldn't allocate her a few hours, regardless.

Babs was delighted with this news and Nate was genuinely happy for her too. Deciding to work and drive had created a sunnier aspect to her life and the independence had turned her into a new woman.

Nate said he was sorry he hadn't supported her sooner. He liked nothing more than Babs driving him around in her car on their days off. He felt like a kept man and he loved it. And, with Babs soon to be promoted to a receptionist in a reputable hotel, he imagined both of them would be perceived as an influential couple.

Babs paused to pull on her rubber gloves before tackling another dirty blouse. Her fingers had turned into prunes after pulverising the first one.

Suddenly Cody let rip outside. She knew his barks and the pitch of this one meant it was a stranger. A knock on the door sounded. Babs cursed as she went to answer it. One of the greatest enemies of womankind was someone calling to the house unannounced. She had a tube of Yardley lipstick on the table in the hall on standby for emergencies. On this inconvenient occasion though, she couldn't be bothered. She looked in the mirror and estimated it would take more than a sliver of lipstick to put all her wrongs to right in this state. Damping down wayward strands of hair with her wet gloves, she swung open the door and got the shock of her life.

"*Babs!*"

"*Rosario!*"

"*Mio Dio, bella, bella, bella! Come stai?*"

Oh my God, he's still as gorgeous as ever, thought Babs in a flash.

"Don't I get a hug?" he asked, extending his two arms. He leant in and gave her a kiss on both cheeks.

She could feel the suds of her laundry dripping down her face and could only imagine the two big wet hand-marks she was leaving on his back when she reciprocated his embrace.

"Rosario!" she said again, stunned at the sight of him at her front door after all these years.

"Well, are you not going to invite me in?"

"Of course. Yes, come on through. The sitting room is on your left."

"No need for formalities. The kitchen is fine," he said and, picking up a leather bag which was at his feet, cheekily walked down the hall.

Babs did a walk of shame behind him. She pulled off the gloves and apron as quick as she could and berated herself for not putting on the lipstick. She invited him to take a seat at the table and sat down opposite him.

She looked at him as he gazed at her. He hadn't changed that much at all, even after thirty years. Slender as ever, not having put on a pound – she didn't know whether to be impressed or jealous, considering he must be fifty-five years of age. His brown hair was the same length, lighter and greyer but he still had those sexy wispy bits that fell naturally around his sallow face. His short-sleeved crisp lemon shirt showed off two arms tanned and radiant from the Mediterranean sun.

"When did Ireland get so warm? It's hot, isn't it?"

"It sure is," replied Babs, not really concentrating on what he had said at all.

"Do you mind? He took off his lightweight gilet and hung it on the back of the chair.

"I'll put the kettle on," said Babs, jumping up and turning to her gas cooker.

"Babs, come and sit down. Relax!" he said.

She returned to her chair.

Rosario looked at her. "I am glad to see that you have not cut your lovely hair," he said. "You look so young! You are the same gorgeous woman I loved all those years ago!"

"What are you doing here?" she asked him, not falling for his palaver.

He gazed into her eyes before taking a deep breath."I feel I owe you an explanation and apology for the ways things turned out."

"You can say that again. You vanished overnight," said Babs, with a surprising return of the anger she thought she had buried years before. "You could have at least written."

"I did! As soon as I went back to Italy. I explained why I had to leave suddenly and how it broke my heart. Did you not get my letter? I sent it to your house in Westport."

"No. I got a job in Castlebar and moved there after you left. My post was forwarded to me but there was *never* a letter from you. I called into the chipper looking for you and all your mother said was that you went back to Italy to run an olive farm."

"Babs, I am so, so sorry. This is like a Greek tragedy. All those years and you thought I abandoned you! Oh, if only you knew!"

"I thought you didn't care about me at all. I felt such a fool."

"I never stopped caring about you," said Rosario.

This made Babs feel uncomfortable. "How did you know where I live now?" she asked, changing the subject.

"My family in Westport send me over the paper – the *Mayo News* – from time to time because I like to see what properties are for sale there. The paper was full of articles about you and your husband being accused for the murder of the postman, about two years ago? But I called to Madge to find out exactly where you live."

"My old friend Madge? But she lives in England now."

"No, she doesn't. She moved back to Westport a year ago. Did you not know?"

"No, I didn't," replied Babs, becoming more confused by the minute.

"But, my God, the murder – you poor thing! What a terrible ordeal for you to go through, no? And your husband, where is he?"

"He's at work. I don't want to talk about the murder." Babs could feel her face flushing. "I want to know why you are here in my kitchen."

"*Dio mio*, where do I start?"

"At the beginning," she proposed flatly. His resurfaced presence was rattling her even more than she could have imagined.

"Okay, let me see. So, sadly I wasn't sent back to my native Naples. I was sent to the island of Sicily. My uncle, Paolo, lived there. He was my mother's brother. They were born on the island and lived near the beautiful town of Taormina. Mama was distraught when I had to go. She had worked so hard to provide a good life for us here in Ireland compared to the impoverished life she had grown up with in Sicily, and she couldn't bear that I was going back there."

"So why did you?" asked Babs impatiently.

Rosario rubbed his head in his hands, again as if not knowing how to continue. He sighed. "Uncle Paolo had an olive farm, just like his father and grandfather before him. The farm has been in our family for generations. Some of our olive trees were hundreds of years old. One of our neighbours claimed his pride and joy was a tree in the middle of his grove, supposedly a thousand years old which, despite its decrepit appearance still produced olives. It was a shrine of the industry. The whole island had a tradition of producing the best olive oil in the Mediterranean and it was mostly thanks to the volcanic beast called Mount Etna. When she spewed her lava across the island over the years, its residue rewarded the land with rich volcanic soil, full of nutrients."

Where was he going with all this, Babs wondered.

"The ash fed the olive groves, making them in turn superior to anywhere else. All the oil producers were able to sustain a harmonious comfortable lifestyle. This content and peaceful existence did not go unnoticed by the scourge of the island – the Sicilian Mafia. Like so many others, my uncle was forced to wet his beak and this is when all the trouble began."

"Wet his beak?"

"It's a phrase to describe the malpractice of the Mafia extorting money out of people. Our neighbours fell like dominos to their threats. All the while my uncle felt the same pressure, but he swore he would not let the Mafia force his hand in the same way and defied them for as long as he could. But my elderly uncle was no match for their unscrupulous regime. Vandalism started to occur on a regular basis at his beautiful shop in the town as well as a few nuisances on the farm. He was *advised* to start paying protection money to the Mafia to ensure that these events would not happen again but the reality of it was that the only people they were protecting him from was themselves. He knew only too well they were the ones perpetrating the crimes in the first place. It was no use telling the police – they were also on the Mafia's payroll, either that or they were afraid to cross them. I don't know if my uncle was brave or stupid but he continued to ignore them. This incensed the organisation even more. One night they physically assaulted him and left him in a bad way. That happened on a Friday, Mama got a call from a hospital in Taormina and by the Sunday I was on my way over there. Babs, if you saw him, you would have understood. He was a broken man – physically and mentally. There was no way he could be left to fend for himself. And so I have spent the last thirty years or so trying to run the farm as efficiently as I could, while at the same time I too have been obligated to pacify these monsters. But then the groves started to fail all over the island and that brought its own set of problems, but that's a different story."

"What happened to your uncle?"

"He died about fifteen years ago, heartbroken."

"I'm very sorry to hear that, Rosario. Sorry to hear about all of it. Here, let me put on the kettle this time."

While it boiled she perused the leather bag of souvenirs he had brought her from Sicily which contained a box of cannoli – which were sweet pastries – a bottle of olive oil from his own farm and box of lemon-scented soaps.

Over tea and biscuits, they recounted how their lives had played out and how they came to be where they were now. Rosario had married a girl called Caterina from the city of Catania and they had two daughters, Sofia and Bianca, who were now young adults. Sadly, Caterina had passed away about three years earlier. He hinted that his marriage had not encapsulated the great love that he thought it would. He said, staring Babs in the eye, that he was meant to have that with someone else.

Babs did not wish to share the shortcomings of Nate and their own relationship being tumultuous from time to time. She changed the subject.

"So what has brought you back now? Are you on holidays? Your family in Ireland must be delighted to see you after all this time."

"It is long overdue. You know, I didn't even come back for Mama's funeral. Sadly, commitments in Italy didn't allow it.

"When did you get here?"

"Last night."

"Gosh, you didn't waste any time!" said Babs, laughing.

Rosario grabbed both her hands in his.

"Babs, we have wasted so much time already. I came back here for you. I want us to be together. Better late than never, no?"

"Rosario, that's very flattering but...I mean...Come on, *it's too late*. I'm married and settled and –"

"Listen to me. I have finally found a way to break free from the fist of the Mafia. I have some money set aside now. I am going to buy a chipper that is up for sale across the street in Westport and set up a trattoria. It will

43

be *bellissima*! Can you imagine it, Babs? You and I running it together. You already told me about working in a hotel's restaurant and soon you'll have your receptionist skills too, so it's like it was meant to be. A dream come true!" He beamed at her.

"A dream come true for who? What about your daughters?"

"I know it's a lot to take in, but you and I are destined to be together. My daughters are adults now, they are happy for me. *Il destino*."

"Destiny? In Westport? My home town. Where all my family and friends live?" Babs was becoming agitated by this nonsensical proposition. "Can you imagine the shame of both of us tearing away and shacking up together in a place where everyone knows us? There would be no happy-ever-after ending with that scenario. Did you think this through at all?"

"I don't care what people think. I have thought of nothing else for years. I have been so unhappy living under the shadows of others. Now it's my time to shine. Look, forget about Westport. We can move far away from here and open up a restaurant somewhere else around Ireland. But, it has to be beside the sea, that is my only condition. I cannot imagine not living beside it, just like Mama. Every wave is like a beat of my heart."

"Rosario, I think under *no* condition can I contemplate what you are asking. It's crazy."

"That's what I used to think but true happiness is a rare thing and, forgive me for saying, but none of us are in... how do you say it ...the flush of youth? Even though you are still as beautiful as ever. But, we are not in the harvest of our lives yet either. So all I ask is that you look truly into your heart and consider what I have said, not with fear, but with courage, to live the life you were meant to, with me."

He put his hand in his pocket and took out a red-velvet box. Inside was a gold heart pendant on a chain. He laid it on table before her.

"I meant to give this to you years ago, just before I left Ireland, but then I was glad I didn't because it felt like I still had your heart even though I was away from you."

With that he got up to leave. He joined his hands together as if in prayer.

"Don't take long, Babs. Like I said, we have wasted so much time already. I am staying in Slattery's Guesthouse."

"In Slattery's? Here in Ballantur?" Babs asked in disbelief as she rose to her feet.

"Yes, I wanted to be near you in case you wanted to ask any more questions. I'm in Room 2."

He kissed her on both cheeks, just as he had when he arrived, and walked out of her house.

Babs stood in the middle of kitchen floor, flabbergasted. She turned back to the sink and finished doing her laundry in a trance. Then she cleared the table, before sitting down with an emergency brandy. She tried to make sense of it all. Was he crazy? She couldn't possibly consider doing something like that. Could she? Her life and marriage was almost ruined already by the consequences of Sammy Joyce's murder, eighteen months before. She felt so lucky to have got a second chance following that sequence of events. What would Nate say? He would go mad. There was no way she was going to tell him about any of this, not about Rosario's visit and certainly not about him wanting to whisk her away. She went over everything Rosario had said to her. Every now and again her conscience flickered by default and she actually did start imagining a life going forward with him, but the price to pay was too high and she came back down to earth. But there again, what if...

Nate's lorry roared into the backyard.

Oh my God, he's home! How long have I been sitting here, she thought in a panic. I've no dinner on.

"*Oh shit!*" She spotted Rosario's forgotten gilet still hanging on the back of the kitchen chair. She grabbed it and the bag of souvenirs and ran upstairs. She shoved the locket into the pocket of the gilet and hung it on the clothes hanger underneath her Sunday coat in her wardrobe. The bag she stashed at the bottom of it.

"Hiya!" greeted a cheery Nate. "How are you? Did you feed the dog? He looks hungry out there. What's for dinner? It must be salad, I can't smell anything."

"I'm sorry, Nate. I've had the worse migraine all day. I couldn't shift it," announced a rash but creative Babs.

"No, no, don't worry. Why don't you go for a lie-down? I'll sort out supper. God, I wish we had a chipper here, they're so handy."

Babs gladly did as she was told. She took advantage of his kind concern which gave her uninterrupted quiet time and space to think this through.

Nate popped his head around the door to see if she wanted something to eat but she genuinely had no appetite.

While Nate slept soundly beside her that night, Babs could find no solace. No matter what way she looked at it, Rosario's dream for both of them was nothing more than a nightmare which would ultimately hurt a lot of people who were not the cause of his long-term suffering. Nor should anyone have to bear the consequences of his unattainable happy ending. It would tarnish all the memories of his own marriage and those of his children. She couldn't leave Nate now. If Rosario had turned up two years earlier when they were going through their rough patch there is no doubt but that she would have been very tempted, but after all they had endured during the course of the murder investigation they had rebuilt their marriage and, with the added liberties of driving and working, since then she hadn't been so content in years. She liked the house they lived in, the close proximity of it to the town and all the lovely neighbours and friends she had around her. No, she was not going to throw all of that away on a whim. Of course she felt sorry for Rosario. Her heart went out to him for the miserable life that had been foisted upon him. But throwing away all the new good things in his life now was not going to right all the wrongs committed against him and she was going to tell him that. At this stage of her middle-of-the-night analysis she concluded that his rash appearance and proposal was nothing more than a cry for help. Maybe it was just a mid-life crisis? In any event she decided she would go to Slattery's first thing in the morning after Nate left for work. She would sit Rosario down, empathise with him about the undoubted injustice he had borne, but make him realise that now he had found the means to free himself at last he should revaluate his goals and ambitions realistically. He should enjoy himself for the first time in a longtime, get to know who he was and what he could do for once without other people telling him what to do.

Babs' fair assessment of the situation relieved her woes and, exhausted from all the anxiety, she finally fell asleep.

Chapter 5

Straight to the heart

A sullen Caitlín arrived into work with her head down. The pain in it
after too many brandies the night before didn't help either. She kept
out of Sergeant Lamb's way but, more worryingly, he kept out of hers.
She continued on with her paperwork, processing the arrest of the
robber from the day before. It turned out he had quite a track record
of robberies and it was a great result to have him off the streets, but her
gallant effort was overshadowed by the way she was accused of going
about it, so any sense of achievement she felt was deflated like a burst
balloon.

Her torment was even more exacerbated when she saw Mr. Pollard's
sublime dark-green Jaguar MK2 slowly drive into the station's yard.

She rose from her desk and stared out the window. Mr. Pollard was
getting out but Mrs. Pollard appeared to be staying put.

Caitlín sat back down at her desk. Her heart was beating at ninety.

Sergeant Lamb came out of his office, while Tully went to open the
door for their visitor. Everyone was on standby and tenterhooks to see
what he was going to say. They could hear his crutches scraping the
pavement on his approach.

Caitlín rose again with her fingers crossed behind her back. *Please God, let it be okay*, she prayed.

Mr. Pollard managed to hobble into reception and even hold on to a bunch of flowers in his hand.

"Good morning, Garda Kennedy. I'm glad you're here."

"Good morning, Mr. Pollard. Careful there. How are you?"

"I'm absolutely fine," he answered, nodding at Sergeant Lamb and Tully in acknowledgement. "I just want to clear the air. I do apologise, on behalf of my wife, for her tantrum and threats yesterday. It's just that she didn't understand that I had given you permission to use the car so she thought you had abducted me and, with my broken leg and the mad chase after the robber and all, well, the poor thing was worried out of her mind. I do hope you'll forgive her?"

"Forgive her? Of course we do," Caitlín said, smiling. She could have hugged him for the sense of relief she had begun to feel. "I hope *you* can forgive me for relying on you in such unusual circumstances and –"

"Thank you, Garda Kennedy," butted in Sergeant Lamb, before she could say anything to incriminate herself. "Mr. Pollard, please let Mrs. Pollard know that we were asking for her and we hope she is much recovered after the shock she got yesterday. Can I say how extremely grateful we are to you for the personal contribution you made, allowing our bangharda here to use your car to pursue this hardened criminal who had been terrorising Ballantur and indeed other towns for a long time. It was a credit to you, sir."

"Well, I don't think I did that much really, but I was glad to help. However, there is one thing that I might ask in return, concerning Garda Kennedy, but only if it's appropriate?"

"Ask away," encouraged Sergeant Lamb. If Wesley Pollard wanted Caitlín to walk barefoot over hot coals right now, Sergeant Lamb would light the fire himself. Anything to get this potential grenade out of the office.

"May I ask what age you are, Garda?" Mr. Pollard asked Caitlín.

"I'm twenty-two," she answered slowly, wondering why he was asking her that.

"Oh sorry! These are for you!" He handed the bunch of flowers to her.

As she accepted she could feel his straying eyes running over her figure.

"*Mmm* . . . and attractive too."

Yuck, thought Caitlín, what's got into him today? Squirming, she threw an alarmed look at Tully who was laughing behind Mr. Pollard.

"Forgive me, my dear. It was not my intention to embarrass you. Caitlín, I have been fortunate to be involved in car racing here in Ireland and on the international circuit for over thirty years. As I already mentioned yesterday, I was a rally driver myself when I was younger. Since then, I have had the privilege of sponsoring several cars and drivers, some of which have been very successful for me. My drivers sometimes practise on that old quarry road we drove along yesterday – that is why I know it so well. Anyway, to make a long story short and not to be taking up your valuable time, let me just tell you how hard it is to find a good driver. Caitlín, that performance you gave yesterday was impressive. You were not afraid to put the foot down. You reacted very well under tremendous pressure and took your instructions accordingly. Crucially, you showed no fear. These are the characteristics of a really good racing driver. All the racing organisations are vying to get more women involved in the sport. So, I'm wondering if you would consider becoming a rally driver? I need a driver for the rally coming up here in Ballantur. A pretty, resourceful young girl such as yourself would be ideal for something like this and you'd be paid. You could do it in your spare time, of course."

Tully was still quietly laughing and Sergeant Lamb let out a snort of laughter too.

Bad cess to them, thought Caitlín, becoming infuriated at their chauvinistic, not to mention unprofessional and immature behaviour. Would they have driven any better themselves yesterday? What was so absurd about Mr. Pollard offering her this exciting and unique opportunity? If she was a man they would already be clapping her on the back. She cleared her throat.

"I would be delighted to participate." She was looking at Mr. Pollard but really talking to Sergeant Lamb and Tully as she continued. "I value your appreciation of what I experienced yesterday, especially when I had little or no training of how to adapt in a pressurised situation like that. Secondly, I respect that you recognise my ability to be a racing driver regardless of me being a woman."

"Splendid, Caitlín! I was hoping you would say yes. That's terrific. We don't have much time to practise so we'll meet up with this evening if that's OK?"

"That's fine, Mr. Pollard."

"Well, I'd better let you good people get back to work. Good day to you all!"

With Tully's help, he limped out of the station.

"Now, who would have thought, Kennedy, after you being at the bottom of the barrel yesterday how quickly you have risen to the top again," cajoled Sergeant Lamb.

"I didn't realise I was at the bottom of anything, but it's amazing how far you can go once someone has a bit of belief in you."

Gobshite, she said to herself as she walked into their pokey kitchen, wondering if there was such a thing as a vase in their misogynist shark tank.

Elsewhere, Babs Wheatley was battling with her own predators which were infesting the waters of her mind, causing her to question if she was making the right choice in settling for a predictable life with Nate over going into the unknown with Rosario. No, she was going to stay with Nate. Only for Rosario coming back on the scene she would not have been contemplating any changes to her life at all.

She had gone over what she was going to say to Rosario in her head a hundred times since she had got up that morning and now she was doing it again walking down the street towards Slattery's. She was going to encourage Rosario to enjoy life, but not with her. Then suddenly she started worrying about how she was going to do that. She didn't want the proprietor, Dennis Slattery, or anyone else to see them talking together. This town had a habit of propagating rumours unlike no other. No one knew that better than Babs as she had been personally persecuted needlessly during the murder investigation eighteen months before.

Thankfully the front door of the guesthouse was wide open to let in some fresh air on this fine summer's morning. Babs slowly tiptoed into the hall and paused to scan the dining room. There was only one other guest seated there with his back to her, about to crack the top off his hard-boiled egg. She stole as lightly as she could up the carpeted stairs.

Recalling that Rosario told her he was staying in Room 2, she peeped around the landing and could see a bag of laundry in the corridor. A humming noise from a vacuum cleaner was circulating from Room 1. It stopped and a cleaning lady came out and shoved the used bed linen into the bag. When she went back into the room Babs made a run for it, hoping the cleaning lady wouldn't come out again. She was about to knock on Rosario's door but was relieved to see it was slightly ajar. She shoved it open and then closed it quietly behind her, delighted she had made it without been seen. Rosario was standing with his back to her. Babs decided to spit it out before he got a chance to sweet-talk her again.

"Rosario. It's me, Babs. I'm not going to make this anymore painful than it has to be, but I'm sorry. I'm not going to break up my marriage or my life to run away with you." She was glad she didn't have to say that to his face.

Slowly Rosario turned around. It looked as if all the blood had been drained from his face at her words. But literally it had. A knife was sticking out of his chest.

"*Babs, Babs, help me!*" he gasped.

Babs ran to him and instinctively pulled the knife out before he slumped to the floor.

A gentle knock could be heard on the door followed by a melodic "*Room Service!*". When the cleaning lady received no answer she opened the door slowly. "*Mr. Fratelli?*" she called.

Then she froze.

"*Aaargh! Aaargh!*" she screamed loudly, dropping a bundle of clean towels from her arms.

Dennis Slattery came running up the stairs.

"What's going on?" he demanded.

Then he beheld his hysterical staff member, a lifeless man dying on the floor with a red-stained shirt and Babs Wheatley standing over him with blood dripping from a knife she was holding in her hand.

Chapter 6

Murder scene

Dennis Slattery rang the ambulance first, then the gardaí. Sergeant Lamb, Caitlín and Tully were on the scene within minutes. On entering the guestroom they saw Babs Wheatley on her knees in an agitated state, leaning over Rosario and shaking him. She repeatedly called out his name while the cleaning lady looked on in horror. The knife lay abandoned on the carpet which was becoming stained with the blood loss.

Tully pulled Babs away and told her to wait outside for the ambulance, thinking a sense of purpose might calm her down.

"Tully, go bring the priest," said Sergeant Lamb.

"Yes, sir," said Tully.

Sergeant Lamb got down on his knees with a groan and pressed two fingers to the side of the victim's neck. "He's alive. I can feel a weak pulse."

Caitlín grabbed the towels the cleaning lady had dropped on the floor and pressed one firmly on Rosario's chest. This was all they could do until the ambulance arrived.

"Dennis, who is this man?" asked Sergeant Lamb.

"Ah, his name is Fratelli – Rosario," replied Dennis as quickly as he could. "He's one of those, you know them, the Fratelli family in Westport who have the chip shop on the main street."

"So why is he staying here with you?" asked Caitlín.

"This chap had gone back to live in Italy and was only here on holidays, although I don't know why he was staying here and not in Westport."

Tully arrived with the priest who knelt by Rosario and began to perform the Last Rites. Caitlín and Sergeant Lamb stood back and watched the life of the fatally wounded man ebb away. Rosario's face appeared to grow whiter and paler as the final diminishing breaths left his body. It was a very sombre experience to witness and no words or actions seemed appropriate. They just had to let it happen and respect the honour a person deserved at that particular moment.

Rosario left them and the priest closed his eyes, granting him pardon and peace.

Sergeant Lamb went downstairs to use the telephone while Tully went to check if there was any sign of the ambulance.

Caitlín was left alone with Rosario.

This was the second dead body in extraordinary circumstances she had been exposed to in her personal and professional young life. Like the other, this victim's face was void of emotion and pain, but you couldn't help imagining what thoughts filled their minds in their final moment of terror. Did they silently call out for God? Think of their spouses and children? Or did the physical action of fighting for their lives leave them without an opportunity to feel anything at all?

Caitlín managed to switch her concentration back to the job. '*The investigation starts where the life ends*' – she remembered that from her training so first she proceeded to bag the murder weapon. She was concerned about keeping minimal disruption at the crime scene but so many people had contaminated it at this stage it would be hard to retrieve vital forensic evidence. She looked again at the face of the victim and noticed that he appeared to have a black eye. She leaned in a little closer. The decolourisation of the bruise on his right eye socket suggested that it was not new and could have been inflicted twelve to twenty-four hours earlier. She had to leave it at that for now as the ambulance had arrived and two paramedics rushed into the room with a stretcher.

In the ladies' toilets in Slattery's, Caitlín stood and looked in the mirror to see if the reflection of what she had just been through was etched on her face. She hated at how gloopy and sticky the blood was on her hands and how it seemed to dry into her skin quicker than she could stand it. She scrubbed her hands hard with the bar of soap and watched Rosario's blood dilute away down the drain, just like his life had dissipated a short time earlier. On her re-entry into the guestroom, she examined its door and its lock. It had not been forced open. She scanned the room. There was no sign of any disturbance. Its contents were neat and tidy. The unused twin bed was perfectly untouched without a crease in its shiny gold eiderdown and matching pillow set. On the nightstand beside the bed stood a glass of untouched water, a pair of sunglasses and a newly purchased jar of Sudocrem which she suspected Rosario may had bought to treat the bruising around his eye. She looked in the wardrobe but there was nothing in it apart from half a dozen rattling clothes hangers and a woolly blanket with a strong smell of mothballs. The floral curtains were drawn open and the top window was open but its small frame would not permit anyone access through it and it was on the first floor after all. His unlocked suitcase lay on his bed with his wash-bag beside it. The wash-bag contained a tub of Brylcreem, a bar of fancy soap (definitely Italian), aftershave, a wet facecloth and a razor. The suitcase held a few plain and patterned short-sleeved cotton shirts, another pair of trousers, socks, underwear and a light jumper. A smaller compartment held his wallet which was fat with an impressive amount of liras and punts. There was a stub of an airline ticket for London to Dublin. However, there did not appear to be a return by any mode of transport. Lying on the bed was an outdated copy of the *Mayo News*, dog-eared and opened at the property section.

Caitlín studied the floor where the body had been. He had fallen where he was stabbed. There were no traces of blood anywhere around the room except the alarmingly large nauseating pool of it seeping into the brown carpet which would stain the wooden floorboards underneath. Its dark foreboding spread was an embodiment of the evil act carried out. Room 2 might never be used again, she thought to herself. She was turning around when she felt something under her foot. Stepping aside, she picked up a black stone but on closer inspection it looked like a broken bead. Seeing that she had little else to show, other than the knife, she bagged it too as evidence. Rosario had used the shared bathroom down the hall and, after checking it, she could not see anything worthwhile noting there either.

In the corridor Caitlín bumped into Detective Brendan Cullen who had just arrived from Castlebar Garda Station. He had been a dominant member of their team on their previous murder investigation. She had seen little of him since but had admired his input the last time. He provided the yin to Sergeant Lamb's yang. In other words, he calmed him down and in general he was a good team leader. And he wasn't that bad-looking either.

They greeted each other warmly.

"Another murder, Garda Kennedy? Unbelievable," he said.

"Isn't it, just?"

He was followed by the forensic personnel, ready to carry out their technical examination. All of a sudden the small guestroom had become overcrowded so she left them to it.

Caitlín went outside for a breath of fresh air and to get a break from the heady atmosphere inside. Babs Wheatley was still there. However, she was bent over with her hands on her knees like someone who was preparing to retch.

"Babs, are you alright?"

Babs looked up at her with pools of tears in her eyes. Then she did what could not be helped so Caitlín held her hair back. While Babs recovered, Caitlín collected a few spent cigarette butts she had spotted on the ground and put them with the other physical evidence she had recovered.

"I'll get you a drink, Babs. Sit down there on the wall. You've had an awful shock."

To give Babs a chance to catch her breath, Caitlín walked back into Slattery's and into the bar where she came upon the tail-end of a conversation between Dennis Slattery and Sergeant Lamb.

"...so that's all I know about him but I couldn't believe it, Sergeant – there she was standing over the poor man with a big knife in her hand and the blood dripping off it. Oh, hello, Garda Kennedy, I didn't see you there. What can I do for you?"

"Can I have a brandy for Babs, please? She's in a bad way outside."

"Garda Kennedy," said Sergeant Lamb, "the only thing you will be getting that wretched woman is a set of handcuffs on her."

"I know, but she's very nauseous at the moment, sir," said Caitlín.

"Well, if you don't, I will," he replied and marched straight out the door.

Caitlín and Tully followed.

"Babs Wheatley, I am arresting you on suspicion of the murder of Rosario Fratelli. You are not obliged to say anything unless you wish to do so, but whatever you say will be taken down in writing and may be given in evidence. Tully, drive her up to the station and process her arrest. Kennedy, you and Detective Cullen can go to inform the next of kin. We can't really kick this off until we inform the family of his death. 'The investigation starts where the life ends.' Did they teach you that in Garda school, Kennedy?"

Sergeant Lamb was all riled up, like he had the case solved already.

Caitlín didn't respond to his insensitive bravado. Instead she sat into the car and waited for Detective Cullen.

Chapter 7

Investigations

During their journey to Westport, Caitlín and Detective Cullen went over the scene in detail and compared it to the last murder investigation they worked on together.

"You did well on the other one, Kennedy," said Detective Cullen. "Your bloodhound nose and instinct closed that case. I don't think we have much to investigate on this one, though – seems to be a fairly open-and-shut case. I know we have no motive yet but murderer and murder weapon were found at the scene. All we need is a confession."

"I don't agree," replied Caitlín, disappointed that he was adopting the same attitude as Sergeant Lamb. "You know from your own experience on the job that sometimes things are not as they seem."

Lucca Fratelli was hard at work behind the counter when they walked into the chipper. The delicious whiff of salty chips made both of them wish they were about to order and the busy fellow was going to ask "Do you want salt and vinegar with that?" rather than anything related to what he was about to hear.

Once they introduced themselves and established that Lucca was the most senior family member present there and that he was privy to his uncle having arrived in Ireland, Caitlín went about relaying the sequence of events to him.

"At approximately half past nine this morning we received a phone call at Ballantur Garda Station, reporting an incident at Slattery's Guesthouse in the town where your uncle was staying. Upon arrival to the room occupied by him, we found Mr. Fratelli in an injured state lying on the floor. He had been the victim of a stabbing and he was losing a lot of blood. An ambulance immediately was called and, in the meantime, my colleague and I continued to keep pressure on the wound to stop the bleeding and comfort him in any way we could. The single stab wound to the chest was quite catastrophic, Lucca. We had a priest present who gave him his Last Rites. When the medical staff arrived they too tried but I'm afraid –"

"Ye couldn't save him. He's dead, isn't he?"

"I'm sorry for your loss, Lucca," said Caitlín. "The wound was fatal. There was nothing anyone could do."

Detective Cullen also sympathised with Lucca before indicating to him the unfortunate necessity of having to identify the body. They gave him some time to tell his family and ring Italy with the news before meeting them at the morgue at Castlebar General Hospital.

Meanwhile, Nate Wheatley took a swerve between the ditches by overstretching across the dashboard to turn up the local radio with the announcement of some breaking news.

"News just reaching us here, folks. A swarm of gardaí and an ambulance have been parked outside Dennis Slattery's pub all morning.

Not sure what is going on there yet, but there is definitely something serious going down. Stay tuned to your local Calico Jack FM and we will keep you updated once we hear more. Now let's get back to the music ..."

Wow, what's all that about? Nate wondered, intrigued. Someone has probably collapsed after finding out how much Dennis charges for a pint! No doubt someone on the rounds will know. He looked forward to finding out what the commotion was all about.

After Lucca carried out his surreal and sad duty at the morgue, Detective Cullen and Caitlín sat him down for a chat in the cold echoing corridor of the grim building.

"We understand that this is a terrible and shocking experience for you but it is imperative that we can establish the last known whereabouts of your uncle before his death," said Detective Cullen.

"I don't know. I don't understand. He only arrived in Ireland on Sunday and now, less than forty-eight hours later, he's dead. Murdered!"

"It's hard to believe, I know that," coaxed Caitlín, "but did you know he was coming to Ireland and why?"

"Yes, we knew he was coming. He had his heart set on buying a property in Westport for ages and when we told him that the property across the street from us was up for sale he travelled to Ireland immediately and arrived here."

"So, do you know what time he went over to Ballantur?"

"*Em...* the first time was around lunchtime yesterday. He borrowed my car –"

"Sorry," interrupted Detective Cullen. "The first time?"

"Yeah, he borrowed my car and drove over, said he was visiting a friend for lunch. He came back to Westport sometime that evening, having visited my grandmother's grave on the way, and then he went back to Ballantur later."

"Do you know why he went back to Ballantur?" asked Caitlín.

"No. Again, he just said he was meeting someone and that he would stay over for the night."

"Was he meeting the same person as he met earlier?" asked Detective Cullen.

"I don't know. He didn't say. To be honest, I'd say he was just glad to get away from Westport because something happened here that you should know about. I think I know who killed him."

"Okay. We'll have to take a written statement from you in that regard, Lucca," said Detective Cullen, throwing a look of surprise at Caitlín.

"That's fine," replied Lucca, who now rushed on to tell them. "Rumour had it for a while that the property across the street was going to be put up for sale and we were delighted to hear it because it's another chip shop. Our competition. It belongs to a guy called Donnacha Finnerty but everyone calls him 'Finn'. I don't know who this guy thinks he is! I mean who would set up another chip shop directly opposite us in the first place? We're an authentic Italian chip shop, and he goes and calls his one 'Rory's Chipper' – I mean, come on! Well, of course that created animosity and fierce competition between us over the years. That's why we opened our adjoining café and thankfully it has been very successful, unlike his chipper which has been lagging behind since, and we think that is why he is selling up. Like I said, my Uncle Rosario had been wanting to buy a similar business in Westport for ages and when he saw this coming on the market he put in an offer to buy it straight away and that's what brought him home. My family and Finn never liked each other because of our competitive businesses, but Finn and my uncle personally did not like each other full stop and that goes back to when they were young. But listen to me – this guy, Finn, he's crazy. He has assaulted people before in Westport – ask the gardaí there, they'll tell you. Anyway, yesterday evening Rosario accidently bumped into Finn on the street just outside our chipper. I heard Finn threaten Rosario. He said the estate agent had told him that Rosario had put in an offer to buy him out. Finn was furious. Our café door was open so I could hear and see everything. Angry words were exchanged then Finn punched Rosario in the face. I ran outside. Finn was standing there, shoving Rosario against the wall. I remember him saying '*You'll never take over my business – over my dead body!*' I bet you he followed Rosario to Ballantur and stabbed him."

"Okay, thank you, Mr. Fratelli," said Detective Cullen. "We'll be in touch with you – rest assured we will look into this altercation without delay."

When Lucca had left the morgue Detective Cullen and Caitlín talked about what they had just heard.

"Well, this Finn guy might not be willing to sell his business over *his* 'dead body' but he might be prepared to sell it over Rosario Fratelli's," said Caitlín.

"I think you're right there, Caitlín. So we're heading back with another possible suspect in the mix."

Tully was itching to hear what took them so long when they arrived back.

"Notifying the next of kin isn't easy," said Caitlín. "We told his nephew Lucca at the chipper and then we had to give him time to tell the family, absorb the bad news and ring the victim's family in Italy. Then we met Lucca at the morgue in Castlebar to identify the body. He had some very interesting information. I think we have another suspect in our sights. What have you been doing?"

"I had to talk to Dennis Slattery, his staff and the only other guest staying there, *blah, blah*."

"So nothing to go on?" guessed Caitlín.

"Wait till you hear this, though – the other guest is a teetotaller."

"So?"

"He's a sales rep for alcoholic spirits," Tully said, laughing, with Caitlín joining in at the irony.

"*What are ye two cackling about?*" shouted Sergeant Lamb. "Kennedy, grab your notebook and get in here. We're going to question Babs Wheatley. Bring her in a glass of water."

"Confirm your name, please."

"Barbara Wheatley. Mrs."

"Mrs. Wheatley, I'm Detective Cullen, this is Sergeant Lamb and Garda Kennedy, although I think we all know each other having been in the same situation, same room, over a year ago in relation to the Sammy Joyce murder investigation. Let's start by you telling us how you knew the victim, Italian national Rosario Fratelli."

Babs took a sip of water and began.

"I'm from Westport originally and I knew Rosario when he lived there. We were going out together for a while until he was sent back to Italy."

"How long ago is this, Mrs. Wheatley?"

"Oh God, about thirty years ago."

"And how long did you go out for?"

"About a year."

"And have you been in contact with him over this thirty-year period?"

"No, I hadn't heard from him at all."

"Until when?"

"Until he turned up on my doorstep yesterday – around midday."

"Were you surprised to see him?"

"Of course I was. He came in, we had tea and just caught up on the way our lives had turned out since then."

"Well, you mustn't have covered everything, Mrs. Wheatley, when he had to stay overnight in Slattery's Guesthouse," stated Sergeant Lamb sarcastically.

"I was surprised he was staying there. I'm sure his family in Westport had plenty of room for him."

"So do you know why he was staying here?"

"He told me he was buying a property in Westport and he was going to turn it into a trattoria – you know, an Italian restaurant."

"Yes, Mrs. Wheatley, I know what a trattoria is," snapped Sergeant Lamb.

"I told him I was working as a waitress in the Humbert Hotel in Castlebar and he said that he might want to ask me more questions about the catering industry here in Ireland."

"His own family own a catering business – why wouldn't he just ask them?" probed Sergeant Lamb.

"Because they run a chipper. He wanted to learn about local produce and local suppliers, like we have at the hotel, that sort of thing."

"What time did he leave your house?" asked Caitlín.

"Probably around four o'clock."

"Did anyone see him arrive or leave your house?"

"No, I don't think so."

"So when did you see him again?" Sergeant Lamb jumped back in.

"Not until this morning, at about half past nine."

"And tell us, Mrs. Wheatley, what was so urgent that you went to meet him so early?" he demanded. "Was he expecting you?"

"No, he wasn't, but I didn't want him wasting any more time on me. I mean, I didn't have any further information really other than what I had told him yesterday. I'm only a waitress. I don't deal with suppliers or 'Cash and Carry' or the like."

"And how did you manage to let yourself in and up and into his bedroom without the proprietor's permission?" Sergeant Lamb asked aggressively.

"The front door was open. There was no one about to ask so I just went on up."

"But how did you know what room he was staying in?" asked Detective Cullen.

"He mentioned it yesterday." She could feel herself blushing.

"And what happened then, Babs?" asked Caitlín, relieving Babs' embarrassment.

"He was standing with his back to me. He turned around." She paused momentarily, realising how difficult it was to retell and relive what she had seen. She exhaled and continued. "He was clasping his chest. That's when I saw the knife." She started crying. "The blood was just pouring out. He looked at me, gasping, and said '*Help me!*' I ran to him and pulled out the knife, I didn't know what else to do, but then he just fell to the floor. I kept shaking him and calling his name but I knew I was losing him."

Babs became visibly upset so Detective Cullen gave her a chance to compose herself by checking his notes and then asked her about the cleaning lady arriving in the room, Dennis arriving in the room and the room itself, but she couldn't remember anything. It was clear her focus was on Rosario and his dying moments.

Detective Cullen then redirected his line of questioning, taking her fragile recall off the table for now.

"How would you describe Mr. Fratelli's demeanour or behaviour yesterday, when he came to see you? Did he appear anxious or troubled to you?"

Babs pulled herself together. She knew she would have to be careful here.

"He was the opposite. He was excited. He told me he had put an offer on the property in Westport and shared his plans to open a proper trattoria. It was going to be his dream come true, considering all he had been through all his life up to now. Well, from the time he returned to Italy."

"Oh yes, you said earlier he had been sent back. Do you know why?" asked Caitlín.

"I didn't get the full story until yesterday, thirty years later," replied Babs. "He left Ireland literally overnight with no warning. He vanished. I asked his mother at the time but all she told me was that he was sent home to help his uncle who ran an olive farm. I never heard from him after that. He came here yesterday to apologise for doing that to me. I guess he wanted to wipe the slate clean before starting a new chapter in his life, here in Ireland. When he explained what actually had happened to him in Italy, it was forgivable."

"And what was that? asked Sergeant Lamb.

"His poor uncle and his business was been extorted by the Sicilian Mafia. They attacked him for not paying them and caused severe injuries. That's when Rosario was sent to Sicily to look after him and take over running his olive groves. But, unfortunately, he too had to succumb to the strong arm of the Mafia and spent his life up to now trying to make the farm marginally profitable to support his own family while handing over substantial undeserved spoils to those awful people."

Sergeant Lamb covered his eyes, wondering how she could fall for such an Al Capone story. Having a conversation about the Italian Mafia in their station in Ballantur was about as rare as fish feathers.

"Okay, Mrs. Wheatley," said Detective Cullen slowly, trying to take in this unusual deposition. "So, if he, as you said, was only making a minimal living from this farm on this rocky island, tell me where he suddenly came up with the money to buy a business in the West of Ireland?"

"I don't know for sure. All he said was that he had found a way to become free from their threats, or something like that. Look, you think I killed him but I didn't. I just told you I hadn't seen him in thirty years until yesterday. Yeah, I was a heartbroken young woman when he left me high and dry all those years ago but, in fairness, I didn't hold a grudge for all that time. I mean, I didn't even know if the man was dead or alive since and when he explained everything to me I actually felt sorry for him and hoped that at last he could have a prosperous future. Maybe he still owes money to those Mafia people and they followed him here and killed him."

"Right, that's enough for now," said Sergeant Lamb who was reluctant to consider that outlandish theory. "Garda Tully will take you back to your cell until further notice, thank you. Kennedy, you wouldn't stick on the kettle and make us a pot of tea like a good girl?"

Chapter 8

Confrontations

Caitlín didn't mind obliging on this occasion because she was dying for a cup herself. In the beginning Sergeant Lamb used to ask her to make him mugs of tea. She made the worst tea imaginable on purpose. A few days later he stopped asking.

When the brew was ready today, Caitlín, Sergeant Lamb, Detective Cullen and Tully sat around the reception room munching digestive biscuits while engaging in an 'off the record' debate about Babs Wheatley.

"So who thinks she did it?" asked Sergeant Lamb, kicking things off.

"I don't," said Caitlín straight away.

"I don't either," said Tully, even though he hadn't been present for the interview. "She'd crack like a twig under the pressure if she had."

"However, I don't think she's told us everything," Caitlín added. "The dots have to be joined up between his alleged involvement with the Mafia and how he had enough money for this proposed purchase. It doesn't add up."

They all sat silently for a bit, contemplating the situation.

"In any event, that doesn't change the fact that she was discovered in the room standing over him with the murder weapon in her hand," said Sergeant Lamb. "Brendan, what do you think?"

"I agree with you. All she said was how sorry she was for the guy, but she could be harbouring a hatred for him. You know, bitter about him leaving her high and dry all those years ago. We have to wait for the forensics and Coroner's reports to come back and see what they throw up. But, in the meantime, we have enough to charge her. She was caught at the scene with the murder weapon in her hand."

While the force was having their tete-á-tete, Babs was having a heart to heart with herself in her cell. She hadn't told the gardaí everything. Sitting alone before her interview, she had decided that she would not tell them anything about the intimate conversation she had with Rosario, with him urging her to run away with him and start a new life together, just the two of them. No, she had been humiliated before by the late Sammy Joyce on whom she had foolishly developed a crush. *There's no fool like an old fool*, as they say, so she was not going to suffer the same shame and embarrassment as before. And, poor Nate – how could she put him through all that, again? He didn't deserve it the first time, never mind having to endure another dose of it now. Besides, it would make no difference to what had happened to Rosario anyway. He was dead and she was certain it was nothing to do with his declaration of love for her. No one else needed to know about that. A truth like that would only ruin her marriage with Nate and ruin the memory of the marriage Rosario had shared with Caterina, presuming they had been happy. And what of his daughters? They would end up with a residue of hatred for him for his betrayal of them and especially their mother. Their lives would be shattered. Too many people were vulnerable to the consequences of such a truth being confessed now. No, she would never tell a soul. She would take it to her grave, just like Rosario did.

"♫ *Calico Jack FM* ♫...*Now, if you're just joining us or if you're waiting for an update on the commotion outside Slattery's this morning, we have found out that shockingly a man who was staying there as a guest was stabbed in the chest and died. Local woman, Babs Wheatley, has been arrested for his murder. And, in case you are wondering, yes, it is the same lady who was questioned before for a different murder. Can you believe it? What is the town coming to at all? First we had the post office robbery, then there was a break-in at Cassie Quirke's house, then separately she was robbed on her way to the bank and now this! The place is completely lawless. Anyway here's a song from Andy Williams, called 'Can't Get Used to Losing You'!*"

Nate Wheatley couldn't believe what he was hearing as he made his way home after fulfilling his rounds for the day. "*Sweet suffering Jesus!*" he said as he put the foot down and headed straight for the Garda Station.

On his arrival, Sergeant Lamb informed him that Babs had been formally charged with the murder of Rosario Fratelli and her arraignment and bail hearing was scheduled for the following morning. Nate was speechless. He barely knew who Rosario Fratelli was and now he wondered if he knew who Babs was either. He didn't want to see her and left the station, banging the door hard behind him.

The following day, Caitlín and Tully were dispatched to Westport to interview Donnacha Finnerty, the man who assaulted Rosario the evening before he died.

"This is the second time in two days I've been in a chipper," said Caitlín as she entered Rory's Chipper.

"Yeah, you'd want to lay off there a bit alright – a moment on the chips – a lifetime on the hips!"

"Do one, Seán."

After being informed that Mr. Finnerty was not presently on the premises they were redirected to his private living quarters down the alleyway at the back of the chipper. Tully went straight out but Caitlín hung back and casually asked the staff if they knew the whereabouts of Mr. Finnerty last Monday night or early yesterday morning. The staff confirmed that he had not been working that night, which was not unusual because he only worked late when he felt like it and, as the chipper only opened at five o'clock daily, they could not account for his movements on any given day.

Caitlín hurried after Tully down the urine-scented alley.

After a few loud knocks on Mr. Finnerty's brown door, he pulled it open abruptly.

"Oh, it's you lot," the middle-aged, grey-haired man said unenthusiastically.

"Mr. Finnerty, I presume? Can we come in to ask you a few questions?" said Tully.

"Do I have a choice?" he answered flatly and stood aside.

He directed them into the kitchen but, once there, he didn't invite them to sit.

"We are here to investigate an altercation witnessed between yourself and a Mr. Rosario Fratelli," said Caitlín, "which took place on the street Monday evening outside Fratelli's Café."

"Oh, that would be right – he's not back in the country five minutes and already he's squealing to Mammy and Daddy."

"You physically harmed Mr. Fratelli," Caitlín said. "You were seen punching him and shoving him against the wall. Can you explain what led to this offence?"

"Yeah, I can. I had just found out that spineless git had put an offer in to buy my chipper. If he was the last person on earth I wouldn't sell it to him and I just wanted to make sure he understood that."

"May we ask why you are so opposed to selling your property to him?"

"If he buys my chipper then that family will have two businesses in the town and, before you know it, that Italian lot will have taken over the whole place."

"Being entrepreneurial is not illegal, Mr. Finnerty," stated Tully, ignoring his discriminatory remark.

"Neither is hating someone."

"We're just trying to hear your side of the story," coaxed Caitlín.

"Oh, I see, he's pressed charges against me, has he?"

"No. I'm afraid he hasn't. I'm surprised you haven't heard. Mr. Fratelli was found dead yesterday. He'd been stabbed." Caitlín tried to read the reaction on his face but he turned around and walked towards his kitchen window. She noticed he had an obvious physical disability in his legs.

"So he's still trying to hog the limelight, even in death."

"Mr. Finnerty, can you confirm where you were Monday night and more importantly where you were yesterday morning at approximately half past nine?" said Caitlín.

"You think I did it? Just because I pulled his hair?"

"Just answer the question," said Tully firmly.

"Monday night I was tucked up in bed alone and I was still glued to the scratcher at that time yesterday morning. Advantages of being your own boss and all that."

"Can anyone verify that?"

"No. I just told you I was on my own."

"Thank you, Mr. Finnerty," said Caitlín, fed up of him.

They left his house.

"That attitude makes me suspicious of him," said Tully.

"You can say that again – but do you know what I really think?"

"What's that?"

"I'd kill someone myself for a bag of chips right now with all the talk of them," she replied, laughing.

"Well, we're not buying them from that asshole. What a weirdo!"

"We can't go to Fratellis' for them. Look at the black ribbon on the door – they're closed. The family is grieving. We could get some in Castlebar on the way back."

"Nah, I don't feel like them," said Tully, changing his mind.

"Oh, forget it so!"

And so while Caitlín and Tully continued to bicker about where to have their lunch that afternoon, it was nothing compared to the colossal showdown about to take place in the Wheatley household after Babs was released on bail.

Nate collected her from the Garda Station but he didn't speak to her on the way home. She could tell he was mad.

He stormed into the house and paced up and down the sitting-room floor, swung around and tore into a tirade.

"I mean, for fuck sake, Babs! Jesus Christ! Is this a joke? How on earth are we back at this junction, again?"

"Please calm down, Nate. You know well I didn't kill him. I'm not capable of such a thing."

"I know you didn't kill him! But I want to know what the hell you were doing caught in a guest-bedroom with a strange man! Let me guess! The hot-press was occupied so you couldn't hide in there like you did the last time with your old bit on the side!"

"Stop, Nate. That's not fair."

"Fair? Will you explain how fair it is on me that my wife has been caught publically with a dead man walking for a second time? And how she has ended up accused of this murder too? I suppose at any minute now the gardaí will come knocking and arrest me as well."

"Don't be ridiculous. You have a solid alibi this time. You were with your customers all morning."

"And what I am to say when I'm serving them tomorrow? This isn't exactly small talk, Babs. It was all over that new local radio. They even gave out your name."

"There you go again, only bothered about what other people think. You didn't even ask me if I was alright, Nate. I just saw someone very dear to me die before my very eyes. Someone who was stabbed to death with a knife. There was so much blood, I couldn't stop the bleeding. Tell that to your cronies." She started to cry, again distraught at the horrid image in her head.

Nate pulled his horns in and felt his own stab of remorse for shouting at her.

"Sorry, Babs. I can only imagine what an awful thing that was to come across."

Both held their fire.

Nate poured himself a glass of whiskey but then changed his mind and handed it to Babs. He poured himself another and sat heavily in the fireside armchair. His bouncing knee reflected his restless mind.

He could feel a sense of betrayal rising in him again. He wanted to know.

"Exactly how 'dear' of a friend was this guy? Who the hell was he? Garda Tully said he was some Italian from Italy."

Babs threw her eyes to heaven at that senseless observation.

"How well did you know him?"

"Rosario Fratelli," she replied slowly and dolefully. "I went out with him years ago when I lived in Westport. I told you about him once or twice."

"The fella from the chipper?"

"Yes, *the fella from the chipper*! God!" She wished people would recognise him for so much more than that.

"Have you been in contact with him?" Nate asked sharply.

"No, I hadn't seen or heard from him for thirty years until he turned up at our front door on Monday."

"*Here?* Why didn't you tell me? I thought you had a migraine? So that was a load of bollix and you let me fuss over you like an idiot!"

Babs knew she was skating on a very perilous surface of thin ice right now and if she didn't choose her words carefully she would sink heavily to the bottom of the murky waters. So she half lied and told him that her migraine was brought on by Rosario's unexpected arrival. She further went on to say how he offloaded so much about his life since they were young that she didn't have the energy to retell it all when Nate came

77

home, opting to lie down instead, but of course she was going to tell him when she was feeling better.

"But you didn't waste any time on your recovery! You skipped down the road to Slattery's first thing this morning. What were you meeting him again so soon for?"

"He was going to open a restaurant in Westport and wanted information from me about suppliers and traders."

"With all due respect, Babs, you're only a waitress."

"With all due respect, Nate, you're only a jacked-up grocery boy on wheels who's frustrated that you are involved in this story so you can't take the piss out of it for your own gratification when you tell everyone else! Why is it, Nate, that every time something bad happens, instead of supporting me, you hang me out on my own to dry?"

"Give me a break! You wanted to work, I got you a job. You wanted to drive, I bought you a car. I thought you were happy and now here you are again cavorting with someone else behind my back. I'm sick of it. I'm going for a pint. Oh fuck it, I can't, sure Slattery's is closed. Because of you!"

"You get your priorities sorted out there, Nate. I'm going for a lie-down and you can go to hell."

Babs sat on the edge of their bed. She took up the book from her bedside locker and pulled out Rosario's postcard. She ran her fingers across the photograph of the azure seacoast in Sicily. Right now, she felt closer to the dead man than to the raging bull in her sitting room.

When Caitlín and Tully arrived back they updated Sergeant Lamb on the outcome of interviewing Donnacha Finnerty.

"Another definite person of interest then," agreed Sergeant Lamb.

He told Caitlín to set up her incident room and silently began to wonder if they were too hasty in charging Babs Wheatley. Nevertheless, he was confident that his dedicated little rural team would persist until they caught the real murderer who brought this unwelcome spectre of tragedy to their town.

Caitlín's temporary 'Incident Room' was basic and in definite need of funding. During the last investigation she'd stuck all her suspect-notes, photos, maps and timeline to the wall with red electrical insulating tape. Embarrassingly, when she took it all down the tape took the paint with it. On one of her quieter days she tried to paint over spots with old paint she found under the kitchen sink. As a result, the paint didn't match and the room now looked like it had a bad dose of measles. Ignoring her lack of interior-design skills, today she went on to draw a new timeline on a blackboard with chalk. She also drew an information table with all the victim and suspects' particulars inserted. She used masking tape this time to stick up any ancillary notes she had.

Sergeant Lamb had received the forensic and Coroner's reports that morning so, once Caitlín had set up her stall, she let her colleagues know.

With cups of tea brewed and instant coffee available, the team convened. Detective Cullen kicked things off by summarising the victim's profile.

"Rosario Fratelli, fifty-five years of age. Italian National who had lived in Ireland during his formative years from fourteen to twenty-three. He attended the local secondary school in Westport and worked in the family chip shop until he was sent back home to run his uncle's olive farm on the island of Sicily. He and his uncle were the victims of extortion at the hands of the local Mafia, allegedly. Rosario remained there until now. He married a woman called Caterina who is deceased and they had two daughters, now adults. He had returned to Ireland on Sunday last to buy a property in Westport and set up an Italian restaurant. Sadly, he was stabbed Tuesday morning, while staying as a guest in Slattery's B&B and died a short time later. Frank, both the forensic and Coroner's reports are in now, I believe?"

"Yes, they are," replied Sergeant Lamb. "And, unfortunately, there really is not a lot to go on. Between Babs Wheatley, the hotel staff, ourselves and the medical staff who attended the crime scene, it was unavoidably contaminated. Forensics describes the murder weapon as being a steak-knife, with a five-inch blade inserted into a brown wooden handle embedded with rivets. The serrated blade is approximately half an inch at the base finishing in a tip at the top. The fingerprints on it are a match to our suspect number one, Mrs. Barbara Wheatley. Garda Kennedy also collected a stone or a bead, or I don't know what you'd call it from the scene as well as a few cigarette butts." He looked at the bagged evidence. "Not sure what you think you'll deduce from those but, anyway, moving on."

Sergeant Lamb paused and changed to the Coroner's report.

"And then, the Coroner in *his* report states: '*The impact of the single stab that lacerated the heart was sufficient for the injury to prove fatal. The point of entry of the wound was a half to an inch wide from a diagonal motion and penetrated deep into the coronary artery.*' He goes on to say: '*Such an infliction could not have been operable or remedied by any physician or emergency department.*' Basically, he's saying it was curtains for the guy. Finally, he also notes the victim's right eye-socket had significant bruising. Probable cause is likely to it having been hit by something forceful. However, he states that injury was sustained at an earlier time not concurrent with the stab wound as the colourisation of the bruising suggests it happened at least twelve to twenty-four hours before that."

"Compliments of Donnacha Finnerty, no doubt," said Caitlín.

"Dennis Slattery said he did not recognise the knife or own anything like it in their kitchen," said Tully.

"Which brings us on to our suspects and why they wanted to kill him. Kennedy?" Sergeant Lamb nodded at Caitlín, handing over the gauntlet.

Caitlín cleared her throat and began. "Suspect Number One: Barbara, otherwise Babs, Wheatley, local woman, married to Ignatius, otherwise Nate, Wheatley. She's fifty-two years of age and works part-time as a waitress in the Humbert Hotel. She claims she had not seen the victim since they were in a relationship about thirty years ago, which ended abruptly when he went off to Sicily without saying goodbye –this may have led to some bitterness on Mrs. Wheatley's behalf. She said he turned up on her doorstep out of the blue on Monday last to catch up on old times and also, according to Mrs. Wheatley, he enquired whether she was knowledgeable about the catering industry here in Ireland. She does not appear to possess any animosity towards the deceased, nor have we, as of yet, established a motive for her to kill him. However, she certainly was in the wrong place at the wrong time and –"

"Kennedy, you have not been asked to present your biased conclusions about her guilt or innocence!" barked Sergeant Lamb.

Caitlín gave him a straight look and continued. "And, as we already heard, her fingerprints are on the knife – but she claims she came upon him after he was stabbed and extracted the knife from his chest in order to help him. She did say in her statement that the victim had confided in her that he is, or he was, having difficulties back home where he was been extorted by the Mafia. Whether that is relevant here or not remains to be seen."

"Tully, talk us through Suspect Number Two," directed Sergeant Lamb.

"Donnacha Finnerty, aged fifty-four, is a native of Westport. He is the proprietor of the second chip shop in Westport which is currently up for sale. He admitted having a business rivalry with the Fratellis but he has more than one enemy by the sound of things. I rang our boys in the Westport Station and they confirmed that he has been convicted of a GBH in the past. He caught some poor unfortunate stealing a bag of potatoes from his shed. The thief won't do that again, that's for sure – Mr. Finnerty broke his hand with a hammer. The garda I spoke to said he was a bit of an oddball. Monday evening he assaulted our victim and punched him in the face. This, technically, would correspond with the bruising of Mr. Fratelli's eye. The assault was witnessed by Lucca Fratelli, Rosario's nephew, who claims Finnerty said: '*You'll never take over my business – over my dead body!*' When we interviewed Mr. Finnerty about this assault, he was adamant that under no circumstances would he sell his property to Mr. Fratelli. Whether that was enough to kill him over, or there was more going on, we don't know. We will have to investigate further in order to establish a definitive motive. Unsurprisingly, he denied murdering Rosario but did admit physically assaulting him Monday evening. He has no alibi for the morning of the murder. He claims that he was in bed."

"So that's all we have?" asked Sergeant Lamb, rubbing his face which wore a much-unenlightened look.

"One more thing, guys," said Detective Cullen. "His two daughters are aware of the death of their father – they have been contacted by the police in Italy. I wonder if we should contact the police there too?"

"I thought you already did?" said Tully.

"Our contact in the Embassy in Rome is going to do it on our behalf but I wonder if we should touch base with them ourselves directly?"

"The Cabonara?" asked Sergeant Lamb

"The Carabinieri. Cabonara is a pasta dish," corrected Detective Cullen. "We can't ignore what Babs Wheatley told us about Mr. Fratelli being mixed up with the Mafia. We'll tell them but they can deal with that end of things, not us."

"Ah, good luck with that!" Sergeant Lamb said with a laugh. "Sure you have no Italian."

"If ye want someone to go over to that beautiful sunny island, I'll go," teased Tully. "I promise to keep the expenses down. I hear that wine is cheap."

"You don't have any Italian either," said Caitlín.

"No, but I have a dictionary."

"Well, you can buy a pillow for that dream, Tully. Now back to work, everyone," ordered Sergeant Lamb. "Kennedy, return to Westport in the morning and find out more about Rosario's Fratelli's past and his relationship with the handy man with the hammer. You can take Dream Boy there with you."

Thursday morning was already a warm one. Caitlín and Tully gladly threw their jackets into the back seat of the car.

"What a fab day to be going to Westport! We could go out to Silver Strand after," said Tully gleefully as they sat in and rolled down the windows. "What do you think? Go for a paddle?"

Caitlín never knew whether Tully was joking or not.

"We're at work, Seán. We can't be taking off like that. We need to uncover something which would make Finn a definite suspect and the Mafia theory a wildcard."

"Lighten up, Caitlín. Sergeant Lamb won't know how long this interview is going to take. I might even buy you a 99."

"We'll see. I still have to study that information pack we got for the President's visit."

"You're such a swot. It's a load of palava if you ask me. But I suppose you fancy J.F.K. like all the other women?"

"He's a good-looking man, but I wouldn't take a bullet for him," said Caitlín, laughing.

"Would you take one for me?"

"I already make you tea, Seán, so I might draw the line there."

"Not good enough, Caitlín – besides, Sergeant Lamb will soon be making tea for me. I think he fancies me."

"How do you make that out?"

"You heard him, calling me 'Dream Boy'."

"I think that was in a different context. What's the story about his marriage anyway – why did his wife leave him?"

"She did the dirt on him, I think, but I'm not sure. I heard one of the old lads on about it once at the station."

"That explains a lot, though. One, why he's miserable all the time and, two, why he's down on Babs Wheatley so much. He sees her as a scarlet woman."

"There's a professional, single, older man for you."

"You should take him to the Fla with you – the two of you could go on the pull."

"That guy couldn't pull a pair of curtains."

"You're hilarious," said Caitlín, "Have you ever thought about being a sit-down comedian?"

"What do you mean, sit-down?"

"You'd be so long waiting for your audience to laugh that you'd need a chair."

"*Ha!* Look, who's trying to be the comedian now!"

Lucca Fratelli had a beautiful small back garden at his townhouse. As they sat in its suntrap, he served Caitlín and Tully bottles of a drink called 'Fanta', straight from the fridge. He had popped a straw into each bottle and for a while the two born-again six-year-olds didn't hear a word he said because they were hypnotised by this new fizzy sensation.

Rosario was revered by Lucca – that was obvious when he described him as being an honourable and hard-working man who had turned his uncle's ailing farm around and making it into a successful business in Sicily. But, despite this, he said Rosario's heart was still in Ireland. He was always keen to know the news from home and they used to send the local newspapers over to him.

"He used to pay particular attention to our local football team 'Westport Cove', having played with them as a youngster–he was a bit of a legend by all accounts! My grandmother was so proud of him. She said he would make something of himself. Even when the odds were stacked against him he found a way to persevere, make his fortune and follow his dreams. I was very excited at the prospect of him returning from Italy and setting up the trattoria here – and finding out the whole story of his life since he left Ireland."

PART 2

Chapter 9

Under the Sicilian sun

Sicily 1933

Rosario sat on a craggy grey rock by the shore and looked out at the beautiful Ionian Sea. A strong wind was blowing and he wished it would sweep away these new responsibilities in his life. He felt he had woken up in the middle of a nightmare, even though he had not been to bed yet. Yesterday he was in Westport, in love with life and with Babs –now he felt he was incarcerated. It might not have been so bad if he had been sent back to his native Naples but he had been exiled to an island that was unfamiliar to him, apart from been there on holidays with his family when he was younger.

There was no tiredness in him. It had held off, despite the fact he had spent the whole night sitting by his Uncle Paolo's bed in a hospital in Taormina. His uncle recognised him straight away, which is more than could be said for Rosario. The poor man was unable to speak due to his swollen facial injuries and he appeared to be in a great deal of discomfort. What kind of monsters are these people? Rosario wondered.

While Rosario lamented for his life back home in Ireland, he had to concede that his uncle needed him more. He would stay for a few months to help him get back on his feet and then maybe together they could find a way to pacify the circulating vultures and generate a modest profit from the farm so that he could return home with confidence, knowing that his uncle would be alright and able to survive on his own.

Rosario walked back to the farm. Anxious faces on staff he barely remembered stared back at him, looking for news.

"He'll be in hospital for a couple of days," he told them. "He's badly bruised and has a broken rib but he'll be alright."

The senior staff advised Rosario of what needed prioritising. They could have stuck their hands in their pockets and taken the high road, paying little heed to Rosario, but those pockets were empty and, besides, they were loyal to Paolo who had never let them down before, so now was the time to return the favour.

When Paolo came home from hospital, he and Rosario sat on the front porch of their ancestral home.

The house was very old but well taken care of. The roof had a neat cap of orange terracotta tiles peeping over its powdery-pink external walls. The windows were flanked each side by mint-green shutters that were aesthetically pleasing to look at and matched by a beautiful mint-green double front door, nicely decorated with lace curtains on the glass pane each side. A pergola had been erected on the entrance porch and it was covered with exuberant rambling pink clematis. Rosario stared at the posts of the pergola and suddenly a memory came flooding back.

"I don't believe it. The tooth-marks are still in it," he said, laughing. "It's so chewed, I'm surprised the post is still standing. This was eaten by the fox, yes?"

"The tooth-marks are still there but the fox is long, long gone," Paolo said, smiling. "You remember the story then? About the time when we were kids and we found a baby fox cub in the fields? Your mother brought it home and kept in one of the enclosures out the back. She fed him every day with milk and stale bread and the odd egg if she could get away with it. We used to tie him at different locations around the farm but your mother loved to tie him here on the porch and rub his rich fur coat. Your grandmother used to be angry because he loved chewing the timber of the pergola."

"Pity he wasn't cute enough to chew through his rope," Rosario said, laughing.

"Ah, but he *was* cute. One day, I don't know how it happened, but the first chance he got to escape, he did, and we never saw him again."

"What did you expect? If you were tied up every day and got the chance to run away, wouldn't you?"

"Of course. But it just goes to show the primitive nature he still possessed, despite having been reared by humans for nearly three years. He had the instincts to know he was not one of us and wanted to be with his own kind."

Over a glass of Chianti wine they enjoyed the beautiful vista of the endless olive groves that ran ahead out of sight down to the sea under the cantankerous eye of Mount Etna but, as beautiful as that picture was, Rosario was concerned and anxious to find out the unfortunate chain of events that had recently beset his uncle. He asked Paolo how it all began.

Paolo straightened up in his chair. "Life had always been passive for us and indeed for our predecessors too. Well, apart from the historic ferocious conquests from outside attackers for sovereign control of the island of Sicily for thousands of years that left its people mostly aimless, poor and without leadership. But that was nothing compared to one unique threat created on our own soil that caused the most undue hardship and misery of all: the Costa Nostra – 'Our Thing' – more widely known as the Sicilian Mafia. Tired of the numerous battles to rule Sicily by colonies and empires, the indigenous people grew wary of everyone else trying to take over their homeland. It may have been born out of self-preservation that they felt they needed to build a militia of their own. However, over the years the power and the greed of such an organisation sadly outweighed the benefits of its origin and a brutal regime grew out of control. Your mother was right to get out when she did. The grip of the Costa Nostra was getting stronger and more widespread. Poverty was rife, there were no jobs, especially for young women on the island. Your mother had no choice but to leave. She was going to emigrate to America but she met your father on the mainland, in Naples, got married and then all you little ones came along. Several of your father's family members had emigrated to England and set up a few successful chip shops but these gradually became more and more plentiful so that's why they encouraged all of you to go to Ireland and start there, where chip shops were still relatively scarce – apart from some in Dublin. So to monopolise they moved to a place called Navan. But, as you know, your mother loved the sea and missed it so much. It was in her blood. She could not settle in the landlocked town. The craggy windswept west coast of Ireland appealed to her and she seemed so much happier when you all relocated there. The seaside town of Westport proved very popular for your chip shop – she used to say it must be something to do with the salty air."

"Or, it could be more to do with their huge appetite for potatoes!" said Rosario, laughing. "But, that aside, when did the Mafia start threatening you?"

"Our part of town was not largely influenced by them until one day, out of the blue, a team of construction workers arrived at the Merchant Hall opposite our shop in town. Do you remember it? It looked like a tower, built by the Romans. That beautiful building was older than time itself and it had been a central Mecca for traders, both domestic and beyond, for centuries. Well, I couldn't believe my eyes. They started to demolish it. Myself and some other shop owners ran out to protest and asked them what they were doing. They said it was being torn down and replaced with flats. 'How could this be?' we asked. Surely the authorities would not allow such a thing? But they said that was where the go-ahead came from. Over the next few days and after futile campaigning, it became clear what was going on. That was apparent when the people saw the *select builders* who were appearing on site. Oh my God, I wouldn't ask them to build a sand castle, never mind somewhere for people to live in. They were nothing more than a pack of vagabonds and known nuts-and-bolts of the Mafia. Needless to say, the building turned out to be an eyesore and nothing more than a pitiful tenement. The poor people who ended up dwelling there were probably tricked into paying for something not much better than what they left. But, boy, the Mafia were clever and the tenacity of their long-term planning would pay off. This new residence created a nesting ground of destitution. Which of course it was bound to do – that was the idea. They used it to take advantage of the tenants' perilous conditions and the effect it would have on the rest of us. That's when sinister events started happening to me. I was doing well, Rosario. Your mother was proud of me. We sold our produce from the farm in our lovely artisan shop in town. We had an abundance of yellow lemons, beautiful red tomatoes – fresh and sundried. Fresh olives and bottles of the finest olive oil. Hens' eggs and cheese. Herbs such as basil, rosemary and parsley. Our store was more fragrant than any perfumery. But it was the lemons in particular that were doing well at the time. Sicilian lemons had a good reputation and our orchard yields were healthy and high, resulting in a good demand for them on the mainland by all the hotels, bars and restaurants. I had a big supply of them all ready to go, waiting at the harbour for their deportation. A small thin boy came into the shop – well, he was small for his age. He told me there had been an accident down at the quays and my consignment of lemons had fallen into the water and floated away. I ran to the harbour as quickly as I could and all I could see was a shoal of yellow, bobbing away out in the evening tide. There was nothing I could do. Any effort to retrieve them wasn't worth it. The Harbour Master told me the ropes broke when they were lifting the cargo onto the boat and the wooden crates smashed to the ground sending lemons rolling in every direction, but mainly into the sea. Not long after that it was a supplier who came to all of the shop owners on the street that ran into trouble. Again, the thin boy appeared and told me the supplier's truck had overturned and all the goods he was carrying were destroyed because the oil and diesel had leaked all over them from the crashed vehicle. The next thing that happened was getting closer to home, well, at least to the shop in town. I was distraught one morning when I arrived to find my front window had been smashed and our lovely shop looted on the inside. Rosario, it bled my heart. It was such an awful sight to see. Glass everywhere, the place turned upside down. The money box was broken even though I had left no money in it. But surprisingly, on closer inspection, nothing had been taken at all. I couldn't understand it, except to realise that all these disasters were far too much of a coincidence. I started sweeping up the broken glass, the noise of which rang like an alarm and brought a few people to stand outside gaping in, including none other than the thin boy. 'So, I suppose you know what happened here too?' I asked him. He nodded. 'Yes, sir,' he said. 'I saw a few vandals hanging around your shop last night alright. They had a shifty look about them – they were up to no good.' I asked him his name. He told me it was Saverio Filosa. I asked him where he lived. 'Across the street, sir. That's why I can see everything that is going on.' I bet you do, I thought."

Paolo fell silent at this point, his thoughts in the past, his face twisted in grief. Rosario stayed silent too, reluctant to disturb his uncle.

Eventually, Paolo continued with his tragic tale . . .

Later that evening, after Paolo had put some order back on the shop and boarded up the window with the help of a few neighbours, it was time to go home. Exhausted, he had picked up his straw trilby hat and was about to open the door when he heard a knock.

"*We're closed!*" he shouted.

He'd never looked so closed in his life. What's the matter with people? he thought.

There was a second knock on the door, this time louder.

"*I said, we're closed!*"

"Mr. Lamberti, can you open the door? It's important," said a man's voice from the other side.

Paolo opened the door in some annoyance. He wasn't in the mood for any more nonsense.

"Good evening. Let me introduce myself. I'm Rocco Berrino." The man removed his expensive felt hat in a mannerly fashion.

Paolo didn't know the face but he certainly knew the name and now what he had been dreading was standing in front of him like the devil himself. He realised that this wretched man was responsible for all the unfortunate events that had happened to him, and what was to follow had the potential to forge a ball and chain around his neck indefinitely.

Rocco moved inside. Firstly, he empathised with Paolo for all the "bad luck" as he called it that he'd had and pointed out that they were acts of sabotage due to the lawless society their town had become and said he could not see the situation improving. In fact, he predicted, it was only going to get worse.

Paolo could read between the lines and knew exactly what Rocco was telling him.

"We need to protect ourselves," claimed Rocco.

He went on to describe an *"alliance"* he had formed of local people to conduct a discreet service of security and surveillance which had become very popular and said that many of the local businessmen had already signed up to it for a nominal fee.

Paolo was inwardly furious. How dare this thug come into his shop and start threatening him! He disguised his anger. "Thank you for your concern, Mr. Berrino, but I have looked after my own business since it opened and have never encountered any difficulties until recently – which is a bit of a coincidence, don't you think? I'm sure once these vandals realise there is nothing here for them they will move on and treat someone else unfairly for a while – isn't that how they get their kicks? There is no reason why we can't all work in harmony without any one person losing or gaining more than the other. Now, if you'll excuse me, I've had a very depressing day and I want to go home."

"Very well, I respect your optimistic view, Mr. Lamberti, but if I were you I would seriously consider your options. There is no guarantee these mishaps won't continue, or God forbid, something worse. Good evening."

Rocco donned his hat and left the shop.

Paolo stood behind the closed door with his arm stretched against it to steady himself and his beating heart. He had just stood firm with the local Mafia boss. He had heard about him, read about him, but had never encountered him before, personally. He could only imagine what demands he might foist upon him now like so many of his friends and neighbours had been subjected too. Deep down he knew it was only going to be a matter of time but he was defiant – determined that the hands of this clock were not going to move too quickly.

Over the next few days Paolo spoke to some of the other street traders who had already succumbed to this intimidation. They sadly advised him that he had no choice, that these people would make his life hell if he did not start paying them – ironically – to leave him alone.

After three weeks of peace, trouble flared up again. The tenement building across the narrow street went up in flames. While not directly the fault of the Mafia, it was they who had employed renegade tradesmen to build it in the first place and then discouraged the qualified personnel to check its safety standards and regulations. And here again they profited on the misfortune of its residents. Despite all the smoke damage and soot-cloaked walls, the people moved back in because they simply had nowhere else to go and faced an increase in their rents by their Mafia landlord under the guise of a 'Repair Fund'.

The dense black plumes of smoke had blown indiscriminately onto the facade of Paolo's shop. He hardly recognised it when he saw it. The black soot had covered the yellow exterior walls and the new window so thickly that people had started writing on it. One chilling message read: '*YOU'RE ONLY A SPARK AWAY!*'

He hauled out his ladder, climbed upon it and tried to wash down the walls to the best of his limited ability, using brushes and rags, but didn't achieve much success.

"I'm too old for this," he confided to his neighbour who was holding the ladder for him.

Then he looked behind him. The thin boy was sitting on the step at the front of his apartment block. There was something uneasy about that child that Paolo didn't like. He felt he had a vindictive nature and he half expected him to come over and pull the ladder out from under him.

But suddenly he had to contend with a much bigger bully. Rocco Berrino had arrived back. His black salubrious car came to a silent halt. He got out and mingled with the tenants of the apartments and shop owners who had gathered around him.

Paolo kept his back to him and continued on with his washing. When he came down to fetch another bucket of clean water, Rocco approached him.

"Mr. Lamberti, a lucky escape for you, no? Now you can understand what I was trying to tell you. Even indirect atrocities such as this can have dire consequences for you too. Look at your beautiful shop!" He pressed his hands together in a praying motion. "That's why I urge you to let us help you so this pestilence can be controlled."

Paolo spat at the ground. Then, pointing his finger at Rocco, he lost his temper.

"*This is all your doing!*"

A hush overcame the bystanders.

"Mr. Lamberti, please, is it my fault that the direction of the wind blew the smoke onto your shop?" Rocco laughed, making all sorts of gestures with his hands like a farcical conductor.

"No," said Paolo. "But it is your fault that building behind you went on fire due to the shoddy builders you hired to construct it after you criminally demolished the beautiful Merchant Hall that stood there before it. And are the people not suffering enough with the unlawful inhumane living conditions you put them in and now you have the audacity to raise the rent on them? When all they have done is moved out of the mud and into the gutter. Look at that poor child sitting there on the steps of his home because the air is cleaner outside than it is inside. You should be ashamed of yourself. *You disgust me!*"

Paolo picked up his bucket and threw the dirty contents to the ground near Rocco, splashing his suede shoes on purpose. He walked into his shop and bolted the door behind him.

The people on the street looked down at the ground. They secretly marvelled at Paolo's courage for sticking up to Rocco but feared the price he was going to pay for it.

Paolo worked on late that evening despite being tired from all his cleaning earlier that day, but his mind was unsettled, remembering the confrontation he had with Rocco. Maybe he should have kept his mouth shut. The reality was that he knew he would have to oblige him sooner or later and start an unspecified open-ended indebtedness to him. But at least he had tried to impress upon him that he was not going to be a walk-over and was going to concede defeat with a bit of dignity and try and give a voice to those who were silenced.

As expected, the dreaded knock came on the front door. He stood still in the middle of the floor behind the bread-stand not making a sound, thinking about what to do. He wouldn't answer. He would go to the police tomorrow and hope there was still one honest official among them who could help him.

What Paolo had not thought to do though was lock the back door and suddenly Rocco and two henchmen were circling around him like a shiver of sharks. They beat him savagely.

———— ❈ ————

Rosario tried to absorb this terrible story and he admired his uncle greatly for standing up to the regime. He shook his head in disbelief, thinking how lucky his uncle was to be alive.

"If you cross them again, Uncle, you know they might kill you."

"I know. I requested the police to come to see me in the hospital. Unsurprisingly, it was clear the two officers who did were in the back pocket of the Mafia. They advised me to start paying up for my own sake. Can you believe that!"

"So, have you approached them yet?"

"Yes, I've sent word."

"How?"

"The thin boy."

"But, Uncle, now that I am here maybe we can find a way to isolate them and mind our own business."

"Ah, you have no idea what you are dealing with. Now, your presence will be another red flag to them. I'm an old man now, Rosario. You have your whole life ahead of you. I'd never forgive myself if something happened to you. It's the only way to protect all of us, *huh*, protecting ourselves from the threat that is meant to defend us. No, we'll focus on the farm and turn it around. You can give it the necessary attention now that I am unable to anymore. With my brains and your brawn, we'll be soaring as high as an eagle before you know it."

They raised their glasses and made a toast.

"*Saluti – Ad Maiora Semper!" Always towards greater things!*

Whatever about the eagle, Rosario couldn't stop thinking about the elephant in the room, as he sat back quietly on the porch and watched the beautiful Sicilian sunset descend against the backdrop of the blue horizon.

Chapter 10

New beginnings

A crowing rooster woke Rosario up at the crack of dawn so he went for a wander around the farm before anyone else was about. It was so quiet and peaceful. Walking out through the yard, he met his alarm clock and his flock of scruffy old hens which he immediately knew would have to be replaced. A bee rested on the wooden handle of the gate he was about to open which made him think of honey, a natural accompaniment to the lemons. But Paolo felt that the citrus income was about to slump due to all the competition on the island so Rosario tried to brainstorm other sources of revenue. Paolo kept a few sheep for their own brand of cheese and, having sampled it with much tasty satisfaction the night before, Rosario couldn't see why they shouldn't try and produce more of it.

After a magical walk through the fragrant lemon orchard still shrouded in a morning mist, he came to the boundary of the olive groves. The trees still produced oil but overall looked in a sorrowful state and this is where he noted they needed to make the biggest investment of all.

Like Alice in Wonderland he meandered aimlessly through the groves until he had arrived by the edge of the sea. Two beautiful mute swans bobbed on the waves, rifling for food in the water underneath them.

He stared at them for a while, jealous of their eternal unity, suddenly reminded of Babs. But there was work to be done and no shortage of it.

Rosario was on a mission, inspired by all beauty around him vying to be adored. The natural environment which surrounded him was like paradise. It was suddenly difficult to imagine retuning to a job where he spent all day staring into a vat of boiling oil.

After a few weeks Paolo had made a good recovery and took a trip into town to see how Rosario was managing at running the shop. He sat at the side of the glass cheese cabinet and chatted with his customers who were delighted to see him again.

Suddenly, the thin boy stretched his neck around the corner of the front door.

"*You! Get out! Shoo!*" shouted Paolo like he was banishing a stray cat.

Saverio quickly tried to retreat but instantly was shoved back in, under the big looming shadow of Rocco Berrino, who nabbed Saverio by the scruff of the neck and kept him close to him.

"Ah, Paolo, my old friend! I am so glad to see that you have made a swift recovery. You made the right decision. I will help stabilize your recent turbulence. And who's this?" he asked, nodding in Rosario's direction. "I had heard that you had taken on an assistant." He tapped Saverio on the head, grateful for the tip-off.

"He's not an assistant. He's my nephew, Rosario. He has sacrificed everything, to do for me what I cannot do for myself as a result of a senseless and unjustified assault," replied Paolo, still full of nerve.

Of course, Rocco was not going to publically incriminate himself in front of the customers and changed the subject by delivering the real reason he came to see Paolo.

"Welcome to our little community, Rosario. I am surprised that your uncle's business appears to be prosperous enough to take on another employee. Despite everything that has happened, business must be booming! I know that you are a charitable man, Paolo, so I'm sure you'll find another position for Saverio here, or 'Savi' as we call him."

"Are you crazy? My nephew is not even drawing a wage here yet because of all the expenses I've had to fork out for the criminal damage in 'our little community'. How can you ask me such a thing?"

"I'm not asking you. I'm telling you." At that Rocco shoved the boy in the back, causing him to land hard on his knees before Paolo. "You were the one on the soapbox campaigning on behalf of these disadvantaged people and how unfairly they were being treated. We all heard you, remember? Now here's a chance for you to save one of your wretched souls and, if you don't reserve your opinions this time, maybe this won't be the first of many vulnerable souls who come crashing through your door. I will leave you to get on with it and hopefully I will not have to call upon you personally again."

So Rosario got to witness at first-hand how deep this cut had the potential to go. It was like watching one hyena taking a bite of their prey one way, and another in the opposite way, when eventually after all the pulling and dragging there was nothing left only the skeleton of dignity. Damned if you do and damned if you don't.

Over the years, when it came to Rocco and his life-sucking demands, Rosario learnt to keep his head down, hoping that his subliminal presence might make him invisible. His unobtrusive compliance was successful to a point, until Rocco came calling again for an increase in his dues. It always happened just when they had a good run or a good surplus in their profits, but how did he know? Saverio. The boy had been planted in their shop as a watchdog and spy, not just on them, but on their customers and suppliers too who frequented the business. Surely the boy knew he was nothing more than a pawn being groomed to participate in a vicious circle, destined to a life of subordination. Defenceless because of his age and hapless youth, for now he could not bite that hand that fed him and his family.

The farm's activities were constantly monitored as were those of their neighbours. All their harvests and their economic gains were scrutinised by the Mafia who demanded a cut of a livelihood that was already borderline surviving. Savi was sent out to Paolo's farm to help out, as they called it, from time to time and despite his ominous presence the difference in him was unquestionable. When the shackles of his allegiance were not called upon, he was as carefree as any other boy and loved the freedom and genuine camaraderie of the farm. Paolo always wondered if his soul could be redeemed before it was too late.

Rosario tried to teach him to speak English and encouraged him to travel the world, hoping the boy would open his eyes and see that he could escape his entrapment and live a better life. He never did and Rosario pitied him for not trying anything else other than what he knew.

Despite all the shadows, there was sunshine too. Rosario was running the farm like a natural. He had so much to learn from his uncle and, while Paolo was eager to pass down his knowledge, Rosario suspected there must be new technologies and innovative ideas to modernise an old homestead such as this. In fact, he felt the whole region was a step back in time, which sometimes he loved and sometimes he hated. He tried to talk to the owners of the neighbouring farms and, while they were friendly at the outset, any forthcoming information was limited as nobody wanted to share the secrets of their success.

As well as getting to know the workings of the farm, Rosario learned so much about himself during the first few years in Sicily. The absence of this challenge had he stayed in Ireland would have meant that he would never have realised what he was capable of and, for that alone, he was grateful to be here. He hadn't known what a progressive aptitude he possessed towards enterprise and development.

He enrolled in a college in Palermo and completed a part-time course in horticulture. Absorbing all this new information, he relished it. It gave him a steely determination to incorporate a natural and organic approach to readapting the farm to its full potential. He paid particular attention to the rejuvenation of the olive groves to maximise their potential. He visited other olive farms on the mainland and through a subsided grant he got the opportunity to travel to Spain and see how they managed their olives there. It was on this trip he met Caterina, another like-minded olive enthusiast, whom he went on to marry and have two daughters with, Bianca and Sofia.

On the whole, Rosario thrust himself into a long-term plan to get the olives up and running. Through on-going educational schemes he became a horticulture representative as appointed by the Department of Agriculture and followed its guidelines, making his own farm a case study. Diligently he documented in his diaries how the littlest change could make a significant difference resulting in a noted series of successes and regressions.

1940: After years of neglect the trees have grown wayward. We have pruned them all, having to precariously use a ladder and handsaw to encourage the branches to grow out rather than up so we can reach the olives. The weeds were extremely overgrown so we dug them all out. This will allow

the rain to access the roots quicker and not have to compete with any other plants.

1942: The removal of the weeds has been a disaster. It has caused acute soil erosion at the base of the trees. Our comrades at high altitude who did the same as me have reported significance root damage due to exposure to frost and snow as a result of not having any overgrowth as a protective layer.

1944: We have had great success this year. I pioneered a project to encourage all farmers to use mulch around their trees as the protective layer instead of weeds competing for water. We used the clippings from when we were pruning the trees this year. Imagine the answer was literally under our feet!

1946: A disappointing harvest. While the yield was average, the oil content was poor. We shouldn't have watered the trees so near harvest. Lesson learned. N.B. This needs more research.

1948: A terrible year. The olive fly has decimated our harvest and that of our neighbours. The flies laid their eggs and the grub burrowed its way into the olives. Disaster. Currently corresponding with the Department to see how we can eradicate them.

1950: I'm so frustrated. The queues at the Frantoio where we bring the olives to be crushed are negatively affecting the freshness of the olives going to press, reducing their liquid return. This will have to be addressed by the Department.

1952: Labour issues this year. The unusually hot weather made it very challenging to pick the olives during the glaring heat. The 'tourist pickers' didn't approach us this year, preferring to go to the beach instead. The heat didn't help the preservation of what we had picked either.

1954: After a collaborative effort this year we were victorious against our enemy – the olive fly. Government guidelines encouraged all the farmers to terminate the fly swarms together, as individual farms would not be capable of preventing widespread damage. Using makeshift containers that we hung on every tree, we filled them with a little drop of wine or vinegar then sealed them before boring some small holes in the top of the vessel allowing the flies to get in – but they didn't have the brain power to get out which was also influenced of course by them getting drunk or drowning in the liquid inside. All the farms participated so this remedy was a regional success, keeping these pests to a minimum.

1956: While the yield was again average this year we were commended for the quality of the oil. I had campaigned for the last couple years for changes to be adapted at the Frantoio. Instead of having to wait in a queue for all our olives to be pressed at the same time we are now able to bring in a load daily. This ensures the olives are pressed within 24 hours of being picked. Another thing I tried, even though my workers were not enthusiastic about it, was picking the berries at night. There is no doubt the cooler temperatures preserved their aromatic flavour.

1958: A very good year for us. We added some phosphate to the soil earlier in the year and this appeared to have provided much needed nutrients that perhaps our rich but very old volcanic soil is beginning to lack. Note: send soil samples to Department for analysing.

1959: A disappointing yield and quality of oil this year despite doing everything right.

1960: Another very bad harvest which is hard to fathom because we had brought the groves on so much over the last few years.

1961: Heartbreak. Something sinister is going on within all the groves in the region. There is something unidentified ailing the trees. Several Department officials have come to see us and have taken away numerous samples to be examined. I fear the outcome. The trees are sick.

———— ❁ ————

This disaster in 1961 was very unsettling for all the farmers on the island. Every day one of them came to see Rosario, because he was the local representative of the Olive Farmers Federation. It was he who pioneered all the changes in the past and, while some were a failure, a significant amount were successful, and for a bunch of farmers who were originally very discreet about their respective olive productions, they had openly participated in Rosario's recommendations and reaped the benefits as a result. By now they looked up to him as an advisor and an expert so unsurprisingly they came to him for answers and they wanted them quickly.

One farmer, Marco Carbone, was particularly anxious. His farm was the most popular with the tourists who came to visit the olive groves because, for one thing, it was the oldest on the island and, more importantly, it had the oldest tree growing on it. The tree was fondly named 'Mirabella' meaning 'wondrous beauty', from the Italian and Latin *bella* meaning 'beautiful' and the Latin *mirablis* meaning 'marvellous', and that she was. At nearly one thousand years old, she still stood proudly and serenely like a queen. She had outlived droughts, floods, erupting volcanoes, wars and of course centuries of mankind. She was a shrine in the region whereby visitors described standing in her presence as a humbling experience. She had a calming effect on people when they reflected on all the nonsense going on in their lives, compared to the tumultuous history she had overcome and yet her strong branches did not weaken with all the burdens she must have endured. She was always there like a grounded dignified Northern Star.

Unfortunately, this serenity was not currently enchanting her owner, Marco. He was irate with Rosario for the demise of the groves and genuinely upset that Mirabella, despite her spectacular longevity, was too becoming a victim of this mystery illness. "Man is no match for Mother Nature," he said, and he told Rosario that he should have left well enough alone. He accused Rosario, saying all his meddling with the groves over the years had evidently proved that all this change was not a good thing. He questioned the fact that Mirabella survived nearly a millennium without any horticultural modifications to her existence, so why was it only now that she and several of the other older trees were suddenly being affected?

Rosario could not answer that but tried to reassure Marco that he would try and get to the bottom of it as soon as he could and instigate another programme to reinstate the growth. Marco told him to shove his programme up his 'sedere'.

When the results came from the laboratory they were inconclusive. In other words, they could not determine for certain the cause of the deterioration and therefore the Department of Agriculture officials were not very vocal about advising a corrective course of action. The Department eventually issued a devastating statement, estimating a total decay of all the groves within a two to three-year period. One harsh and unpopular plan was to completely destroy any severely infected farms to stop the spread of the contagion.

Sadly, Marco Carbone's farm was singled out as being significantly contaminated and so a Government Order was issued that his groves were to be destroyed. Marco immediately objected, pointing out that his farm had been in his family for generations, he owned the oldest tree on the island, how this farm was his livelihood and all the other valid reasons why he should fight to save it. But deep down Marco knew he had already lost. Every morning for the last year he felt like he was walking through a graveyard when he entered his groves. All the trees were getting stiller and greyer, like a cloud of ash had fallen upon them. An eerie quietness was present, the wildlife had left. The branches snapped like matches, all the succulence drained from their veins. Collectively the trees stood together like statutes from an evil spell some sorcerer had cast upon them. A malevolent atmosphere that gave Marco a chill hung in the air. He knew it was time to say to goodbye to Mirabella. With a lump in his throat he placed his hand on her trunk, asked God to spare her and take him instead. He wished for a will or a power so he could draw the sickness out of her and replace it with a new vitality. It's hard to watch something that is dying. It diminishes your own purpose in life because it leaves you helpless to provide any kind of benefit to theirs. Marco wept.

"Goodbye my old friend, Mirabella the Wonderful. I know God has a spot for you in his Garden of Paradise and it's no more than you deserve. I'm sorry I could not save you."

The day the bulldozers arrived Marco could only watch from his porch at a distance. The destructive crunching sound of timber breaking was like hearing their cry of torment. He couldn't watch their slaughter. He went inside and closed his door.

Rosario's farm and that of some of his neighbours were spared the cull. Their groves were left alone as they were not as tainted as some of the others. However, another Government Order prohibited them from carrying out any kind of activity until they figured out what to do. As a result of such dire consequences, Rosario felt like his left hand had been cut off and the farm was at a huge loss economically. He was devastated. He would have to find a new enterprise to support his family and others.

He needed time to think so he was drawn to where and what had become his favourite spot. This was down at the sea coast beyond the olive groves where he would frequently nestle in between the craggy rocks for shelter. The swans had got used to him. The cob hissed at him in the beginning but Rosario hissed back so one could say they kind of developed a mutual respect for one another. He missed them in the winter when they migrated. He wasn't sure where they went but he presumed they flew inland for kinder climatic and nutritious conditions. Watching them idle the day away, he envied their gentle oblivious existence compared to the trials and tribulations of his own. He sighed and wondered if he would ever catch a break. He was acutely aware again of the sacrifices he had made by coming back to Italy in the first place. Blood, sweat and tears were the physical stains he had borne, while hopelessness, frustration and doubt were the emotions he overcame to turn the olive groves successfully into his greatest achievement to date. And now all his hard work lay in ruins. Guilt burrowed into his mind now. Perhaps all his new farming methods were a step too far and a pirate's plank on which all the other farmers had trod to the demise of their respective businesses. He should have left well enough alone. These negative thoughts were going around and around on a loop in his head. He knew he would need a significant amount of capital to reinstate the olives but without their turnover in profit he had no idea how he was going to raise it. Both his daughters had aspirations to go to college and he had strived to make sure that was going to happen, until now. How would he support his family from now on?

Floundering in his current predicament, he wondered who was more merciless, the Mafia or God? For a brief moment he thought about making one set of footprints into the sea. However, his colourless kaleidoscope of pessimism ceased when he heard a commotion being made by the swans. One of them appeared to be swimming with difficulty but did manage to wrangle itself free by the time Rosario had walked to the water's edge. There he saw a floating garment which had encumbered his feathered friend. Using a piece of driftwood he scooped it out of the water so it would cause no more danger. But during this effort he noticed several other belongings strewn on the upper side of the beach. He quickened his step with a foreboding feeling gripping him. Scanning the sand he could see children's shoes, shirts, empty bags and water containers, but no people, only an overturned ramshackle boat barely waterproof due to its wooden structure which was perished and warped. A human tragedy of unknown loss of life, young and old, of those who were trying to migrate to Italy to make a new start in life but sadly not even making it to the shore. No matter how bad things are, there is always someone worse off than you, and that is the sentiment Rosario took away. Straight away he alerted the authorities about the washed-up boat and when he went home he gave his family a big hug, vowing to find a way to start over with a stoic resilience not to fail.

Part 3

Chapter 11

Ne'er cast a clout

After leaving Lucca's house, Caitlín and Tully called into the Westport Garda Station to see if they could find out more information about Donnacha 'Finn' Finnerty. They were introduced to a senior garda who was privy to a few unfortunate events that Finn experienced throughout his young adult life and said he could only imagine what a negative impact they would have made to it. There were a few things on record, he said, but those were brief notes which raised more questions than they answered.

They listened attentively as he did his best to retrieve as much relevant information as he could from decades-old memories.

Young Donnacha Finnerty's alarm clock rang at half past seven. It was still too early to get up for school which he had a severe dislike for. This fourteen-year-old boy's passion was athletic and not academic. He lived for playing soccer. Every morning after breakfast and before lessons would be spent kicking a ball around in the small concrete back yard of his home. It drove his single mother, Joan, crazy, as the incessant kicking was knocking the pebble dash off the wall of the house. She bit her tongue, though, because she was relieved that his energy was going into this rather than something else more troublesome that a teenager might be influenced to do. Besides, she had been told for a long time now that he had a "natural talent". She wasn't sure where that talent would lead but for now he was happy and that was enough for her.

There was no doubt about Finn being a gifted player but this brought its own set of problems. Firstly, soccer was seen as a 'foreign' sport and some of his few friends and peers expected his first love to be Gaelic football not soccer, so they took ample opportunities to remind him of this and not in a nice way. Secondly, his obvious talent and skills were envied which caused him to be treated as a bit of an outsider by the other schoolboys. But his infatuation with the game protected him from their pettiness. He devoured every out-of-date football magazine his uncle managed to procure and send to him from Liverpool. The letters in these publications from fans expressed the same adoration that he felt for the game and he covered his wall with the pull-out posters. His uncle had emigrated to England and on his eagerly anticipated annual visit home to Ireland, he fascinated Finn by telling him about all the games he had gone to see in Anfield to watch Liverpool play there. On one lucky occasion he gave Finn a Liverpool Jersey and when Finn put it on he felt like he had been canonised.

"Someday, when you're older, I'll take you there to watch them play," his uncle used to say.

"Someday, when *you're* older I'll take you there to watch *me* play," Finn replied resolutely.

So Finn's future had the potential to be in the back of the net until the following autumn when a new boy from Italy enrolled at the secondary school Finn was attending. His name was Rosario Fratelli and he instantly received a lot of attention. His longer hair, brown eyes and brown skin labelled him as a 'foreigner' straight away. The boys were playing it cool in their attitude towards him until they noticed that all the girls were very *flaithiúil* with their '*Céad míle fáilte*'. However, both adolescent genders drifted away from Rosario because his lack of English created a barrier. The Fratellis had spent six months in England with family there for the purpose of learning as much English as possible before moving to Ireland, but despite the best efforts of Rosario the short attention span of his fellow scholars did not afford him the patience to express himself and so their new curiosity abated after a while and they lost interest in him. Fortunately, it's not love that makes the world go around – it's sport – and it wasn't long before the universal language of soccer brought the two outsiders, Finn and Rosario, together. Finn was already playing for Westport Cove, a new up and coming junior team and it wasn't long before Rosario joined them too. Rosario already loved the English football clubs. At least his six months in England were useful for something and he returned that homage into an exchange of information, telling Finn all about the wonderful clubs they had in their 'Serie A' National football league in Italy. Of course his allegiance was to his native Napoli, but like a lot of closet fans he had a penchant for Associazione Calcio Milano, or as the boys knew it AC Milan, obviously.

For hours they would knock the ball about between them. Rosario's family in Italy would send him newspaper clippings and football magazines in the post and he would translate the articles into English as best he could for Finn.

Apart from their interest in football, the two of them bonded very well together. They would frequently go swimming, to the cinema and the odd school dance where Rosario was popular with the girls which did not go unnoticed by Finn, who was teased by the other boys and asked if he had a crush on Rosario too. But there was no doubt that he was certainly influenced by Rosario, especially when Finn started to grow his red hair longer and wear cooler-patterned shirts. The breezy and devil-may-care attitude of Rosario neither flattered nor addled him. The only thing that rattled Rosario's pedestal as far as Finn was concerned was his soccer skills. Rosario was the better player. Natural flair and a steadfast composure on the ball made him a pleasure to watch. It unsettled Finn but, in fairness, Rosario had been playing soccer since he was a small child in a country where the game was revered and an expected given that every boy there would aspire to be a great player, just like the youngsters in Ireland would for the GAA.

For the most part, Finn and Rosario played in harmony and often relied on each other's strengths, producing nice set pieces of play between them and set-ups for targets on goal. All was cordial in the Stadium of Paradise until a talent scout turned up.

The coach announced one evening to the team that this individual would be present for the upcoming match between themselves and Ballina. A murmur of excitement whizzed through the dressing room. The scout was a representative from the Irish Football Association on a mission to recruit a national youth team from all over the country. While all the boys dreamt of winning a coveted spot, truthfully and rightfully they knew that spot should go to Finn. His commitment and obvious growing talent made him the deserving choice. But, historical performance was not going to be considered and the fear of Rosario outshining him on the day was a real threat. In the run-up to this precious game, they both handled it as best they could, by not talking about it at all.

On the evening of the match Finn was nervous as hell but Rosario adopted his '*Que sera, sera*' approach. Finn played out of his skin, ran himself to death. He showed good tackling and execution on the ball and even had a shot on goal but sadly it was just about saved by the keeper. Rosario scored. It was a class goal right in the back of the net. Then he effortlessly got another. After the match, the talent scout and the coach spoke at length. The tension in the dressing room was inward with no one speaking. The players had already forgotten about the match they just won – their eyes were on the other prize. Finally, the talent scout left and the coach announced that "the exciting young Italian player" had caught the eye of their visitor who was recommending Rosario for selection. Immediately he received a cheer from the other boys and several claps on the back but genuinely they were sad for Finn and spent more time commiserating with him than with Glory Boy. Despite that, Rosario hung back and waited for him outside the clubhouse. He sympathised with Finn because he knew how much this chance had meant to him. Finn could feel the lump in his throat rising so he just nodded and walked away.

That night Finn cried into his pillow. No boy in the County of Mayo had wanted that spot more.

Avoiding Rosario over the weekend gave Finn a lot of time to think about how he was going to deal with this awkward situation, cumulating in his most mature decision to date. Truthfully, he did not want to end his attachment to his best friend, his only friend. Who else would he talk to about football and share that passion with? That loss was a sacrifice he didn't want to make. Besides, the coach had told his mother that he would get the talent scout back again next year and how this disappointment should not have any effect on Finn's determination to make it as a professional player if that was what he really wanted. So the first fracture of the fellowship was repaired but lay dormant until Rosario's commitment to the coveted selection became questionable.

The training took place in Athlone at monthly intervals. However, to Finn's astonishment, Rosario had not attended some of them, flippantly admitting he had to work in the chipper instead. A shameful waste, Finn thought to himself. He would have walked to Athlone if he had to. He couldn't let it go so he wrote a letter to the Irish Football Association requesting that they put him on standby in the event of a player not being able to make the commitment as required. They never wrote back.

In the meantime life encouraged the two boys to continue growing up together and participating in all the good things it had to offer. Apart from the soccer, Rosario loved swimming in the sea and he had just discovered a new place to swim that he was eager to show to Finn. It was still only the month of May and Finn's mother cautioned him not to go near the water until after Pentecost or the Whit weekend in June when the water was blessed and safe to enter. Finn couldn't be bothered listening to all the superstitions and headed out the door, throwing a stripy bath towel over his shoulder.

"*Ne'er cast a clout till May be out!*" his mother shouted after him, laughing.

Finn had been swimming in the sea a few times already that year. It was cold but invigorating. He wasn't sure exactly where this new location was but Rosario's directions were to go along the walkway on the top of the cliff right down to the stone wall with the stile. Eventually, he spotted Rosario's bike abandoned in the long grass. He could see a lifebuoy attached to a stake in the ground further on so he knew he must be near. This path was frequented by hill walkers and people walking their dogs. He looked out to sea. The tide was in and the calm conditions made for very still waters. The scenery was very tranquil and picturesque. The only activity he could see was the dark head of his friend bobbing in the water nearby. After a quick shy glance around he stripped down to his cotton shorts and made for the edge of the cliff, cursing the thistly grass underneath his bare feet.

"*Ow!*" Rosario shouted suddenly from the water.

"Over here, Ros!" responded Finn, waving his arms. "What's wrong?"

"Leg cramp! Help me! I can't stay afloat," Rosario shouted, thrashing about in the water.

Finn panicked. He didn't know where exactly to get in but didn't want his friend to drown. Looking down at the deep water which must have been twenty feet below, he took a deep breath and braced himself to jump.

"*No! Don't jump in there!*" cried Rosario.

But it was too late. Finn had jumped off the edge with his knees up.

He landed straight onto a jagged rock that was hidden by the tide and its smooth water. He resurfaced and roared out in pain. "*Help!*" he managed to yelp before the water swallowed him up again.

A fourteen-year-old boy and his sister walking on the cliff top, accompanied by their young collie dog, had heard the shouting and witnessed Finn's jump of horror to save Rosario.

The young boy knew he was the only one near enough to make any sort of attempt to rescue them.

"*Quick, go and get help!*" he instructed his sister.

The little girl took off like a bolt with their dog barking by her side, the dog enjoying the excitement but oblivious as to what was causing it.

The boy grabbed the lifebuoy and threw it to Rosario who was then able to stabilise himself in the water. Then the boy ran down a little sandy slipway, on to the staggered flagged rocks and slid smoothly into the water – where Finn should have got in. He swam over to Finn who surfaced and sank again, his pain incapacitating him. The boy took a deep breath and ducked underneath, successfully pulling Finn back up with him. But he struggled to keep both of them afloat. Finn's weight was a lot to bear.

Then, thankfully, above him he could hear the voice of a man yelling *"Hang on, lad, we'll get the pair of ye out!"*

After kicking off their boots two men plunged into the water. One of them immediately went to Rosario's aid while the other took Finn from the boy who was shaking now both from the cold water and his weakened muscles which had just about tolerated his gallant rescue. Despite this, he was one of the last to get out of the water, his good nature compelling him to help carry Finn out and carefully back across the rocks.

Finn was alive. The ambulance had been called from the nearest house when the little girl sounded the alarm but, in the meantime, all they could do was turn him over to make sure there was no water in his lungs. They winced when they saw a lengthy open wound on his back which was bleeding.

The little girl returned with her mother and a bundle of towels and woollen blankets. They put one over him and used another to comfort his head. Rosario knelt beside him, crying. Between the sobs he tried to talk to Finn but the injured boy continued to drift in and out of consciousness. Two ambulances arrived as close to the scene as they could. Finn was taken away by one while the medical staff in the other examined everyone else. The young rescuer was highly praised for saving Finn and, apart from feeling very cold, he had come away unscathed except for a cut on the bottom of his foot from the sharp rocks.

The shock of what happened to Finn made Rosario forget about his leg cramp altogether.

After an initial examination in the Accident and Emergency Department at Castlebar General Hospital, Finn was diagnosed with having a spinal injury, the extent of which could not be determined accurately there. So, out of grave concern, he was immediately transferred to a hospital in Dublin. Following a very anxious wait for his mother over the next twenty-four hours, the doctors explained that Finn's collision with the submerged rock had damaged his spine and it would take more than one operation to repair and realign it. Even with that challenge, there was no guarantee the operations would be successful. For now, Finn was unable to walk.

With all the to-ing and fro-ing to the hospital, the question of what had actually caused the accident was disregarded at this stage. Rosario and his family constantly asked after Finn's condition and said that they would pray for him. The first operation was more of an exploration to see exactly what the surgeons were dealing with and gave them an opportunity to repair what they could there and then. The second operation was more challenging and disappointingly only confirmed there was much they couldn't repair despite their best efforts. Six weeks later and a more perilous operation left them with no choice but to put steel plates and rods into his spine to compensate for what they could not salvage at all. All of these physically demanding operations meant that Finn spent five months in hospital.

On one occasion Rosario and his mother travelled to Dublin especially to visit him. Finn's mother, Joan, was already in the ward. Ordinarily this should have been a cordial exchange of good wishes but this was the first time the two families had come face to face since Finn's horrific fall.

Finn and Rosario were too shy to speak freely in front of their mothers but it didn't take long for the two women to start liberating the tension. After setting down the compulsory bottle of Lucozade and the pound of grapes, Mrs. Fratelli began by asking Finn how he was doing. Finn's mother tried to bite her tongue but couldn't help getting her teeth stuck into Mrs. Fratelli's benevolent platitudes.

"Well, you have the neck of a giraffe coming up here asking him how he is when it was your spawn that put him here in the first place!"

"*Excuse me?* How can you greet us like that? We travelled all this way specially to see the boy," replied a shocked Mrs. Fratelli, who was not expecting this hostile reaction. "Rosario misses him terribly and we have prayed every single day for him."

"To relieve your guilt, I presume, considering what he did to him!"

"Please, Joan, it was an accident!"

"Accidents don't happen – they're caused. And I am looking at that cause right now," she replied, glaring at Rosario.

"Why don't we leave the boys to chat and you and I go for a cup of tea?"

"No, thank you."

"I beg you, Joan, can we talk about this?" pleaded Mrs. Fratelli.

"Sure," said Joan, sarcastically. "What do you want to discuss first? Operation one? Two? Or three? The steel inserts in his back or the fact that he will never walk properly again?"

"Maybe it was too soon to visit. I can see this is still a very difficult time for you. We will continue to think of you both in our prayers."

"I don't want your pity or your prayers –*you're not welcome here.*"

"Come on, Rosario, we'll go," said a scorned Mrs. Fratelli quietly.

Finn felt sorry for Mrs. Fratelli and Rosario. He wasn't sure they deserved that. But his mother didn't deserve any of this either. If it wasn't for Rosario and his stupid leg cramp this would never have happened. He could see that his mother was not coping and this made him feel guilty. She was exhausted from all the worry, the travelling up and down, and taking all this time off work to be with him was causing problems with her employer. Despite everything, she tried to hold down her job so she could attempt to pay some of the mounting hospital bills.

When all was said and done, his mother kissed him goodbye and told him she would see him again in a few days. So once again he was alone and isolated with only misery for company. Rosario had left a football magazine on the bed. Finn didn't know whether to love it or loathe it. After flicking through a few pages he slammed it shut and started to cry, knowing he would never play football again. At this stage, he was getting physiotherapy every day, learning how to put one foot in front of the other. Every step he took was clumsy, painful and slow. He couldn't stop thinking about the metal plates in his back. They made him feel like Frankenstein or the Elephant Man and he imagined everyone staring at him for the rest of his life at the sight of his calamitous walk of shame.

"Recovery from an illness can be a very solitary experience," so the hospital's chaplain told him. "No one else can do it for you. You sit or lie there and spend every waking minute of every day literally waiting to get better. And every day you wake up, immediately hoping for a dramatic improvement, but the change can be so gradual you disappointingly don't even notice it and that's why one can feel a great sense of hopelessness at a time like this."

The hospital's chaplain also tried to give Finn some peace of mind by telling him that life was a journey and we all had our crosses to bear and how Jesus would be there to help him along the way. Which was all very well, but a recurring obstacle to Finn's mental recovery was that everyone was telling him what to do: the doctors, the physiotherapists, his mother, his relatives. No one was asking him what *he* wanted to do, or talked about what happened to him and how to deal with it, until one day inadvertently the hospital porter came into his room and picked a book up off the floor.

"Hiya, Finn. Let me get that for you," he said kindly, putting the book on the bedside table.

"I don't want it."

"Somebody's in a bad mood, again," the man said, sitting on the side of the bed. "Do you want to talk about it?"

"No."

"I come in here every day and I still don't know what happened to you. Must have been something bad," he coaxed.

"I dived onto a rock that was submerged under water," Finn replied, hoping his no-nonsense reply might shut the man up and make him leave him alone.

"*Ouch!* Did you not know the rock was there?"

"No. But my friend did."

"Oh boy, some friend he was. Did he not warn you?"

"He was already in the water, seizing up with a leg cramp."

"Jeepers, so what happened?"

"I jumped in straight away to help him but at the wrong place."

"Oh dear, so it wasn't really his fault then?"

Finn flashed him a look of annoyance.

"Well, your friend didn't deliberately want you to crash onto the rock, did he?"

"I suppose not," Finn responded quietly.

"Sounds like an accident to me. Finn, you're going to have to let that blame go. People don't live long enough to correct all the mistakes and regrets they have harboured in their lives. You're going to have to accept what has happened to you. And, yes, this may feel like a sign of weakness or defeat, not to mention feeling like shite. The mental scar will be painful at first but it will disappear when the next one comes along. And then the next one, and then the one after that. Life's a bitch. But depending on how you deal with this blow could make the rest of them more tolerable. This is what people don't tell you: the reality is that no one really cares at the end of the day. Sure people will say 'Poor Finn, isn't it awful what happened to him', but two minutes later they will have forgotten all about you because they're too busy thinking about what they are going to have for their dinner. Move on with ignorance, if you ask me. Seriously, what's the alternative? I hear you have steel rods in your back – now imagine them around your heart. You'll have to toughen up, sonny boy. You have a long, lonely and hard journey ahead of you and you won't survive it unless you start fighting back."

Then the hospital porter got up, swished his brush briefly around the floor and left the ward.

Finn sat there, blinking. Whatever happened to me, what the hell happened to him? he wondered. His advice was harsh but for the first time in a long time Finn felt stronger about his situation, rather than the usual sucker-punch of despair. He began to realise he was going to have to accept this huge change to his life if he were to have any chance to enjoy anything again.

One weekday evening, Finn was sitting out of the bed at his hospital window. The physiotherapist had made him do a lot of walking and repetitive exercises earlier that day and now he was feeling sore and tired. Out of the blue, Rosario popped his head around the curtain of the bed.

Finn smiled even though he wasn't sure if he should show it.

"Finn, I can't stay for long, someone is outside waiting for me. My family don't know I'm here. I just wanted to say...well, I'm sorry and I didn't get the chance to say that to you the last time because your mother was so... well, you know what I mean." He was trying not to offend him. "I never meant any of this to happen to you, of course I didn't. I miss you, bro, I don't have anyone to talk football with."

"I don't want to talk about football anymore, it's over for me."

"Right," responded Rosario, not knowing what to say now. "Well, we'll find something new to talk about when you come home. How about that?"

"I don't know when I'm coming home."

"Would it be alright if I come and visit you when you do?"

"Maybe."

Rosario left, not knowing if his honest effort to reconcile had made things better or worse.

Finn was left wondering if he should have done more to encourage him, or less to protect himself.

While Finn's mother was open with him about all the aspects of his operations and their limitations, there was one truth she was not prepared to tell him yet. The young boy who came to Finn's rescue was hailed a hero. His name was Rory Costigan. The incident was reported on the national news and ran in all the newspapers. But sadly his valiant rescue was overshadowed a few days later by his sudden and tragic death. Despite being treated at the scene of the accident for the cut on the bottom of his foot, the wound became infected. He became very unwell and was admitted to hospital. He was diagnosed with septicaemia and despite the best efforts of the doctors, his body went into septic shock and he died.

When Finn eventually returned home, his mother sat him down that evening and told him what happened to Rory. She knew he was too vulnerable to hear it insensitively from someone else. Earnestly she told him that under no circumstances was he to blame himself for the tragic death of the boy.

"It was an infection that killed him, there was nothing anyone could have done for him, and don't let anyone else tell you otherwise."

She told him to go for a lie-down following his long journey home while she cooked his favourite dinner: lamb cutlets, fried onions and mashed potatoes.

Finn sat up in his bed and thought about what he had just been told. He was shocked but, as his mother had just said, it was not his fault that Rory had died. This led him to rethink his own stalemate relationship with Rosario. He realised now he could not blame Rosario for what happened to him either.

Chapter 12

A tortured soul

Over the course of the next few weeks and months Finn and Rosario rebuilt their friendship. It was slow and awkward at first. Finn was still physically dealing with the trauma he had endured. It took him a long time to trust Rosario again because he had to stop looking at him as a reminder of what happened to him and start seeing him as someone he could share things with again. It was never going to be the same as before but, considering everything that had happened, their friendship was in a reasonably trustworthy place once more.

One evening Mrs. Fratelli called upon Finn and his mother. There was no denying that she felt remorse for Finn's accident and the holy woman volunteered to pay for Rosario and Finn to go on a Christian retreat together. Finn's mother, Joan, who was sceptical about this trip, demanded to know the devil in the detail. It was led by a Brother Anthony in a monastery in Enniscorthy, County Wexford. The boys would spend a week there and their stay would centre upon prayer and meditation. They also would be requested to work for a few hours daily, picking strawberries in the fields that were cultivated by the monks, which in turn meant that the monks only charged a nominal fee for the retreat which Mrs. Fratelli was happy to meet. She gave a brochure to Joan detailing the practicalities and ethos of it. Joan became a little bit uncomfortable when she quoted aloud *"An opportunity for wayward young men to steady themselves"* and immediately voiced her concerns, pointing out that their two sons might return more corrupted than when they left. They decided to let the boys choose for themselves but, just as Joan feared, they were keen on the idea. She knew well it was not the decades of the rosary that were tempting them. It was a week away in a different part of the country and a chance to see and do something new. She didn't want to diminish the curiosity of their youth and begrudgingly agreed to let Finn go.

Buses, trains and a bumpy trailer-ride later they arrived at the old stone monastery called St. Fiachre's which they and six other boys were immediately told all about during their induction in the communal hall. Their waning interest must have become evident on their faces and Brother Anthony knew it had been overpowered by the hunger that had manifested over their long journeys. He told the boys to follow him into the dining room. A broad wooden table in the centre of the room was partially hidden by four rather portly monks standing in front of it.

"An empty sack cannot stand," Brother Anthony announced before nodding to his colleagues who receded from the table to reveal the biggest white enamel basin of freshly picked strawberries the boys had ever seen. Their intoxicating sweet smell and vibrant red colour put the new arrivals under a spell. The generous display was accompanied by several bowls of

fresh cream, whipped to perfection by the monks. The boys salivated in a trance.

"Well, what are you waiting for? Get stuck in!" encouraged Brother Anthony coyly.

Of course experience had taught Brother Anthony that liberty to gorge on something so tantalising without cost or limit was the one way to ensure that this new crop of pickers would not resort to thieving and feasting in the fields when they were sent there to help with the harvesting.

"*A full stack cannot bend*," he declared mischievously when the groans of their over-indulgence began to sound. "Time for bed now. We'll have an early start in the morning with prayers before breakfast and then we'll spend a few hours in the fresh air, working in the fields. Late afternoon we will practise some meditation and then you will have some leisure time after supper before lights out."

And this was the repeated itinerary for the week. The second night the boys were still a bit wary of one another and stuck within their own circles formed by recognition or locality. On night three they all became more courageous and mingled with one another, inquisitive to find out each other's stories. Joan's suspicions were realised as most of the boys revealed troublesome backgrounds with minor offences already perpetrated. Without any sensitivity, they asked Finn straight out what happened to him. Finn humorously told them that he had an accident at sea – just like the *Titanic*, he didn't see the iceberg either. When Rosario was asked why he was there, he simply replied he was here to support his friend.

"Are ye boyfriend and boyfriend?" asked one Smart Aleck.

"No, but we're '*fuck you*' and '*fuck off*'!" replied Rosario in a no-nonsense tone.

The boys probed no further.

Night four involved the boys playing cards, rings, darts and various other board games and jigsaws available. Night five was a very pleasant balmy autumnal evening and the boys arranged a football match which the monks were delighted to be asked to join in. Finn watched from the side-lines and, even though it was Gaelic, Rosario's handy footwork earned him a goal with his team winning. Night six brought a sense of boredom within the group. They felt they had exhausted the enjoyment of the basic entertainment as provided by the monks on site. A convincing pitch from one of the 'not backward in going forward' boys granted them permission to walk into Enniscorthy town as "It would be such a shame to come this far and not see it," as he pitifully put it. With a curfew to be obeyed for half past nine the boys scurried into town where they completely disregarded all the cultural attractions Brother Anthony had recommended them to see.

While feasting on a sugar rush of minerals, sweets and crisps the boys sat on the wall of the bridge, watching the world go by. Finn and Rosario were happy to sit in contentment but a sense of devilment was beginning to stir in some of the others. A game of truth or dare was suggested and on commencement the initial challenges were more humorous than bold, so after that wore off they decided to raise the bar.

An ambulance was parked on the other side of the street and appeared to have been left unattended for some time now. One of the more brass-necked boys dared the others to break into the vehicle and steal some medicines, bragging that he would sell them when he went back to Dublin.

This made Finn uncomfortable. "That's a stupid idea – as if," he whispered to Rosario.

"I don't think he's looking for something for a broken toenail, Finn. He'll be after painkillers, penicillin, antiseptic, scissors, bandages – he could make a few bob for sure."

"That's no good to us,"

"Oh, lighten up, Finn, it's only a bit of fun."

So with one chap on the lookout, the evidently more experienced opportunist jimmied open the back door of the ambulance and hopped inside. A minute later he returned with an armful of medical necessities. His partner in crime did the same and another then until their watchman suddenly yelled at them to scram because the ambulance drivers were coming back. All the boys fled like a swarm, apart from Finn who did his best to keep up. Wolf cries howled from the boys when they got a safe distance away. They were exhilarated by their brazen undertaking and the sheer thrill of getting away with it.

Back at the monastery, not being able to bring their haul into their sleeping quarters for fear of being sprung by the monks, they quickly signalled to each other to hide it all in one of the old unused picking containers in a barn. They were still laughing when they went to bed.

The following morning the bravado of the Crime Crusaders had come down a gear. It was their last day so they lazily gathered around the outdoor table for their rustic lunch – a hearty serving of Scotch broth and wholemeal brown bread. The subdued atmosphere was suddenly interrupted by one of the boys who dashed around the corner and informed everyone that the gardaí had arrived and how he had overheard them saying that they would start by checking the sheds. They knew now they hadn't got away with last night's robbery as lightly as they thought.

The ringleader told everyone to 'abort the mission' and throw everything over the big wall in the walled garden, saying the gardaí wouldn't find it there.

"Yeah, but the monks will," said one concerned boy.

"But we'll be well gone by then, sunshine," winked the mercenary.

They all ran into the barn through its back door and frantically started shoving as much of the medicines into their trousers, jackets and arms as they could before fleeing to the walled garden and firing it all over.

Finn was reluctant but didn't want his new friends to get caught so he helped them.

"Hurry up, lads, they're coming!"

Finn and Rosario were the last to leave the barn. Finn's efforts were in vain. Despite doing his best, his getaway was not going to be lively as the rest.

"Rosario, you have to help me!" he pleaded.

"I can't, Finn. If I get a criminal record I'll never be able to play professional football."

Finn looked at him in astonishment. "But you hardly play anymore anyway."

"I'm sorry, man, you're on your own. You'll have to fend for yourself." And with that Rosario scurried off.

Fend for himself was exactly what Finn had to do when he faced six weeks in a Juvenile Detention Centre in Sligo, following his arrest when he was caught red-handed in the barn at the monastery with the stolen goods. No was else was caught or admitted to the crime. Because it was Finn's first offence, he could have got off with a warning but the seriousness of the crime of robbing a State-owned vehicle used in accidents and emergencies assisting vulnerable people could not go unpunished.

His mother was incensed, knowing that her son was not solely responsible for robbing the ambulance but yet he took the fall for everyone else.

Mrs. Fratelli had to lie down for a while.

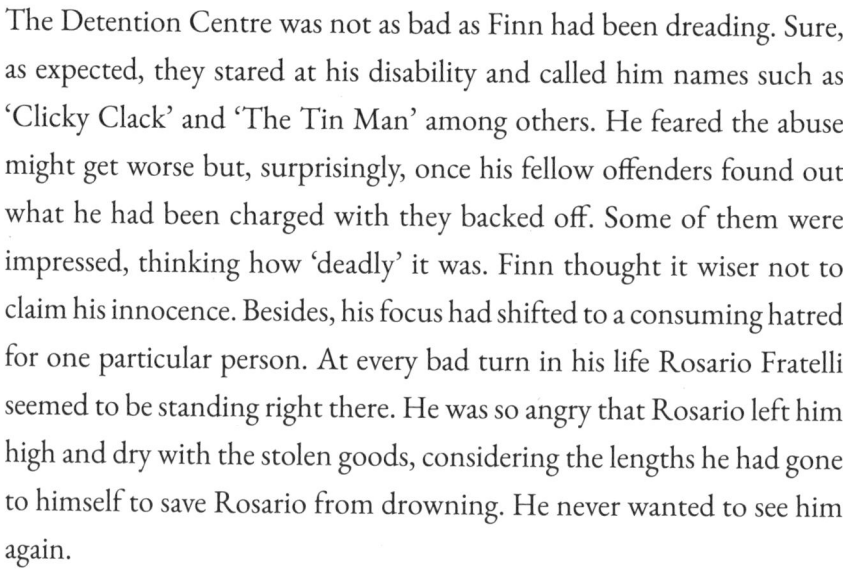

The Detention Centre was not as bad as Finn had been dreading. Sure, as expected, they stared at his disability and called him names such as 'Clicky Clack' and 'The Tin Man' among others. He feared the abuse might get worse but, surprisingly, once his fellow offenders found out what he had been charged with they backed off. Some of them were impressed, thinking how 'deadly' it was. Finn thought it wiser not to claim his innocence. Besides, his focus had shifted to a consuming hatred for one particular person. At every bad turn in his life Rosario Fratelli seemed to be standing right there. He was so angry that Rosario left him high and dry with the stolen goods, considering the lengths he had gone to himself to save Rosario from drowning. He never wanted to see him again.

Like most young men at the time, Finn emigrated to England when he finished school and he was excited as the next to see what prosperity it would bring him. All his healthy counterparts headed off to various parts of Britain, getting copious amounts of work in construction and trades. Unfortunately, Finn's disability limited his options greatly. "Neither use nor ornament – what good is a man who cannot lift anything?" one un-potential employer told him. But he remembered his mother telling him *"Brains are always stronger than brawn,"* and with that in his heart he persevered.

One night, in a pub in Ruislip in London, he heard how a bookie was looking to hire someone. On the day of the interview he was amazed by the amount of men going for the same job. But his knowledge of sports, especially soccer, not only in England but also on the Continent, gave him a competitive edge over his fellow candidates and he was offered the job there and then.

Bookies were still illegal therefore his 'bartender' wages were dubiously put through the books to his advantage, by stating less than he was actually earning. Over the years he worked in the same job and saved a decent amount of money. Sadly his hoarding was not by choice. His physical disability shamed him into a reclusive existence, not allowing him to enjoy the social aspects of life. Children often mimicked his walk and whispered behind his back, while the adults said nothing, but the look of pity on their faces said enough.

He frequently bought his dinner from one of the many takeaway outlets on the street where he worked. It never ceased to amaze him how popular a practice this had become and one that ordinary people could afford. This view was shared by a colleague he worked with. Both of them were delighted with the ease of being able to have your dinner cooked and ready to eat straight away. The fish and chip shops were proving to be the favourite but they were coming under pressure from the Chinese and Indian takeaways too.

"Who would have thought that the humble spud could taste so good?" his workmate cooed as he shoved a large chip into his mouth one day at lunchtime. "Do you have many takeaways where you're from in Ireland, Finn?"

"Yes, we have one," he replied, not wanting to be drawn on that touchy subject.

"Just one? In the whole place? Isn't that a seaside town you come from? God, there's a golden opportunity for someone to share a slice of that lucrative fish pie!"

"Oh yeah, a 'Golden Wonder'," said Finn with a laugh.

"Actually, I think it is the Maris Piper variety that makes the best chips. Nice and floury."

"Maybe you should open one then? You seem to know a lot about them," said Finn with a smile.

"Nah, that's not for me but there is a new one opening up on Victoria Street. You should pop in and sweet-talk the tradesmen to find out how much they cost to set up. You've always said that you would love to return to Ireland. It's just an idea, mate."

Finn dismissed his friend's business plan and went back to work but, later that night, when he was sitting alone in his one-bed ground-floor flat, he started thinking about it. Hand on heart, he, like every other emigrant, would love to return home but the job prospects were as scarce as hen's teeth and his disability meant that he would even have fewer possibilities. Then he began to imagine the advantages of his friend's idea, like being his own boss, choosing his own hours and setting up something that currently was not overdone so there was potential for it to be successful. But his conflicted conscience would not settle for long enough to ask himself if he was considering this for the great opportunity it could be, or if it would be an act of revenge on the Fratellis.

One way to put a halt to his intentions, good or bad, was to find out how much it would cost to open such a business. The next day, after finding a bit of courage, he went to the new fish and chip shop that was under construction and quizzed the tradesmen about the fit-out.

Encouraged by their estimates, his savings and the sale proceeds of the house he had been bequeathed from his late mother, Joan, he felt that he was in a financially strong enough position to pull this off.

Over the next few months Finn kept changing his mind about committing to this new venture until an estate agent from Westport rang and told him about a property that had come on the market favourable to his budget. The premises was small but described as being located in a prime business location which Finn came to realise was situated on the main street, right opposite Fratellis'.

He convinced himself that if several of these similar shops could survive on the one street in Ruislip, then surely there was enough room for one more in the whole town of Westport? The only thorn in his tyre was the owners of the actual competition. Rosario's presence in his life had brought nothing but destruction on more than one occasion. But, the more he thought about it, the more he asked himself why should he once again miss out and watch the Fratellis reap the rewards? Besides, Rosario was living in Italy now so there was nothing to stop him.

Within six months, Finn had packed up and moved home. His new shop was proudly fitted out and opened. He called it 'Rory's Chipper' in memory of the young boy who saved his life.

Caitlín and Tully didn't go for their paddle but they did get two 99's and went for a walk down by the quays instead. They sat on the wall in the sun and relaxed. Lost in their thoughts, they both absorbed what they had heard. Tully was the first to break the silence.

"After hearing all of that I feel sorry now for Finn. He didn't have an easy life."

"I suppose he's selling up to enjoy what he can with the rest of it," said Caitlín.

"But there must be so much anger there," Tully said between licks.

"And so much hatred," agreed Caitlín, trying to eat hers before it melted.

"So a definite suspect then," affirmed Tully.

"No doubt about it. We'll have to bring him in for questioning."

"Do you want to organise it this evening?"

"No. I said I'd call up to visit Pa and Elsie Leonard. I haven't seen them in ages. Then I have to wash my camogie kit and I also have to telephone Wesley Pollard about doing another rally-training session."

"Are you still going ahead with that?"

"Like a bat out of hell. What are you getting up to this evening?"

"I'm not doing a tap and I'm looking forward to every second of it. You're like a Tasmanian Devil."

She jumped off the wall. "And you're like tumbleweed, Seán. Now tumble yourself off that wall and come on."

PART 4

Chapter 13

Visiting

Babs Wheatley filled the tin watering can in the kitchen sink and went outside to water the flowers in her window boxes. The current dry spell had caused her lovely red geraniums to droop and she hadn't tended to them over the past few days because she had been afraid to show her face outside the door since the humiliation of her arrest. Nate's anger had abated, albeit it was mainly due to his customers reassuring him that Babs was a good woman. It disappointed her greatly though that it took his customers to convince him rather than the character of his own wife, whom he had known for so long. But she knew the prickly part was not really due to her arrest – it was the yet another publicised entanglement she had shared with another man that had hurt him the most. But at least they were on speaking terms again and this encouraged her to think that things could return to normal.

"Hello, Mrs. Wheatley, how are you?" came a friendly voice over the wall behind her.

"Good, Garda Kennedy," replied Babs, turning round. "But, please, call me Babs. Mrs. Wheatley makes me feel old."

"Only if you agree to call me Caitlín. If you ever want to talk, Babs, just give me a shout. I mean that as a friend not just as a garda. Sorry, I'll have to keep going. I'm off up to the Leonards for a long overdue visit."

"No problem at all, Caitlín – give Pa and Elsie my regards."

The sound of children laughing made Caitlín smile as she knocked on Leonards' front door. Pa opened it and invited her inside to the rowdy atmosphere.

Calm ensued as she made her way into the kitchen where a warm welcome greeted her.

"Caitlín!" called out Elsie, Pa's wife. "Sit down there. Will you have a cup of tea?"

"I'd love one. And I'm going to take further advantage of you, Elsie. You wouldn't be able to fix my jacket? I've ripped it here under the arm." Caitlín didn't divulge that this occurred from tackling Cassie's robber to the ground. Elsie was known for being a competent seamstress and had many calling on her to do various alterations and repairs.

"I don't think you have ever met our daughter, Grace," said Elsie.

One of two daughters of Pa and Elsie, Grace had the misfortunate of having cancer but was putting up a brave fight for the past few years. Her frequent admittance to hospital meant her children, Molly aged ten and Tadgh aged thirteen, spent a lot of time with their grandparents, Pa and Elsie. The children's father ran out on them when the going got tough – right at the onset of Grace's diagnosis. Grace's sister, Claire, was married with three children and lived in Dublin so the duty of care fell on Pa and Elsie to look after them when necessary. Caitlín had never met Grace before and was taken aback at the poor woman's frail demeanour, despite her best efforts to appear in good spirits.

After their acknowledgment of one another, Caitlín turned her attention to the two youngsters who she was familiar with and out of her bag she produced a marble cake, two bottles of Fanta and two straws. The children's eyes glazed over and Caitlín knew herself what a treat they were in for.

"Will you have a cup of tea?" Elsie asked a second time.

"I've already given one her one, missus," said a patient Pa.

Over the course of this visit they discussed all the local trivia including the murder, which Caitlín could not really comment on, so she changed the subject by telling them about the upcoming car race. Pa piffled at the nuisance of it all but the children were enthusiastic about it, especially Tadgh, who made it clear he definitely wanted to see it. They could hardly believe that Caitlín herself would be driving a racing car and wished her well.

All that was left to talk about then was the bigger show coming to Ireland: the four-day visit of President Kennedy on the 26th of June. Caitlín also got to reveal that she would be working for the Galway leg of his visit, how she and five hundred and ninety-nine gardaí were being collated to provide tight security while he was in the city and how they had to attend a two-day training event in Galway which was commencing the next morning.

Elsie was much more animated about that than the car race. She was a huge admirer of the President. At this stage the kids tuned out, not wanting to listen to her gush about him again. Instead they watched *Jackpot* on the television, a popular quiz show presented by Gay Byrne.

"Did you know John F. Kennedy was the second of nine children and came from a place called Brookline in Boston?" Elsie enthused. "He graduated from Harvard University before fighting in the Second World War. He was a lieutenant with the Navy in the South Pacific. The ship he was on was sunk by the Japanese and he bravely saved the lives of many of his comrades during that terrorising ordeal. He was made a War Hero for that. When he returned home he went into politics and represented the State of Massachusetts as a Democrat. Despite being the 35th President of the United States, he is the youngest and the first Catholic President. He hasn't had it easy – he's been in the news nearly every day because of that Cuban Missile Crisis last year and the Cold War with the Soviet Union."

"Thank God they sorted that out," exhaled Pa with a sigh of relief. "It was a bit close for comfort."

"I notice that you never mention his beautiful wife, Mam. Or the fact that he's married," teased Grace.

"I don't think an old one like me would be good competition against the lovely Jackie."

"I'm stuck with you so for another while," mocked Pa.

"The debonair Mrs. Kennedy is not travelling with her husband on this trip so don't count your chickens yet, dear. Will you have a cup of tea, Caitlín?" Elsie asked again.

"No, thanks," replied Caitlín, confused as she had just finished one.

Pa winked at her and then she realised it was Elsie's dementia that was making her forget her previous offers of hospitality.

"I apologise for the brief visit, folks, but I better go – early start tomorrow!"

"We might see you on the television during the visit," said Elsie.

"No fear of you seeing me at all, Elsie, I'll probably be behind a wall or down a side street doing the boring stuff."

Chapter 14

Road Trip

Tully was already outside his house the next morning waiting for Caitlín who eventually tore into his drive in her Morris Minor. Taking advantage of the sunshine she had rolled down convertible roof.

"You're late," he reprimanded her as he got in.

"Well, good morning to you too! I'm sorry. It was late when I went to bed, I was faffing around the house. I went to visit the Leonards, as I told you. The kids were there with their mother, Grace."

"How did that go?"

"Fine. Of course they were looking for the scoop on the murder. Why don't people understand that we cannot discuss that kind of thing?"

"Friendship can blur the boundaries, you need to remember that. Did you know Sergeant Lamb and Detective Cullen are bringing Donnacha Finnerty in for questioning today?"

"What?" asked Caitlín, disappointed they were doing it without her.

"Relax – I'm sure they're well capable of interviewing him in your absence. To be honest, he's such cool customer I don't think they'll get anymore out of him than we did. How's Grace Leonard anyway?"

"I don't know. I mean, I never met her before but she didn't look very well to me."

"Poor woman. That's sad." He paused and then tried to lighten the mood. "Maybe we'll have a bit of craic at these JFK training days."

"Two days of it, with an overnight at the barracks, sounds like a lot of fuss over one man."

"Well, he is the President of the United States of America," said Tully, as he foostered with the dial on the radio, trying to find a suitable station. "Oh, I like this song! 'From a Jack to a King'!"

When the music faded out, the radio presenter came back in, announcing the local gig guide for the weekend, which caught Caitlín's attention.

"That guy sounds exactly like our local bad boy, Waxy Carolan."

"It *is* Waxy!" confirmed Tully.

"How on earth did he get on the radio?" she asked incredulously. "He's not at all legit."

"Neither is the radio station," smirked Tully.

"What are you on about?"

"It's a pirate radio station – Calico Jack FM. Have you been living under a rock? Everyone around the place knows about it and has been tuning in. He's really good at it."

"Where is he broadcasting from? It can't be from his house."

"Knowing sly dog Waxy, probably Mars. It won't be anywhere obvious, that's for sure."

"I can't believe we have to stay over in an army Barracks," said Caitlín, returning to the thorn in her side. "The President gets a five-star suite in a hotel and all I get is a mothball bed in a dorm."

"I thought you were dying to do this?"

"I am. Truth is, I just don't like being away from the murder investigation."

"Sergeant Lamb and Detective Cullen will manage fine. They have a lot more mileage under their belts than we have – they know what they're at."

"But we'll be away again for the actual JFK visit."

"Well, you better hurry up and solve the murder then," retorted Tully, getting a bit fed up with her. "What did you pack for your stay over?" he asked, trying to change the subject. "I bought my own hot water bottle, hairnet and face cream."

"You're so full of bull. By the looks of your tiny little bag, I'd say all you packed was a clean pair of jocks and your toothbrush. Oh shit! I forgot mine – my toothbrush. Stop looking at me like that."

"I'm not sitting beside your smelly breath for the next two days. The Secret Service will arrest you for emanating poisonous gases."

Caitlín laughed off Tully's joke but inside she was frustrated that she was not going to be there when Sergeant Lamb and Detective Cullen were bringing Donnacha Finnerty in for questioning.

During the journey Caitlín became pensive about her job and recalled how the previous murder inquiry had lit a baptismal fire to her fledging career. She had received a motivation from it that lasted a long time but, unfortunately, that was beginning to extinguish. Within her first week of being assigned to Ballantur Garda Station she had cracked the case, resulting in much praise and recommendation from her peers. Personally, her ambition grew and she dreamt of becoming a detective but she knew that was only a fantasy. Women were only allowed to join An Garda Síochána in 1958, so other than presently being a poster girl for recruitment her long-term goal did not appear to be very promising. One day the world is your oyster, the next day it's nothing more than a damp squid. Mundane duties such as renewing gun licences, liquor licences, setting up road blocks, inspecting tax and insurance on vehicles were de rigueur, while trying to convince drivers that seat belts really were a good idea and that five or six kids all piled into the back seat was not. These duties were not giving her the buzz she craved. When she did get a call out to something, frequently her exuberance was frustrated by the '*But you're a woman*' response or '*We were expecting a Garda*' because to some a woman was not a real garda. It was even sadder when she got this response from other women. She missed being on the same shift with her colleague, Tully. The pair of them had got on great but all the laughing and the messing had not had gone unnoticed by Sergeant Lamb, who put an end to them having the craic by assigning them to opposite rosters. Now they were like ships in the night. Occasionally they would meet at the change-over but, with one hardly awake yet and the other trying not to fall asleep, their interactions were passive. She couldn't make up her mind whether she fancied him or not. His boyish appearance came from the gap between his two front teeth, suggesting a sense of immaturity and devilment about him which was further enhanced by wild brown curly hair that always tried to spring out from under his cap. But with her no longer seeing him that much anymore, that notion was going nowhere.

But for now, this new murder case was going to occupy all of Caitlín's time and, while she would never say it out loud, it had brought a reprieve from the amount of paperwork she was currently buried in for the upcoming rally. There was no doubt she was thrilled to be taking part, she just wished she didn't have to do the donkey work for it. The amount of forms and permits to be done in advance with the race organisers, town committee, Mayo County Council and the Emergency Services was staggering. It all related to crowd control, rights of way, temporary road closures, animal safety, diversions and any other head-frying element one could think of.

Tully picked up on her discontentment on the rare chats they had of late. He pointed out to her that solving a murder case when she started here was an exception and not the norm. The day-to-day duties of a garda in a small rural town were never going to be of any great significance and the chances of another murder happening here were between zilch and zero. In the nicest way possible, he was telling Caitlín to get over it.

But now there *was* another murder and she nearly cursed the President of America for his bad timing.

While the two gardaí were lost in their thoughts on the road to Galway, Babs Wheatley was debating to herself whether or not she should go and see her old friend Madge. The two of them were best friends growing up and Madge's mother had arranged for both of them to live with her sister, Aggie, in Westport town so they could attend the secondary school there. But Babs was still puzzled why Madge never contacted her since she had moved home from England. Secondly, Rosario had said that he wrote to her after his return to Italy all those years ago. Why hadn't Madge passed the letter on to her after she had moved to Castlebar to start work as a waitress? And thirdly and more importantly, what did she and Rosario talk about when he called to see her? She would have been one of the last people to see him alive. Would there be some clues, anything at all to get the gardaí off her back? Awkward and all as it might be, she would have to grasp the nettle.

Chapter 15

Training Camp

The scene at the barracks in Galway City was lively. Multiple members of An Garda Síochána were circulating in all directions. At the '*Induction Wing*' all the gardaí were required to sign in and confirm their member number. Then they were given a handbook of instructions, their dormitory location and their meal times before receiving a complimentary cup of tea in the catering building. When a sharp bell rang out all the participants were directed to a large assembly hall where Caitlín and Tully sat beside one another.

"*Right, a bit of hush, ladies and gentlemen, please!*" was announced by someone from a line of officials that had gathered at the top of the room, some in uniform, others in civilian suits. One man heavily laden in medals tapped the microphone and addressed the room.

"My name is Chief Inspector Russell Brogan and I am heading up the contribution of security measures from the resources of An Garda Síochána. To my right is a team of security men from the Secret Service at Pennsylvania Avenue, Washington, better known as the White House. There have been approximately three thousand gardaí deployed around the country for the several locations the President will visit. In particular, there are six hundred gardaí being drafted in to provide security for the Galway visit. One hundred of you are to receive training which you will get today and tomorrow. This afternoon we will focus on the schedule, routes, town maps, plans etc. Tomorrow, we will partake in a physical walkabout of the route. Please pay attention. This is a unique opportunity in your professional careers to be part of something very special. It is the first time a serving President of the United States of America has come to Ireland and arguably the most famous of any dignitary to come to our shores. So, as per your handbooks, he arrives in Ireland on Wednesday June 26th, flying into Dublin. On Thursday he is travelling to County Wexford – Danganstown to be exact, to visit his ancestral home. On Friday he is scheduled to go to Cork City and will return to Dublin that evening. Saturday, June 29th is D-Day for us here in Galway. You will see on page four that he is due to arrive here by helicopter at quarter past eleven, landing at the sportsground on College Road. This will be a giddy touchdown for over three hundred schoolchildren draped in the colours of our national flag, to make an impressive visual from the air. After a bit of social gathering there he will travel by an open-top car in an entourage flanked by our Garda motorbikes to Eyre Square. We will need strong crowd control on this route – we don't know how many for sure but we are expecting thousands of people to turn out. Our dignitaries will make a speech, then he will make a speech, and after that he will be presented with the Freedom of the City. Various gifts will be presented to him, such as some Irish linen, a handwoven woollen blanket, those kinds of indigenous things. Then he will be entertained by a performance of Irish dancing and singing and we will allow for more back-clapping and handshaking before he returns to his car and the cavalcade drives slowly down Shop Street, Quay Street, over Wolfe Tone Bridge and so on until he gets out to Salthill where his helicopter will be waiting for him to fly him to

Limerick to visit his other ancestral home. You will now all be asked to choose an area of deployment to be tasked with and we have no doubt that you will be absolutely committed to ensure you use it to your best ability. Thank you for your co-operation and my team and I look forward to working with you all."

Caitlín and Tully exhaled at the thought of the responsibility ahead of them.

"Give me a murder enquiry any day!" joked Tully as they walked over to the 'Task Hall'.

The Task Hall was a hive of activity with members of the Force buzzing from outlet to outlet, signing up to their speciality of choice. Tully immediately joined the queue for the motorcycle conclave.

Caitlín felt she was burning enough rubber with her rally driving so had no interest in taking on a bike. Keeping an open mind, she stopped at the armoury depot. Scanning her eyes across the handguns and rifles her gaze was interrupted by the American security guard manning the stand.

"Anything here take your fancy, sweetheart?" he asked, with smile of amusement on his face.

Sweetheart, how patronising, thought Caitlin to herself. "I'm not sure."

"Have you ever handled one of these before?"

"Not since my training in college," she replied, becoming conscious of her own accent for no particular reason.

"No offence, darling, but we'd prefer if you were more familiar with these arms on a regular basis."

"But An Garda Síochána is an unarmed force, sir."

"I understand, but we are looking for someone with a . . . what's the word I'm looking for?"

"A knob," she replied sarcastically. "Don't worry, I'll take my knockers away to find a more suitable gender-related duty."

She turned around and walked towards the motorcycle station, bumping into a giddy Tully.

"*Whoo-whoo!* I got the last bike," he gloated. "Where did you go?"

"I got blind-sighted by the guns but apparently I don't have the balls to use one."

"You're running out of options. There's only 'Crowd Control' and 'Observation' left."

"Spare me, I've done so much planning for crowd control for the rally I'm sick of it already so I guess all that's left is observation. Oh look, they're handing out binoculars! Well, if things go belly-up, at least I could stare someone to death."

"It's only for one day – you'll survive. There's a few of us going for a pint this evening –I'll see you later."

Like most of the other banghardaí present, Caitlín signed up for Observation.

"Do you wear glasses, Garda? How's your eyesight?" asked the security guard.

"I could see a fly on the top of Croagh Patrick."

The US official didn't know what that meant but took it as a statement of affirmation so he passed her a pair of binoculars.

"You're not going to the races. Do you understand what I am saying? You will have to be vigilant at all times, primarily looking for snipers on rooftops and behind windows. You also will monitor the unfolding scene as a whole but, as well as the present status, keep your eyes on where he is going next and equally important watch the activity in the location he is leaving behind. You and the other 'Obs' will have your own specialised tuition in the morning and we will go through all of this with you in detail."

When all the gardaí present appeared to have been tasked, the Chief Inspector addressed the attendees again.

"You can take yourselves off now to the catering hall where supper will be served. You have free time after that and, if you do venture into town, please take note that the curfew is ten o'clock sharp. You are not here to party. If you are not back by then the front gate will be locked. You will not be permitted entry. In fact, you will be asked to go home."

Chapter 16

Lessons in love

Babs walked apprehensively up the stone path to the house where she and Madge used to live in Westport town. The two-storey terraced house was not as pretty as it used to be but at least it had the appearance of it still being occupied. After knocking the brass lion's head on the blue front door, Madge opened it. The colour ran from her face when she saw Babs standing there.

"We need to talk," Babs said firmly and stuck her foot in the door. She was not taking no for an answer.

While Madge clattered around the kitchen making the obligatory pot of tea, Babs snooped around the dark old sitting room. There were three picture frames standing on the walnut cabinet with sliding glass doors. The first one held a photo of Madge and her husband, Ron, on their wedding day. The second was of Madge, Ron and a little boy and the third was one of the little boy all grown up. The rattling of the tea tray made Babs jump back over to the settee and sit rigidly.

After some silence and sipping, Babs cut to chase.

"I don't know where to begin, Madge. When did you come back to Ireland and why didn't you get in touch with me? I don't understand—we used to be great friends."

"I was too busy looking after my crazy mother," Madge replied, not making eye contact with Babs.

"My sister only told me lately that she died – it was her heart?"

"Yeah, an undiagnosed broken one. She never got over my brother's death." Madge got up and sat on the oblong window seat and looked out. "She was fine for years. But time doesn't heal, that's rubbish. You just find a way to push the pain away but for Mam it just boomeranged right back. She always became depressed around his birthdays and Christmas. A neighbour from home wrote to me telling me that they were worried about her. So I came back and luckily I convinced Aunt Aggie to let her live here with her – you know, so Aggie could keep an eye on her. Unfortunately, Aggie, who was the eldest of them, had her own physical medical conditions and, looking back on it now, I shouldn't have done that. It was too much to ask of her. The responsibility took its toll on her health and she died. So Mam was on her own again. Then the neighbours here started writing to me. They were worried about Mam's mental health. They said she had been seen up the town in the middle of the day in her nightdress. She went to bed another night, leaving the front door wide open. Myself, Ron and my son Andrew came home for a fortnight but it soon became clear that it was going to take a lot longer than that to sort her out. Ron went back to London – he had to. He had a good job in the bank and Andrew, bless him, decided to stay here with myself and Mam. He enrolled in St. Pat's Secondary School but the scumbags up there bullied him over his accent. My heart broke when he couldn't take it anymore and he returned home to live with his father in London. That was six months ago. In the meantime, I tried every avenue I could, to get Mam the proper help she needed. *Ha!* This backwater hasn't changed much, that's for sure. Basically my crazy mother wasn't crazy enough to receive any long-term residential psychiatric care in a hospital. They told me to *administer* her pills every day. She hated taking them. I hated giving them to her. She would doze all day when she was on them and when she wouldn't take them it was the exact opposite. The minute my back turned she was gone. And I always found her in the same place. The graveyard. Where, of course, all roads meet anyway. I couldn't get her to eat, she used to get so agitated or else she was completely out of it. The Western Health Board didn't want to know. She died quick at the end."

Madge returned to the coffee table and topped up her tea.

Babs tried to absorb this sad story but felt uncomfortable at Madge's tone which seemed to lack empathy for her mother's suffering.

"So why haven't you gone back to England, then?"

"Because a month ago Ron wrote to me asking for divorce. He said I had been away for so long he had met someone else. Even Andrew has a girlfriend, can you believe it? So he has eyes for only one woman now and it's not his mother anymore. I can't even remember when I had a proper chat with him last. So that's what you get. You sacrifice your life for someone else's and have nothing to show for it in the end. Hardly seems fair, does it?"

Madge sighed, clearly feeling betrayed by all she held so dear.

"God, I'm really sorry, Madge, I had no idea things were so tough for you," said a genuinely remorseful Babs.

They sat in silence again but Babs was still determined to get the answers she came for. "So...I presume you heard about poor Rosario? You must have got a shock when he turned up at your door, just like mine?"

"So that's what really brought you here! Sorry to have bored you with my foreplay of misfortune for the past ten minutes. Little loss he's gone. He brought nothing but misery."

Trying to ignore that heartless remark, Babs calmly continued. "What did ye talk about?"

"*Huh*, I didn't entertain that jackass for long. He asked me where you were living exactly. Then he told me he was going to buy Finn's chip shop. The bloody cheek of him! I had no notion of indulging him so he could commence another reign of terror on us."

"Steady on, that's a bit strong," Babs protested.

"Love is still blind, I see."

"What's that supposed to mean?"

"The minute you met that guy you dropped me like a hot poker and, of course, the minute you broke up you were back straight away crying on my shoulder."

"I'm sorry, Madge. I didn't see it like that. He told me why he went back to Italy. He hasn't had an easy life."

"Oh, cry me a river! Having to live on a beautiful sunny island in Southern Italy picking berries for a living must have been pure hell."

"Hang on, Madge. Rosario said that he wrote me a letter and sent it here, to this house when he returned to Italy. Was that true? Did a letter come here?"

"Yes, I did. I read it and then I burned it."

"*What?*"

"Oh, don't look so shocked! He was droning on about how difficult it was for him over there. I knew well you would believe all that rubbish and probably spend the rest of your life wallowing over him. You were better off without him."

"*That letter was private! You had no right to open it. It explained why he couldn't come back!*"

"How can you keep defending him?"

"*Because he didn't do anything wrong,*" said Babs strongly.

Madge stood up. She was angry.

"What's the matter with you? Look at all the lives he ruined from the minute he and his family moved here. The dogs in the street knew that football scholarship, or whatever it was called, should have gone to Finn and not to 'Mr. Blow-in Fancy Footwork'. And he abandoned Finn at the retreat in Wexford when he was arrested. Finn took the fall for it. And what about the swimming incident at the cliff? Finn could have died. He nearly ended up paralysed. His back and legs were so fucked-up after it, he probably wished that he had."

"Jesus, how many times has it to be said? *It was an accident. That was Finn's own fault for jumping in at the wrong spot!*"

"Oh right, and I suppose it was my brother Rory's fault for dying after he jumped in to save him? Causing years of anguish for my mother which nailed me to the cross as well! Not to mention the breakdown of my marriage and a redundant relationship with my only child who lives in another country!"

"I'm not trying to hang anyone," said Babs. "And I'm not looking for a scapegoat for my own misery. If we continue to circle the wagons of blame, Madge, we'll never find a way out."

"With Rosario Fratelli back in town there was only one direction he was going and that was straight to hell – and if you are too dozy to see that I think we have nothing else to talk about."

Babs sat in her car, trying to rationalise all she had just heard. But she couldn't. Madge's anger and resentment of Rosario was shocking. Like her poor mother, Madge sounded like a woman on the edge of her sanity. The unfortunate chain of events and losses she had suffered had certainly affected her mental health and had the potential to drive her to despair.

Alarm bells went off in Babs' head. She would have to tell Garda Kennedy her fears that her old friend had numerous motivations for murder.

A pub on Forster Street was the location for the next task to be tried out by the off-duty gardaí in training.

"It's a pity there's no music," said Caitlín as they walked in the door.

"We have to be back by ten so we'll just have to concentrate on the drinking instead," said Tully, getting his priorities in order.

A chatty evening was shared by the many gardaí who gathered there, all eager to know where everyone else was stationed and how they were finding the job. It wasn't long until their curfew loomed and it was time to get back to base.

Caitlín and Tully were the last to walk up the long drive to the barracks. A shower of rain made them dash to shelter under a big horse-chestnut tree.

"That was fun," said Tully.

"Yes, they're a nice bunch. By the way, one of the ladies doing observation with me was enquiring about you."

"Observing me, *eh*? Which one was that?"

"Aisling, the girl from Salthill? Good-looking blonde?" prompted Caitlín, trying to break through Tully's beer fog.

"Why would I be bothering with her when I have a good-looking brunette from Clare here beside me?"

This made Caitlín blush. It was the strongest indication so far that Tully liked her. They leaned their heads in for a kiss but didn't quite make it.

A metal monster started screeching nearby.

"Shit! They're closing the gate! Run, Caitlín, or we'll be locked out!"

Fuzzy heads was the common denominator at the breakfast table the following morning. Caitlín and Tully managed to share a subtle smile while sitting among their colleagues. But they were not allowed to languish there for long as they were directed to go to their respective taskmasters. Tully got to go off and be a Hell's Angel for the morning while Caitlín got a lecture about points of view and suspect profiles. Her post was regarded as *"vital"* for the safety of the on-going security of the President. She was told it was the window to all abnormalities, providing surveillance in the event of any opportunistic snipers. Her instructions were to follow a strict BDA: scan the area *Before* the president arrives, scan the area *During* his presence there and finally, scan the area *After* he has left to monitor any untoward follow-up. Finally the location of her surveillance was revealed. She was to be deployed to a room on the second floor over a shop at the corner of Williamsgate Street and Eyre Square. Not being from Galway the exclusivity of this spot didn't register with her until Aisling explained to her how lucky she was. She would be able to see the President arrive in the square, watch the presentations and speeches there and also get the chance to see his entourage go down some of Shop Street. Feeling very chuffed about that, she couldn't wait to ring her mother when she got home to tell her.

Caitlín and Tully met up again after a hardly digested lunch. He raved about how cool the motorbikes were and how sorry he was not to have brought his camera for a photograph. Caitlín joked and described her role as being *insightful*. Then they were driven in an army lorry to commence a walk-about of the pre-planned route, commencing at the sportsground where the president was landing. Following that, they walked down Forster Street and up towards the top of Eyre Square. Everything was explained to them: who sat where, the position of the podium, where the dancers and musicians would perform and how the presentation table would be set up at the side of the stage displaying the numerous gifts to be presented on the day. Then they followed their leader and walked on towards Shop Street. Caitlín's taskmaster took her and three of her colleagues aside and took them to No. 1 Williamsgate Street and in particular the second and third floors where they would establish their look-outs.

Aisling was right on the money, Caitlín thought to herself. It looked like she had bagged the best seat in the house. Looking out she realised she would be able to see the entire ceremony taking place in Eyre Square.

Despite all the excitement over the last two days, that evening Caitlín was never so glad to get home. Who knew the visit of an international dignitary could be so exhausting? Her housemate, Shelly, was gone out for the night so she had the whole house to herself. Taking advantage of the solitude she soaked in a bath of lavender oil and Epsom salts to relieve her tired tense muscles and applied a ghastly organic homemade face mask consisting of oatmeal, brown sugar and honey. She then lay full stretch on the couch and relaxed in peace. The only thing she could hear was the ticking of the clock on the mantelpiece.

She was just about to nod off when someone came thumping on her front door. Startled, she opened her eyes. She was not going to open it, knowing how she looked, under any circumstances. She told herself it would go away, and it did go away – to the window.

Babs Wheatley was staring in at her though the glass. Seeing Caitlín, she beckoned to her to open the door.

For frig sake, I don't believe this, Caitlín said to herself as she grudgingly made her way to the front door.

"I'm so sorry to bother you, Caitlín, but I have some important information for you about the murder. Oh, what's wrong with your face?"

"Nothing! It's a face mask. Babs, if you have information on the case you really should go to the station and make a statement."

"I know, but I would like you to hear it first. Sergeant Lamb wants my head on a plate. I know that he doesn't like me and you only said the other evening that if I ever needed to talk . . ." She trailed off, shrugging her shoulders.

"Fine so, come in. Can I get you a cup of tea?"

"You wouldn't have anything stronger?"

After rattling around in the kitchen, Caitlín returned with a glass of port and set it down before Babs.

"Well, the thing is, Caitlín . . . the thing is . . ."

"*The thing is* . . ." repeated Caitlín, using a winding motion with her hand to encourage Babs to spit it out.

"Yes, the thing is . . . Oh for God's sake, I can't take you seriously with that stuff on your face! Can you take it off?"

Some minutes later, a fresh-faced but cranky Caitlín returned from the bathroom.

"Right, I've had a very long tiring day. Can you please tell me what is bothering you?"

"I think I know who murdered Rosario."

Time suddenly stood still in Caitlín's universe. "Who?" she asked eagerly.

"Madge Costigan, or Walters, which is her married name. She and I were great friends years ago. She was a sister of poor little Rory –"

"Costigan," interjected Caitlín, immediately joining the dots together.

"Oh, you know about that."

"Yes – I know about Rory Costigan's tragic death following the near-drowning of Donnacha Finnerty when they were young."

"Right, well, I hope you are also aware that some people unfairly blamed Rosario for Finn's misguided jump off the cliff and Madge Costigan is definitely one of them. She blames Rosario for Rory's death."

"You're going to have to have more than that," said Caitlín.

"Oh, I can give you much more than that," Babs said enthusiastically. "Rosario called to her house in Westport the day before he died. Madge and I used to live in that house with her aunt when we were younger. Anyway, Madge had been living in England for years since then, she had a job, got married and had a son. I didn't even know she had come back to Ireland and that was a year ago! She said her mother had some sort of mental breakdown and how she returned to Ireland to mind her but she was so long here her husband met someone else and has asked her for a divorce and it sounds like her son hasn't been in touch with her either."

"Okay, okay," said Caitlín in a hurry, raising her hand up to stall Babs who was talking at a mile a minute. "How do you know all of this?"

"I called to see her earlier today at that same house we used to live in."

"And you hadn't seen her for a while?"

"Not for years. I suspected Rosario just took a chance to see if she did still live there. He wouldn't have known that she went to England. Rosario told me the last day that he had sent me a letter all those years ago explaining what happened to him, but I never got it because it turns out that stupid cow kept it from me. In fact, she *burned* it."

"Why did he go to see her?"

"Rosario knew I lived in Ballantur now, but needed to ask Madge exactly where. Madge and I used to write to each other so she knew exactly where I lived."

"So, what makes you think she killed him?"

"You should have heard her, Caitlín. She was spitting poison. She blames him for Rory's death, Finn's accident, Finn's arrest, all leading to her mother's breakdown and the breakdown of her marriage not to mention the lack of communication with her son. She was saying awful things like '*he deserved it*', '*no loss he's gone*' and '*he's gone to hell*' all sorts. Honestly, she was fit to be tied. She's a woman on the edge and I think she is capable of hurting someone to avenge all of the hurt she has suffered herself. I know Sergeant Lamb would think I was stitching her up to take the heat off myself but you have to believe me, Caitlín, I seriously think she could have done it."

Caitlín went over this revelation again with Babs in more detail and assured her that she would look into it first thing in the morning.

When Babs had left she sat back down again in her tranquil house but all serenity had left her mind. Now the prospect of another valid murder suspect had come to light, she couldn't deny that her suspicions were equally heightened to those of Babs.

Chapter 17

Overdue

Babs wasn't working until three o'clock but awoke early at the usual time anyway. Nate was already faffing around the bedroom, getting dressed for work. She pulled herself up in the bed and yawned.

"You're awake? I thought you might have had a lie-in," said Nate.

"I can't seem to sleep right at all these days with so much going on."

"Don't get up yet, stay as you are and I'll bring you in a cuppa."

"Thanks, Nate," replied Babs, heartened by his kind consideration. She reached across to get her book off the bedside table but it wasn't there.

Jumping out of the bed, she started to search for it frantically around the room which unnerved Nate when he returned holding a steaming cup of tea and two slices of liberally buttered toast.

"Babs, what's wrong?"

"My book, the book on the stand I was reading. Did you see it?"

"I took it back to the library yesterday with my one – it was overdue," he replied, wondering what all the fuss was over.

"But I haven't finished reading it yet!"

"Calm down, woman – if it's that good you can get it out again. Are you sure you're alright?" he said, confused by her extreme reaction.

The loss of Rosario's postcard hidden inside the book made her despair. Gathering her senses, she knew she needed to rein in her anxiety to prevent Nate becoming suspicious.

"I'm sorry, Nate. My head is all over the place. Not to worry. Here, hand me over that breakfast, thanks, and I won't be delaying you."

Once she heard Nate driving off, she dressed quickly and jumped into her car. Twenty minutes later she screeched to a halt outside the County Library in Castlebar. With the front doors barely open, she scurried inside and went straight up to the librarian.

"I'm terribly sorry to bother you first thing but I am on my way home from my night shift and I am looking for a copy of *The Feminine Mystique*."

"Just a moment," replied the obliging woman, looking through her tickets. "Sorry, love, I'm afraid it's out on the loan."

"Is it just the one copy you have?"

"I'm afraid so."

"No, that's good," said Babs aloud to herself, confusing the clerk. "Can you tell me who has taken it out. I need it immediately."

"I'm sorry, madam, but we are not allowed to give out that information," the librarian said, starting to wonder about Bab's insistence.

Babs realised she was coming across as peculiar so she needed to be creative and plead her case more convincingly. "I'm sorry, you must think I'm nuts," she said with a false laugh. "You see ...let me explain ..." She was suddenly inspired, remembering something that had actually happened to her a few years before, though the book involved wasn't a library book – just one she'd mislaid. "I have a family wedding coming up next week and I spent the guts of my wages on a dress I bought in Switzers in Dublin."

"*Oooh*, very nice!" replied the librarian, becoming more interested.

"Well, wait till you hear this! When I brought it home and tried it on again didn't the flipping zipper break on me."

"Oh, that's awful!"

"I know. The problem is I was using the receipt for it as a bookmark in that book and now I need it to take the dress back. I was going to go to Dublin again tomorrow with it because it's my day off, but I'm afraid they won't do anything for me if I don't have the receipt and it was so expensive in the first place."

"Indeed, dear, they might not take it back if you don't have the receipt," agreed the sympathetic woman. "Let me see who the library number is assigned to."

She left and returned from the back office a few moments later. She glanced from left to right to ensure no one was listening, even though there was no one else in the library.

You'd think she was revealing the seventh secret of Fatima, thought Babs.

The librarian leaned forward and whispered, "It's a Frieda Huber – she lives in Ballantur."

"No way! That's fantastic! I'm from Ballantur. Frieda is a friend of mine. I have to go. Thank you so much."

"*Enjoy the wedding!*" the unsuspecting woman shouted after her.

"*Oh yeah, thanks,*" returned Babs, who had already forgotten about her web of matrimonial lies.

Babs thumped the steering wheel of the car when she sat back into it.

"Unbelievable! Why does it have to be her of all people? Frieda Huber. I swear to God! That two-faced cow!"

Babs knew she would have to grovel to her nemesis. They already had history and this originated from both of them having feelings for the same man. Now this additional "man trouble" would surely only bring glee to Frieda but Babs had no choice but to don her amour and take her punishment.

Luckily, Frieda was at home. Babs could hear Beethoven's Symphony No.5 coming from the open window of the German woman's sitting room, its foreboding frantic violins escalating her dread even more.

Frieda promptly answered her front door and was visibly surprised to see Babs standing there.

"Hello, Frieda. This may come across as a bit odd but I understand that you have a copy of *The Feminine Mystique* on loan from the library and I need to look at it for a minute," said Babs, blushing, knowing well that Frieda could see through her thin veil of deception.

"Oh? I don't have it. I returned it to the library this morning."

"But you only took it out yesterday!"

"It was a stimulating read. I devoured it."

"Did you notice the postcard in it?"

"Yes, I did."

"Oh, great. Did you keep it for me?"

"No, why would I? Neither the book nor the postcard were my property so I gave it back just as I got it."

Babs' heart sank. "You see, Nate returned the book on me and I hadn't finished it so my *bookmark*, so to speak, was still in it."

"Do you not mean your love note?" smirked Frieda.

Babs nearly died on the spot. "It was sent to me by the late Rosario Fratelli, who was a dear friend of mine. How would you feel if someone had something personal belonging to you? Wouldn't you wish that, if they had the means to return it, they would?"

Frieda suddenly felt guilty. She felt she had allowed her animosity for Babs to cloud her better judgement.

"It will be okay. I only took it back to the library this morning."

"But I've just come from the County Library – the librarian said you have it."

"No, Babs, I dropped it back to the mobile library. It was here in Ballantur earlier. Come on, I'll help you. It's not even ten o'clock, he can't have gone far. We'll ring the library in Castlebar and see what his route is for the day."

Frieda had to come up with a creative story this time and told the librarian that she was going on holidays so she wanted to know where the mobile library was stopping today so she could return her books before they were due. They discovered that, after the square in Ballantur, it was going to the Secondary School and then on to Claremorris to repeat the same itinerary there.

Arriving on the main street in Claremorris, they weren't long spotting the brightly coloured lorry parked up a side street with 'Leabharlann' printed on each side. There was nobody sitting in front so they expected the library to be open at the back, but when they opened the door they were surprised to see no one at all inside.

Frieda looked at her watch. "It's nearly eleven o'clock – maybe he's gone on a tea break?"

"Leaving the door open?" asked Babs incredulously.

"You're in Claremorris, not a ghetto in the Bronx. He'll be back in few minutes."

"I'm not waiting around. It's my first day back to work since Rosario died and I don't want to be late. It's hard enough showing my face there as it is," said Babs as she jumped into the back. "Are you going to help me or not?"

Frieda jumped in too and closed the door behind them. With the treasure hunters starting at either end they left no book unturned till Frieda found their prize.

Babs held the postcard to her chest and let out a sigh of relief. "Right, let's get out of here!"

Frieda grasped the handle of the door but it wouldn't budge.

"We're locked in!" she cried. "I don't think you can open it from the inside."

"Let me try. That's stupid – you can break in but you can't break out?"

"Guess they had a security plan after all," retorted Frieda.

Suddenly the lorry rocked and so did the radio. Loud music blared and the engine started. The jolt of the moving vehicle caused the two women to fall over. Each of them grabbed onto the timber shelving and pulled themselves up. Frieda, shaking with the motion, managed to move slowly upwards to the front of the vehicle and banged on the cabin.

"*Stop! Stop! Let us out!*"

The lorry screeched to a halt, sending both women flying to the floor for a second time.

The driver alighted and walked to the back of his vehicle. Slowly, he opened the door, not knowing what was going to greet him.

"*Frieda!*" he said.

"Oh, hello again. I'm so sorry about this, We can explain –"

"No, we can't," butted in Babs. "It would take too long. All you need to know is that nothing has been lost, stolen or damaged – apart from my head when I banged it off the shelf. You really need to slow down. Go easy with the other man's donkey – did anyone ever tell you that?"

She grabbed Frieda by the arm and pulled her away with her.

"Babs, that was rude!"

"He doesn't need to know why we were in there. Do you not think this is embarrassing enough? We did no harm."

They walked back to the car in silence.

"Maybe you should improve your own driving skills," remarked Frieda, pulling a parking ticket off Bab's windscreen.

"What a day and I haven't even got to work yet!"

Caitlín's day hadn't started off much better. Despite being hanging tired when she went to bed, she had slept very poorly. When the shrill alarm clock went off she nearly needed someone with a crowbar to get her out of the bed. At least Tully had the kettle on when she arrived into work.

In the meantime, she went straight into Sergeant Lamb's office to tell him the suspicions Babs had about Madge Costigan.

"Ah, Kennedy, how was your training?" asked the Sergeant when she approached him. "Tully said it was intensive."

"You can say that again. Any developments in the murder investigation?"

"Detective Cullen and I brought Donnacha Finnerty in for questioning yesterday. There is real motivation there but for now we don't have any hard evidence so we need to start building a case. He's definitely another suspect."

"He's mightn't be the only one. I received new information about someone else late last night, sir."

"Who?"

Caitlín explained. Wisely, she withheld the source of this 'intelligence' until she had convinced Sergeant Lamb on the merit of her suspicions, leaving him with little choice but to consider Madge Costigan seriously too.

"Right, we'll pick her up as soon as possible," he said.

"But why not now?"

"Because while you were learning your ABC's in Galway, I got a letter from Mayo County Council inviting us and the other emergency services to a meeting today to start co-ordinating our plans with each other for the upcoming rally. And it's on this afternoon."

"Could Detective Brendan Cullen and Tully not question her?" asked a persistent Caitlín.

"Brendan is giving evidence in court today for another case of his so he is not available."

"And tomorrow is the President's visit. Tully and I won't be here."

"I know that. Do you not trust myself or Brendan to do the interview without you? Maybe you want to check our notes from yesterday following our questioning of Donnacha Finnerty, in case we missed anything?" he said sarcastically.

"No, sir," said Caitlín quickly, even though she really wanted to say "*Yes, sir,*" knowing she would look at them at the first opportunity she got.

"Besides, I've asked Tully to provide a Garda escort from the morgue to the airport. Rosario Fratelli's body is being repatriated back to Italy today."

Tully was flailing his arms about when she stepped out of the sergeant's office.

"*Code Red, Code Red!*" he called out to Caitlín, who went straight to his aid.

"What's wrong?"

"I was dunking my biscuit into my tea and it broke off. Get me a spoon quick!"

"Tully, if that is your emergency, you need a transfer."

"Code Red is the most serious thing that can happen to an officer. Biscuit-dunking is a minefield," he said, walking into the kitchen.

Caitlín sat down at her desk, ignoring Tully's immaturity. The last thing she wanted was a three-hour stagnant meeting shuffling paper about with the Council. She didn't feel she had the energy for discussing roads closures and diversions. All she really wanted to do was divert back to bed.

The rest of the day passed off quietly enough for most until Nate Wheatley went to the pub that Friday night and told everyone there that Doctor Quinlan had been to the Leonards' house earlier that evening. Grace Leonard had taken a turn and an ambulance had to be called to take her to hospital. Sentiments of good wishes and a speedy recovery were expressed by all.

Then on a lighter note, Nate informed everyone that he and Babs were driving to Galway in the morning to see JFK. They all agreed it was a great showcase for the country and would certainly put it on map, considering that the President of America was spending four days here under the glare of the international media. They all looked forward to hearing Nate's personal review of the visit on his return.

Chapter 18

The President

The Leonard family were up bright and early the next morning. Pa and Elsie wanted to take the grandchildren's minds off the sudden but necessary removal of their mother to hospital so Pa was taking them to the cattle mart. Naturally, they were not very excited about that, especially Molly, but with an unseasonably cold day forecast they were limited as to what activity they could enjoy indoors. Pa promised Elsie that they would be back within an hour or two and she retorted that she would be glad of the peace and quiet. He worried about leaving her on her own but he was struggling trying to please everyone. He cautioned her not to go anywhere and he prayed to God she'd remember to comply.

Elsie shooed them out the door, made a cup of tea before settling down to read the open newspaper on the kitchen table.

Caitlín took up her post good and early at No.1 Williamsgate Street on the second floor, which she shared with a Garda Robert Burke who was a fortnight shy of retiring and couldn't believe how lucky he was to finish his career on such a high. Caitlín took advantage of this veteran and picked his brains about his experience in murder investigations, especially those in which a stabbing had been the cause of death. Garda Burke had served his duty in all the major cities – Dublin, Limerick, Cork and Galway – and had investigated some violent incidents during this time. In relation to Rosario Fratelli's murder he told Caitlín that he thought it strange that the knife was left inserted in the victim as claimed by Babs Wheatley. Generally, he said, the murderer would remove it, to dispose or destroy it. He suspected that the victim might have tried to defend himself, therefore obstructing his attacker's attempts to retrieve the knife, or the attacker was startled by something else imminent and had to leave without it. He also pointed out how a killer did more damage removing the knife than leaving it in for a surgical team to deal with it, explaining how the blade would have caused more internal incisions while it was being pulled out which would result in a heavy loss of blood.

That gave Caitlín something to think about, but for now early anticipation was apparent as loads of people had started to gather around Eyre Square, determined to get a good view. Caitlín was more than satisfied with her own. She realised she definitely underrated the binoculars. The magnification was a novelty – everyone and everything so clear and so near! Scanning the accumulating crowd, she laughed out loud.

"*Ha!* Robert, I can see my neighbours in Eyre Square, Nate and Babs Wheatley."

"I've spotted a few people I know from back home too," he said.

Caitlín continued to watch Nate and Babs, she couldn't help it. Again she laughed when she saw Nate lay a red-and-yellow plaid blanket on the grassy part of the square and Babs produce a flask, two cups and biscuit box full of sandwiches and treats. The pair of them then sat down in contentment and watched the crowd gather.

Pa Leonard, Tadgh and Molly came home early from the smelly mart. Predictably, it had not entertained the children as much as Pa hoped it would.

"Where's Granma?" asked Tadgh, coming back down after he had run upstairs.

"Isn't she upstairs?" Pa asked, pulling off his second Wellington boot.

"No."

"She must be."

"She isn't – honest, Granda – I looked in all the rooms."

"Tadgh, go outside," Pa said urgently. "Look around the yard, the barns and don't forget the henhouse."

Tadgh ran outside.

"Her tea is gone cold," said Molly. "She's left it on the table."

"What?" Pa stood at the kitchen table, staring at the half-full mug. Then he shifted his gaze to the open newspaper beside it.

"Maybe she's gone down to the shops," Molly said.

Pa lifted his eyes from the headline in the paper which read: **'BIG CROWDS EXPECTED TO SEE PRESIDENT KENNEDY IN GALWAY.'**

"I have a feeling she's gone further than that," he said regretfully. "Get Tadgh. We have to go and see Sergeant Lamb."

Initially Sergeant Lamb was reluctant to take Pa seriously about Elsie being missing. So far she'd only been gone for the best part of two hours.

However, when Pa informed him of Elsie's progressive dementia and her fixation on President Kennedy, he understood why Pa was worried.

"In all the years I have known her, she has never left a cup of tea after her. I know that sounds stupid but it's out of character. It's like something has snapped in her head and she felt compelled to go to Galway. She has watched every step of Kennedy's rise to fame. I'm so afraid she'll forget her whereabouts suddenly and God knows what could happen."

"I understand. There are loads of extra buses and trains laid on especially for this – it would be relatively easy for her to travel there. She could have taken the bus from Ballantur. What about her coat? Shoes? Handbag? Are they missing?"

"Oh God, I never thought to check."

"Go home and see – and let me know – we'll need to provide a description. I'll put out a call to all transport and emergency services and make sure they are put on alert to be on the lookout for her. In the meantime, I suggest that you and the kids keep searching locally. I'll come and find you if I hear anything."

Pa knew Sergeant Lamb was going to do to his best but he was terribly worried that Elsie was out there on her own, completely vulnerable in an environment that might suddenly become very foreign to her – and that scared the hell out of him.

Caitlín continued to observe the ever-increasing crowd and could feel a sense of excitement from both young and old. At this stage, herself and Robert had seen loads of people that they knew attending. Another garda popped his head in to see them and confirmed that the President's helicopter had touched down at the sportsground. It had been greeted by the three hundred schoolchildren draped head to toe in the colours of the Irish flag, which must have looked very impressive from the air. Most of the adults and children there had never seen a helicopter before so the teachers' orders to the children to keep their heads down for the visual effect from above was ignored when all the children wanted to do was look up!

After alighting from his aircraft the same children welcomed him by singing 'Galway Bay'. The delighted President rubbed heads and shook hands with many of his little star-struck entertainers to the alarm of his security men, before they managed to get him into his open-top car to start his journey down College Road. The car was flanked either side by multiple Garda motorcycles which provided a barrier from the hundreds of people lining the streets.

Caitlín could tell the President was getting nearer. The people turned in unison at the bottom of the square, anticipating the first glimpse of the main man. Caitlín scanned left to right, then immediately left again.

Well, I'll be damned, no better woman, she said to herself when she spotted Elsie Leonard and wondered if she had travelled up with Nate and Babs.

However, Elsie was not feeling any empowerment at all. She felt very confused all of a sudden, not knowing where she was and why there was such a large crowd of people gathered around. The crowd was now surging towards the corner. She was jostled unintentionally by a horde of people towards the gate.

And then she saw him – President John F. Kennedy.

"Excuse me, ma'am, please step back," said a Secret Service Agent briskly to Elsie.

Elsie stood in awe, looking at the President.

"I'm sorry, ma'am, you have to move out of the way. Now!" said the agent again but more aggressively and shoved her back.

"But he's the only one I know," she said quietly then got upset because she didn't understand what was going on or why this other man was shouting at her.

The crowd shuffled forward again, catching Elsie unaware and she tripped, falling to the ground.

"*No, no!*" said Caitlín, who was still watching Elsie. She knew she was in difficulty for more reasons than one. "Robert, my elderly neighbour has fallen in the crowd. What will I do?"

"Run downstairs and tell one of our lads outside to go and help her," suggested Robert.

"No, you don't understand, she needs to see someone she knows, she's confused," said Caitlín and took off down the stairs.

"*We're not supposed to leave our posts!*" Robert yelled after her.

Caitlín saw a sergeant on the street and immediately voiced her concern about Elsie. The sergeant wasn't happy about it but summoned another garda to take her place upstairs to allow her temporary leave. He shouted after her not to be long.

Caitlín was a woman with a purpose and barged her way across the square through the mass of people until she reached Elsie, who now had been helped back on her feet.

"Elsie, Elsie, it's me, Caitlín!"

"Caitlín? Yes, Caitlín," said Elsie slowly and then the fog began to lift.

Wondering about Elsie's fragile state of mind, Caitlín casually asked, "Have you come up to see the President?"

"I ... have," she replied, but with some uncertainty.

"Was it the bus or the train you got?"

"I'm not sure."

"That's alright, love," Caitlín assured her, noticing some distress in Elsie's voice. "Maybe you came here with Nate and Babs?"

"Are they here?"

"They are. I'll take you over to them. You had a bit of a fall there – look, your palm is bleeding – are you okay?"

"I'm fine. Where's Nate and Babs?"

"Does Pa know you're here?"

Elsie's silence conveyed that she didn't know that either.

Unsurprisingly, Nate and Babs were equally bewildered at the sight of their local garda and neighbour coming towards them. Babs kindly tended to Elsie's hand straight away while Caitlín quietly took Nate aside, telling him that she suspected Elsie had suffered an episode of her forgetfulness and was feeling very unsure of herself. She told Nate to ring the Garda Station in Ballantur straight away to get word to Pa that she was safe. Both of them felt that Pa might not even know where she was.

Elsie looked very shook and fragile. Nate and Babs offered to take her home straight away but she protested. She didn't want to ruin their day. Besides, the President would be making his speech soon so she insisted that they hang on. Caitlín thought about how she could keep everyone happy so she brought them up to the stage. She knew Aisling, the bangharda from Salthill, was deployed to carry out her duties there so, when she found her, she told her that her elderly neighbour was feeling unwell. After a bit of colluding between the security staff, Elsie was offered a chair to sit down out of the way at the side of the stage, the far side of the presentation table. Nate and Babs were happy to stand – in fact, they were delighted to have a closer view now themselves rather than where they were originally. Babs fussed over Elsie, tucking their blanket over her legs to keep her warm. Reliable Nate assured Caitlín that they would not let Elsie out of their sight and would take her home safely.

Caitlín ran back and resumed her post.

A huge cheer and a round of applause could be heard as the President made his way up onto the stage. First, various speeches were made by local and national dignitaries before he was presented with the Freedom of the City and various gifts such as the Irish linen and the woollen blanket woven specially in the colours of white, pink and purple to represent the wild heather of Connemara. When all gifts were set aside, expectancy rose for the greatest prize of them all: the President of the United States of America addressing this small corner of the world in the west of Ireland. His speech was flattering, uplifting and, to laughter and cheers, he envisaged a view of Boston Harbour from Galway Bay on a clear day when perhaps one could see relatives at work there on the docks. Finally, he extended his own *Céad Míle Fáilte* to all who might emigrate there. The crowd loved him. One of their own who had done good and come home. The goodwill of all then translated into the entertainment and, when an eight-hand reel was performed to the beat of the céilí band, even the President couldn't resist its infectious beat and tapped his feet contentedly.

After that spirited rendition, the President returned to his car with great difficulty due to continued adulation he was receiving from the crowds, with more unavoidable handshaking and waving. Finally, he commenced his journey out to Salthill. The entourage of cars was flanked once again by gardaí on foot and motorbikes as they slowly moved down Shop Street which was lined with spectators.

Caitlín continued her *Before, During and After* observation. The President was gone out of view now from her vantage point but, as instructed, she concentrated on the scene he was leaving behind. The crowd was quickly dispersing, most of them caught up in the excitement and setting out on foot to walk out to Salthill to see the President off. Others, who were satisfied enough with what they had seen and heard already, were happy to go home. Caitlín scanned Eyre Square and was pleased to see that her neighbours had left too. There was no sign of them and she hoped Elsie was feeling better. A security guard was now busy at the presentation table, gathering the President's gifts. It was then Caitlín noticed that Babs and Nate had forgotten their blanket. She could see it on the ground at the side of the table. She wondered if she should collect it and take it home to them. Then the security guard came upon it and beckoned his colleague over to him. Both of them opened it up and examined it. Then, dropping it immediately, they started scouring around the table, chairs and stage like they were looking for something.

Caitlín continued her surveillance around the square and beyond – but then she saw exactly what they were looking for.

"Oh my God, I don't believe this!" she said to herself.

There, walking away up Prospect Hill, was Nate, carrying the bag with the flask, the biscuit box and an umbrella. Babs was behind him carrying her handbag and a raincoat. And behind her was Elsie with the President of America's newly gifted blanket rolled up under her arm! Caitlín could make out the colours clearly.

"*Robert, I have to go!*" she called to her colleague and dashed down the stairs.

This time there was no ranking officer to talk to as they all had moved on with the entourage. She didn't want to waste time going the opposite direction down to the square to tell the security guards what had happened, so she took off running up Prospect Hill herself in pursuit of the precious blanket.

"*Babs, Nate! Hold up!*" she shouted as she came close to her targets.

Her neighbours came to a halt and turned to see who was calling them.

"You forgot your blanket," Caitlín said, completely out of breath.

"What? No, we didn't. We have it, don't we?" said Babs.

"Look! That's not your one," Caitlín said, pointing to the blanket Elsie was clutching. "Your one is still below at the stage. The one under Elsie's arm is the one belonging to the President!"

"Where did you get that, Elsie? I put our one over your knees?" asked Babs, getting cross with her.

"I don't know," replied Elsie, suddenly sounding confused again.

"Oh Jesus," said Nate. "What will we do? We need to get it back to him."

"Give it to me. We'll be lucky to catch him before he leaves," said Caitlín, grabbing the blanket and taking off again.

She knew she never would make it to his point of departure on foot so, when she spotted a stationary garda with a motorbike, she rushed up to him.

"Quick, get us to Salthill! This is the President's blanket! Someone took it by mistake!" she said, jumping on behind the garda.

The garda beeped his horn all the way down Shop Street to clear the street of any cars or pedestrians and continued to do so until they arrived in Salthill.

A massive crowd had accumulated near the waiting helicopter. Every member of the Crowd Control Unit struggled to create a safe space between the horde of people and the aircraft. For the second time today, Caitlín battled through the assembly, although this time she was stopped by the Secret Service who demanded to know where she was trying to go and why.

This caught the attention of the President who was about to board, causing him to turn around.

"Is everything okay? he asked.

"*Yes, sir!*" Caitlín called out. "*You nearly forgot the Connemara blanket, that's all!*"

Caitlín handed the blanket to the security guard.

"It's okay, boys, let her through – it's so cold here, I think I might need it," he said with a chuckle. "Thanks, Garda –?"

"Kennedy, Garda Caitlín Kennedy."

"Kennedy? Are we related?"

"No, I don't think so."

"Well, I'm sure if you go back far enough we must have started out somewhere together, right?"

"Yes, sir," she said, smiling.

The blades of the propeller started to slowly rotate once the President had boarded but the crowd had not the good sense to stand back far enough. This 'Marine One' helicopter was as much of a spectacle as the President himself. Their inexperience was going to teach them an unforgettable but nonetheless humorous lesson. They should have hung onto their hats. Once the powerful propellers got going they swept all the caps and hats high up into the air, causing them to fall at length into the thrashing waters of Galway Bay, never to be found. A cartoonist would later capture the scene of a graceful swam swimming at the Spanish Arch wearing a fashionable purple beret.

———— ❖ ————

The lights were still on in the cottage when Caitlín got home much later but she wasn't in the mood for Shelly and a barrage of questions. All she wanted to do was have a warm bath and go straight to bed.

"Oh my God, you're home, at last! How did you get on? Did you see him?" asked Shelly predictably all at once.

"Shelly, I've had a very long day and I am knackered. Is it alright if we catch up tomorrow?"

"I know. I'm sure you are, but do you know where the Leonards are?"

"Don't ask. Like I said, I'll fill you in tomorrow, okay?"

"No, Caitlín, you don't understand. I've been trying to find them all day on behalf of Doctor Quinlan and the hospital."

"Why, what's wrong?" yawned Caitlín.

"It's their daughter, Grace. She's dead."

Shelly explained the circumstances of the day to Caitlín as they drove to the Leonards' house.

As they knocked on the front door, Caitlín saw Nate and Babs' car parked at the side of the house and was glad of the support they would be able to offer the Leonards.

"Caitlín!" greeted Pa warmly. "I'm so grateful to you for finding Elsie today. You wouldn't believe the shock I got when I heard she had made it to Galway."

"Well, thank God she's okay," said Caitlín, saddened by what she was going to have to tell them.

"Caitlín? I thought it was you I heard. Come in!" said Elsie, joining Pa at the door.

"Yes, come on in!" said Pa. "It turned out to be a great day after all, thanks to you, Caitlín. After the Wheatleys and Elsie got back, we all went into Castlebar for dinner and had a drink in Slattery's on the way home. Well, when we told the others about the craic over the blanket, they just couldn't believe it, it was so funny. Waxy Carolan started singing 'The Blanket on the Ground'!"

Then Pa, still laughing over the debacle, noticed Caitlín and Shelly's grave faces.

"What's wrong?" he asked.

"It's Grace," said Caitlín. "Dr. Quinlan's surgery had the hospital on to them a few times this afternoon. Grace took a bad turn last night and was poorly this morning. She continued to fade on them during the day. I'm so sorry, Mr and Mrs. Leonard. She didn't make it."

Chapter 19

Bittersweet

On the day of Grace's funeral, Caitlín offered to man the station so that Sergeant Lamb and Tully could attend the Mass and burial. She had attended the wake the evening before at Leonards' house to pay her respects. It was a sorrowful home. The children, Tadgh and Molly, never left Elsie's side since receiving the heart-breaking news. Sure, they knew that their mam was sick but they never thought that she would actually ever leave them. Elsie stayed strong for their sake but Pa was very quiet and just went through the motions of accepting condolences distantly. Their other daughter Claire, with her husband and children, had arrived from Dublin and filled in the awkward gaps of the forced conversations.

While Tully waited for Sergeant Lamb to walk to the church he made idle chat with Caitlín.

"So, how is your racing practice going?"

"Oh you know, the usual, a few handbrake turns, burning rubber, you wouldn't see me for dust," she teased.

"What a torment! Where do you practise that around here?"

"The bog road, the back road and there is a good looped circuit through the old quarry. Wesley is a great coach – telling me to take my corners tight, accelerate out of them, gear change versus brake control, all sorts of stuff. Oh," she continued, getting very excited, "he said I'll be driving a different car altogether for the race though. Pity, I just getting used to this one. Anyway I think this car is coming from the UK, sounds like a real racy number. It's a whole new world to me and I'm really enjoying it."

Suddenly, they heard Sergeant Lamb's door open abruptly so they dropped their heads and pretended to be busy.

"I swear to God," said the sergeant, waving a letter in his hand, "if I get another of these frigging letters from the Broadcasting Corporation, I'll go mad! They are still writing to me about that local pirate station, instructing to us to cease its production immediately. Did I not ask you two already to close it down? I know well it's that shyster, Waxy Carolan, who's behind it. What's the name of it?" He scanned the letter. "Cali ... co Jack FM – what does that even mean?"

"Calico Jack was a pirate, Sarge, so I think it's a bit tongue in cheek, it being a *pirate* radio station," explained Caitlín.

"Well, why didn't he call it after a pirate we know like Blue Beard?"

"I think that was *Blackbeard*, sir," corrected Tully.

"Whatever, Tully! Find out where it's being broadcast from and tell him to shut it down. There is a Cease and Desist Notice to be served upon him – failure to do so resulting in a heavy fine and, or, imprisonment. Now come on or we'll be late."

Hundreds of people attended Grace's funeral in the Church of the Holy Rosary in Ballantur. One person for each tear shed by her children. Many of those in the congregation had already paid their respects at the wake the evening before but because words of platitude were meaningless, they turned up again. No verbal expression of sympathy could articulate the tragedy and sadness of the young mother's untimely death and the burden of grief brought upon her unprepared children that would change their lives forever.

The church was straining with people standing down the back and at the side of either aisle.

Father Morrissey delivered a solemn eulogy, telling everyone how he had married Grace and christened her two children in this very church. "Two chapters in her life and she should have been able to enjoy the rewards of happiness they would have given her in return. But her life was cut short, so now her family need to embrace the gift that *her* life brought to them. A life strengthened with courage. She was a very special person who will remain in their hearts forever."

Claire, Grace's sister, sat in the front row. Her husband and three children sat behind her. Claire didn't frequent Ballantur that often anymore. Instead, she was the one who sat beside Grace when she was in hospital in Dublin for her treatment and she wondered if her family knew how difficult that was to do. Seeing Grace at her lowest and weakest points often made her pray that her release would be sooner rather than later. Therefore, her stoic demeanour at the funeral was one of inward relief and acceptance of the inevitable. This in turn allowed her to be of great support to Pa and Elsie and she and her husband tended to all of the funeral arrangements.

Little Molly was known for being a good singer and it was sensitively suggested to her if she wanted to sing at the funeral she could. Father Morrissey was hesitant about her choice of song not being a hymn – "But how do you say no to a heartbroken child?" he conceded. Molly's class at school joined her on the altar for her rendition of 'The Twelfth of Never', a song she remembered her mother humming around the house. Tears were wiped away. Claire crumbled.

Outside, the choral notes of the birds made the sun dance to their tune. It made the quiet funeral procession to the cemetery feel warm and peaceful. After further prayers and the Rosary were recited, Elsie was the last one to leave the grave. Her memory might be fading but she could still clearly remember the first time she saw Grace on the day she was born, the happiness Grace showed in her Communion dress, the radiance in her wedding dress and the joy on her face when she had her own two children. She would always remember her smiling face. Before she left, she bent down and picked two pebbles off the grave and put them in her pocket.

The congregation found their voice again at the afters of the funeral in Slattery's. It was noticed that Grace's estranged husband was not there – however, his elderly parents were and their presence was warmly welcomed.

With Nate and Babs present, the locals were frustrated at not being able to gossip about Rosario's murder and could only smile and nod politely at them. This made Nate and Babs uneasy, especially Nate who seemed to be knocking back the pints. To take the isolated look off the pair of them, he started to talk to Tadgh and Molly who were sitting beside their Aunt Claire.

"Don't you two be worrying now. Your mam is looking down on you – or maybe up! I heard she was a little terror when she was younger!"

"Nate!" scolded Babs, pulling him away. She couldn't believe what he had just said. "Are you drunk? Maybe you're overtired. We've been pillar to post up at Leonards' since Grace died."

"I'm fine," said Nate hastily. "I'm going to buy Sergeant Lamb and Tully a pint. Better to keep on the right side of the law at the rate you're going!"

Caitlín was grateful for the quiet morning she had to herself at the station. And, unsurprisingly, she took this prime opportunity to go over all the notes on the murder without Sergeant Lamb breathing down her neck. She gathered the files and sat in the incident room, taking the radio with her. She boldly turned the dial to Calico Jack's frequency and prayed she'd remember to move it back to Radio 1 again before the Sergeant returned.

Two hours later she banged the last report on the desk and exhaled loudly, frustrated at the lack of seeing anything new or helpful. Sergeant Lamb and Detective Cullen had interviewed Madge Costigan and believed she, like Donnacha Finnerty, had a motive for murder and like him had no witnessed alibis. Caitlín wondered how the case could progress on that point, seeing that both of them lived on their own anyway. She had also dwelled on the forensics about fingerprints, the murder weapon and a foreign-looking cigarette butt she had discovered outside. She held up the clear plastic bag, which contained the odd-looking half a bead she had picked up off the floor in Rosario's room, to the light. It was about an inch long and had a hole going down through the centre of it. It was greyish-black in colour. She didn't think it was very pretty – it reminded her of a pumice stone she had in the bathroom to remove dead skin of her feet.

Casting the hard evidence aside, she asked herself how the killer got in and out of the room without being seen, but there again so did Babs Wheatley, nearly. Cailtín wanted to talk to the salesman and the cleaning lady herself. The salesman was the only guest staying the night before. But there did not appear to have been any addresses recorded for either of them – just Slattery's Guesthouse for the cleaning lady. What was Tully thinking, neglecting to record contact details? Her train of thought was interrupted by Waxy Carolan on the radio saying something about Italy.

"And the correct answer is ... drum roll, please...Palermo! Which is indeed the capital of Sicily. Congratulations to Emily Dolan from Ballyvary, the heart of Mayo, who has just won herself a lovely bottle of Italian wine. I'm reading the back of her postcard here – she says: 'Only found this out myself lately after having a lovely chat with a man from Sicily on the train from Dublin to Westport! P.S. love the station! Keep up the good work and please play a request for everyone who knows me.' Will do, Emily, here is 'Mambo Italiano'!"

"Oh my God, I need to find that woman!" Caitlín said, jumping up off her seat and roughly gathering up all of the reports and shoving them back in the cabinet.

Suddenly, the front door opened and Sergeant Lamb walked in.

"♫ *Calico Jack is back*," aired the jingle.

"Kennedy! Are you playing an illegal radio station in a civic building? What side of the law are you on?" shouted the sergeant as he walked straight over and turned the radio off. *"Taking things easy, were you, while we were out?"*

"No, sir, I was listening to it to see if there were any clues from the presenter about where the station was located," she lied. "Anyway, the presenter is just after announcing the winner of an Italian wine competition. The lady who won it said she was in the company of a man from Sicily on the train from Dublin to Westport recently. It might be a lead."

"A lead with no dog at the end," said Sergeant Lamb. "Westport gets loads of tourists of all nationalities. You're clutching at straws there."

"But this woman is local – it would be no harm to speak to her."

"Right, off you go, so."

"I don't know exactly where she lives."

"Ask Waxy."

"I'll get on it. I might head off for break now if that's okay. Where's Tully?"

"He had to drive Nate and Babs home. Haven't seen Nate that pickled for a long time," chuckled Sergeant Lamb.

Caitlín was about to head out the door but her conscience drew her back.

"Sir, could I bring something else to your attention?"

"*Mmm?*" replied the sergeant who was going through his post.

"I was just going through the murder reports there again while ye were out and –"

"I knew you would," replied Sergeant Lamb, cutting her off.

"If it's okay, I was going to interview the cleaning lady and the salesman again. Now that the shock is over them, maybe there's something that they might have remembered."

"You can if you want, but Tully already interviewed them and said they had nothing to add to what we already know ourselves. No more than the train conspiracy, Kennedy. You need to be coming up with something more promising than those."

Then came the thorny bit for Caitlín. "Yes, of course, but the contact details for these witnesses do not appear to have been recorded in our reports."

"Did Tully not write them up?"

"He put the guesthouse as the address of the cleaning lady which probably will be okay. I mean, I presume she lives around here. Dennis Slattery will know where. But there doesn't appear to be anything inserted for the salesman."

"Bring that report in to me," he said crossly.

When Caitlín left the station she had a sick feeling in her stomach. The last thing she wanted to do was get Tully into trouble but this was a murder investigation with the killer still at large, and it was imperative that all attention to detail was adhered to and she was vexed with him for not paying more attention to it.

It was just as well she didn't feel hungry for she spent most of her break talking to Wesley Pollard who had come to see her about the race. Her jaw dropped when he showed her a magazine with a picture of the car she would be driving. It was a 1961 black Ford Capri with a red-leather interior.

"Oh my God, Wesley! It's amazing!" cooed Caitlín. "Does she drive as fast as she looks?"

"She could shave spots off a cheetah!" responded Wesley proudly.

"*Woo-whoo!* Well, I'll definitely look the part whatever about the driving. I'll need to get as much practice in as I can – when are we getting it?"

"Ah . . . slight problem there, we mightn't get it until a few days before the race."

"*Wesley!* That's no good. I need to be well used to it before then."

"I know, I'm conscious of that too, but I'm waiting for my mechanic to finish a few jobs so he can travel to England to get it."

"England?"

"Yes, it's in Cornwall."

"Could you not get one a bit nearer to home?" asked Caitlín, surprised.

"Oh, not this one – she's a little beauty. I know the chap that is selling it because our garage has bought a few cars from him before. Splendid fellow, like a glass with a good clink! Don't worry, dear, it'll be fine."

Caitlín's anxious feelings did not match his relaxed attitude and she started stressing over her ability to drive a strange car on her first racing debut. It will be a disaster, she thought to herself. I'll be a laughing stock, like a loose saddle on a thoroughbred – completely useless.

"Cheer up – might never happen," said Tully when he saw Caitlín's gloomy face on his return to the station. "Where's the Sarge?"

"Gone to Quirke's for a sandwich. I got disappointing news at lunchtime."

She confided in Tully her apprehension about the new car and not having enough time to practise in it.

"I think you're going to be great. Remember, the day you jumped into Wesley's car and chased the robber you hadn't driven that car either and you mastered it. Look, it's your debut race. Your aim is keep the car between the ditches and get over the finish line."

The front door opened. "You two dossing again, I suppose," said Sergeant Lamb. "I just spotted Waxy Carolan down the street, so you better get off your arse and go after him."

"Yes, sir!" replied Tully dramatically, grabbing his cap.

"Not you, Tully. I want to see you in my office. Wait there a minute, Kennedy."

He strode into his office and emerged again with a paper in his hand.

"Serve him this Cease and Desist immediately."

"Right, sir."

After he went back in, slamming the door behind him, Caitlín delayed, pretending she was looking for an envelope so she could listen. She could hear Sergeant Lamb bring up the issue of Tully's incomplete reports. She felt bad for ratting on him, especially when he had been so supportive towards her about the race. She took an envelope and ran out of the station.

Waxy Carolan walked out of Quirke's shop with two bags of groceries. Caitlín watched him from her car as he sat back into his. She felt uncomfortable at finding him attractive because of his bad reputation and good looks. He was in his late thirties, had wispy ash-coloured hair always escaping from under his flat peaked cap and blue eyes framed by long eyelashes. He was in good shape, considering his only sport was rebelling against authority.

As she had hoped, he didn't drive off in the direction of where he lived. Maybe she'd strike lucky and he'd lead her to the covert location of his illegal makeshift studio. She followed behind at a safe distance for a country mile, up a hill veering out of the town. The road looked more unused after every bend. Eventually, the road ran out and an old disused flax mill came into sight. She had only ever seen it from the main road down below on the outskirts of Ballantur. It was four storeys high and dressed in a heavy coat of ivy that was probably binding its old stone walls together. She parked behind some old outhouses and walked up to the building. Quietly she went around the back and saw Waxy's van parked there.

After climbing up the stone stairs to the fourth floor, she paused and took in Waxy's technical operation before her.

"Do they charge you extra for the views?" she asked him over the loud music being aired.

Her unexpected arrival spooked Waxy and his comrade and they leapt to their feet.

"I thought a fortress like this would allow you to see your enemies approaching?" Caitlín said.

"Well, you must have been camouflaged out there – I didn't see you at all," replied a miffed Waxy.

He beckoned her into another room so they could talk.

"So if you're here the game must be up?"

"Not necessarily. I have a Cease and Desist Notice to be served upon you," she replied, handing him the envelope.

"No, you're alright, thanks. I'm good for toilet paper."

"God, you haven't changed."

"That's why you like me," Waxy replied, winking at her.

"*Ahem*. I have to serve this upon you but I am willing to compromise."

"You? Have you turned to the dark side, Garda Kennedy?"

"The truth is that a lot of people like your station and the service of information it is providing to the local areas."

"Do you like it?"

"I think your choice of music is more progressive that other radio stations," she replied in a haughty voice, trying to disguise the fact that she loved it.

"And does Sergeant Ram like it?"

"Sergeant *Lamb* is of the opinion that you should cease operating this illegal operation immediately or else you may face a hefty fine and, or, imprisonment."

"Sounds like you're the one being compromised, Garda."

"I'll get to the point. Now that I know where you are set up, I will try and keep the dogs off you but I don't know for how long. In the meantime, I need some information from you."

"Oh, this is where I get to scratch your back," replied Waxy in a husky tone.

Caitlín ignored the remark. "The woman who won the bottle of Italian wine today, how does she and other listeners know where to write to you?"

"You obviously don't tune in that much, Garda. We have a designated PO Box."

"I see. Right, well, I need her address from you. She's local?"

"What about client confidentiality?"

"What about I close this station down?"

"What do you want the address for?"

"It's Garda business. You can give it to me the easy way or I can make this very difficult for you."

"Alright, alright," agreed Waxy, who was bemused at Caitlín's unusual underhanded co-operation.

While Waxy went to get the address, Caitlín took in the spectacular scenery. She could see the town of Ballantur down below, its oblivious inhabitants driving their cars and criss-crossing on the roads of its hinterland.

"I have to hand to you, Waxy, the views from up here are something else," she said when he returned and handed her the address. "You can see all around from up here. We better make sure we keep Sergeant Lamb away or he'll want this control centre for himself."

"You keep him busy eating out of his own nosebag and I'll play a special request for you," he said with a wink.

"Oh, you'll do more than that. You owe me big time," she said, winking back.

Caitlín hesitated to resume her lines of inquiry when she returned to the station because the tension between Tully and Sergeant Lamb was palpable. She sat down opposite Tully. Dipping her toe in the water, she leaned over and whispered that she had found the location where Waxy was broadcasting from.

"Are you going to tell Sergeant Lamb?" he asked rather plainly.

"No. I'm not."

"Well, it didn't take you long to tell him about my omissions in the report!" he hissed back at her. "How long were you waiting in the long grass for me to mess up?"

"Tully! It wasn't like that. I was thinking of interviewing the cleaning lady and the salesman again but there are no contact details for them."

"I already interviewed them! Is that not good enough for you?"

"No. Yes, it was. But maybe there's something new that has come back to them now."

"The housemaid lives in Castlebar. Dennis Slattery knows where she lives," said Tully. "And the travelling salesman is on the road all the time – someone like him lives in a suitcase."

"But he must live somewhere," replied Caitlín, getting newly annoyed with his lazy attitude.

"Well, gee, hot-shot investigator, here's an idea – why don't you contact the drinks company that he works for and find out!"

"If you'd done your job right, I wouldn't have to!"

"You know what, Caitlín? Ever since you cracked the last murder case here you think you're smarter than the rest of us. But the reality is you got a lucky break and you've been riding on its coat-tails ever since. Get over yourself!"

Tully walked off.

———— ❦ ————

Caitlín was down at heart when she went home. She and Tully had never had a bad word between them before. She didn't mean to call him out – she just wanted to give the murder investigation the due diligence it deserved. What's more, he was right – the drinks company was the obvious answer. Why hadn't she thought of that?

Her camogie training was on again this evening and she was wasn't in the mood for it. But, she knew she needed to get out of her own head or else she'd dwell on the row all night.

The girls on the team were always a bit of craic. No matter what was ailing Caitlín's mind, or if at any time she was feeling lonely or homesick, the warm blanket of camaraderie shared by the team always gave her a sense of belonging. The physicality of the training twice a week since they joined the league topped up her fitness which she was committed to maintain due to her occupation. But it was her passion for the game that gave her the most satisfaction. Fortunately, this particular evening all her commitment paid off and she finally got her spotlight when the coach announced that she would be playing her first match the next Tuesday evening. She beamed like a seven-year-old and got a cordial cheer of support from the other girls.

She bounced home with her spirits renewed and immediately told Shelly about the new car for the race and her selection on the team. She also told her about her fight with Seán. Shelly could tell that the fight bothered her so she suggested they should go out on the town and celebrate the good news instead of dwelling on the bad.

They went to the Fla but Caitlín turned on her heel when she spotted Tully already there at the bar having a pint.

"This is ridiculous," said Shelly, pushing Caitlín back in the door. "Let me talk to him."

Before Caitlín could protest Shelly had taken off in Tully's direction. Caitlín got herself a vodka and coke and slunk down on a low stool at an empty table, wishing she could disappear altogether. Her wish appeared to be coming true with the length of time Shelly spent talking and laughing with Tully. When the two of them hurried onto the dance floor once the band starting playing 'The Loco-Motion', Caitlín threw back her drink and crushed the ice between her teeth in disgust.

Suddenly, another drink appeared before her on the table.

"Just in the nick of time." It was Detective Brendan Cullen.

"Is there anyone on the Force working tonight?" asked Caitlín.

"Crime numbers are dropping so we thought we'd let the criminals get a head start," he joked.

"Oh right, ever thought about running for Commissioner?" said Caitlín with a laugh.

"There's that lovely smile. You looked like you had the world on your shoulders a few minutes ago. What's the matter?"

"You really *don't* want to talk shop," Caitlín said sadly.

"And what else are we going to talk about? I hate this place. Come on, let's get out of here."

Chapter 20

Settling scores

Caitlín awoke the next morning with an enthusiastic Woody Woodpecker inside her head. It even hurt to open her eyes. Instantly she knew she was not in her own bed and it only took a man's snore beside her to realise she was lying on top of the dapper detective on his couch. Slowly and quietly she slid off him and tried to remember where she left her bag and jacket. A shuffle behind told her she was not going to make the quick getaway she wanted.

"Morning," Detective Cullen managed to say gruffly. "Jesus, how much wine did we get through last night? My head is pounding."

"Join the club."

"Caitlín ..."

"Yes?"

"I think we should keep this on the lowdown."

"Completely," she replied hastily. "I better get going, see you around."

Leaving his house she got flashbacks of kissing her colleague the night before and didn't regret it.

In the Leonard household an equally awkward conversation of a different nature was being poorly attempted. Claire's husband had taken all of the children into town for an ice cream. Pa and Claire already tried to talk, while away from Elsie, about the future welfare of Tadgh and Molly, but now they wanted to include her in an open discussion. With Claire already having three children of her own she was reluctant to take on two more but she knew she couldn't expect her father and mother to look after them. Pa was in his early seventies, suffered from chronic arthritis and was already challenged looking after Elsie and her progressive dementia. She wanted him to enjoy his golden years and not be faced with a situation way beyond his capabilities. He had always been a good provider to his family. They were rich in all aspects of their upbringing apart from money. Pa couldn't afford the cost of two youngsters growing up and going to school, nor could she expect him to weather the storms of their unpredictable teenage tantrums.

"I'll have to take them to live with me," she said, knowing there was no other way around it.

"I don't think they'll want to go and live in Dublin," said Pa.

"You and Mam can't mind them, you know that," Claire said.

"It will break their hearts to move away from here," said Pa.

"Yes, it will, but they're young, they'll adapt."

"Tadgh especially will hate Dublin," continued Pa.

"Dad, I know you'd love to have them here but you have enough on your plate already," said Claire, glancing in the direction of Elsie.

Elsie's silence indicated that she was in agreement with Claire, mindful that she was part of the problem and not part of the solution.

"Dad, I'm sorry but they really can't stay," said Claire firmly. "We'll tell them when they come back and get a few things from their house in Castlebar. We can come down another time for the rest of their stuff."

"You're taking them away today?" asked Pa, not expecting the sudden departure. "Will you not leave them till the end of the summer at least? God love them, their world has been turned upside down and now you're going to spin it on its axis altogether!"

Claire knew this was breaking Pa's heart. "Alright, Dad, we'll leave them here with you for another while but we'll be down for them before the end of August. I want to get them settled before they start school in September."

All Caitlín wanted to do when she got home after her wild night was to go back to bed. She barely had the blankets over her head when Shelly burst into her bedroom.

"So you made it home safely after all?" she asked sternly. "Where the hell did you go last night?"

"Who are you, my mother?" replied a muffled voice from under the blankets.

"You're the one always preaching to me about getting home safely."

"Can we just leave it, Shelly? I have a banging headache."

"You'll have a banging arse-ache in a minute by the time I've finished kicking it. You're not getting off that easily, lady. You went home with that detective fellow, didn't you?"

Caitlín sat up in the bed, knowing that Shelly was not going to let this drop.

"And what if I did? I'm surprised you even noticed, you were so busy flirting with Seán Tully."

"I'm not taking sides, Caitlín."

"Maybe you should! Get off the fence and stop plamausing the two of us – it's two-faced."

"That's not fair. You should have told me you were leaving the Fla and who you were leaving with. I'm the bigger fool for worrying about you."

Shelly left, banging the bedroom door after her.

Now Caitlín felt as sick in her stomach as she did in her head. She regretted being that short with Shelly. Of course she wanted to tell her about Detective Cullen. She wanted to tell her everything.

By the time Caitlín came back on shift one day later, her monstrous hangover had retreated and she was rather looking forward to seeing Detective Cullen again. The timing of her recovery was crucial because she had her first camogie match that evening. She was really psyched up for it and determined to make a good debut so she could make her jersey a permanent fixture on the field and not on the bench.

The day went by without there being any movement on the murder investigation. She told Sergeant Lamb that she had served the notice on Waxy when she met him down at Quirke's but she didn't reveal she'd discovered where he was broadcasting from.

She and Tully were going out of their way to avoid each other. Sergeant Lamb gave her permission to question the woman who had won the competition on Waxy's radio show. Normally, she'd ask Tully to join her to question a witness and typically he would be happy to oblige but today no breaking bread was taking place across the desks.

Emily Dolan lived in Ballyvary, and luckily was at home when Caitlín pulled up outside her door. The lady in question was very compliant and confirmed that she did sit beside a man from Sicily on her train journey from Dublin to Castlebar. Her travelling companion was going on to Westport. The date coincided with the date Rosario travelled. Her description and estimated age of her fellow passenger matched the profile of the deceased. She recalled their pleasant conversation where this 'gentleman', as she referred to him, mesmerized her with his description of his beautiful island, its history, culture and scenery, and that of its capital Palermo. She remembered him telling her that he went to college there. While Caitlín was in no doubt this woman had crossed paths with Rosario Fratelli, other than charming her with the dolce vita of Italy he hadn't revealed anything else worthwhile. The woman asked Caitlín if this was the man that was murdered in Ballantur. Caitlín politely confirmed that, going by her description, it was very likely.

It was only when Caitlín was leaving that the woman suddenly added something else hesitantly, as if what she was about to say was more of an inconvenience than relevant.

"I don't know if this is of any help to you, but when I was getting ready to get off he helped me with my suitcase and he bumped into another Italian man."

"Did they know one another?" asked Caitlín eagerly.

"I couldn't tell you. Sure they were speaking in Italian."

"Yeah, of course, but were they friendly or were they, you know, fraught or serious with each other?"

"I couldn't say, dear. The train had stopped by then and I got off."

"Here's the number of my station. If you remember anything at all, no matter how insignificant it is, please ring and ask for me. Thank you for your help. Enjoy your bottle of wine."

"I don't drink – would you like it?"

"Is it red or white?"

"It's red."

"Oh no, you're grand, thanks. Red wine gets me into all sorts of trouble!"

Caitlín sped back to the station. Her mind was racing faster than the engine as she strained her brain to think how this other Italian man might be a link in the chain of events that led to Rosario's death.

Detective Cullen was at the station when Caitlín arrived back. She was pleased she had this new piece of information to share with everyone, to take the initial awkwardness out of meeting the detective again.

Sergeant Lamb remained sceptical and called it a cul de sac with no way of pursuing anything promising. Detective Cullen, on the other hand, was more open-minded. He was going to ring the gardaí in Westport to open a line of enquiries with the B&B's and hotels to see if any of these establishments accommodated an Italian national of late. Caitlín offered to talk to Lucca again, to see if he could offer any insight into this mystery traveller encountering Rosario in the last few hours of his life. Tully said nothing.

After a fruitless call to Lucca who was unable to identify this passenger, Caitlín returned to the incident room. She sat on the table while looking at the wall which was covered in details of the enquiry. Scrunching her face up, she wondered about the complexities of how this new person of interest might fit in but she didn't even know where to start.

Then Detective Cullen popped his head around the door.

"Hi, Caitlín," he said quietly, "I just wanted to say I had a nice time the last night," before taking off again.

Caitlín jumped off the table and ran after him. "Brendan!" she whispered, bringing him to a halt. "I was wondering if you wanted to go for a drink Friday night?"

"*Em*... right ... sorry, I can't. I'm going to Dublin for the weekend."

"That's okay. How about you call to mine on your way back and I'll cook dinner for us?"

"I can't, Caitlín. I'll take a raincheck for now, if you don't mind."

"Yeah, sure, *no problemo*," said Caitlín, trying to sound cool about it.

"And it's best to refer to me as Detective Cullen when we're at work," he said before hurrying off.

Caitlín was taken aback at his abruptness and further disappointed that he had turned her down, but she had no time to dwell on it. She looked at her watch. It was time to go, kick-off was in an hour.

A loud cheer rang out when the Ballantur ladies' camogie team ran out on the pitch at their local GAA grounds. It was a home game. Caitlín was nervous and justifiably so. It was her first time to play a match with the team in front of the locals so she felt she had a lot to prove. After spotting several friendly faces in the crowd, it reassured her and provided much-needed support on her debut.

Nate and Babs were there and had brought Tadgh and Molly Leonard with them. Local business owners Dennis Slattery and Cassie Quirke were there too, both of whom were sponsors of the home side. A great source of comfort was the presence of Shelly on the sidelines. Caitlín laughed at her homemade flag – despite its team colours, she knew in her heart it was a white one and was happy to acknowledge Shelly with a wave back.

Weather conditions were favourable – there was a light breeze and the sky was overcast. Caitlín patted down her black skirt and red jersey.

The opposition had a strong hand of supporters too. A contingent bearing flags in green and gold occupied one select area of the stand. Being from Castlebar, they didn't have far to travel to support their team, St. Catherine's – a team well known for its success which had won a lot of games so far this year.

"A little bit of fear only makes you braver," so Caitlín's coach, Finbarr McNulty, had told them, reminding them that Ballantur was the underdog so they had nothing to lose.

The local newspaper had sent a photographer. As St. Catherine's composed themselves to say 'cheese' Caitlín had to look twice. She was aghast when she saw Mary Joyce as their No.15. This was the same Mary Joyce she had arrested for stealing Cassie Quirke's jewellery. The case was still pending in the District Court and Caitlín would be giving evidence against her. Caitlín's teammates had constantly given her stick for wearing a helmet but she was glad to be wearing one now and hoped to God that Mary Joyce wouldn't recognise her. Thankfully she was not marking her either, as Caitlín was playing as a right corner back and Mary was a left corner forward.

St. Catherine's got off to a blistering start, just like they planned it. Within five minutes, they were three points up. After fifteen minutes the heat of the game had burned off and everyone settled into their positions.

Those who were unable to attend the match were fortunate to hear it on Calico Jack FM live. The brazen Waxy Carolan commentated from a van at the side of the pitch. With the locals loving his broadcasts, he didn't feel under any threat but at the same time he positioned himself in the driver's seat so he could *vamos* immediately if he needed to.

A listener turned up his radio . . . *"The possession is still with St. Catherine's but Caitlín Kennedy has intercepted and claimed the sliotar! She's pucked it so high in the air God himself will need a camogie stick to rein it in. But, I've spoken too soon. It's a heavenly catch by her teammate, Annie Connor, and she's powering up the field. She shoots! And terrifies the back of the net with a scorcher of a goal! Ballantur are finally squaring up to St. Catherine's! . . . The momentum is back with St. Catherine's. Their No.15 is causing all sorts of trouble at the mouth of Ballantur's goal. They need to clear their line. Nooo! Their defence has been punished, it's a cracker of a goal from Mary Joyce who is running rings around her marker. She's winning all the high ball coming in to her."*

At half time Ballantur were trailing St. Catherine's by five points. Finbarr was all rallied up, convinced or pretending to be that they still had the beating of them. He pointed out that this was what all their hard hours of training was for. This was the payoff. He reminded them of all the evenings they trained in the rain, in the sun and when the sun went down the flash lamps came out and they kept going. "Don't let your mind stop what your body can do," he told them. "Get physical with them. Nice teams don't win trophies. You *must* work as a team to bring this home. Now get out there and show those bitches no mercy!"

"♫*Calico Jack is back ... You're welcome back here to the pitch side at Ballantur where we are live at the game between our Ballantur and St. Catherine's. The visitors are in the lead scoring 1-10 to 1-5. Five points between them which is the tipping point of any game. The teams are making their way back out."*

Coach Finbarr's pep talk had worked – the girls were fired up to win this match, all except Caitlín. Instead, she was weighed down by the fact that Finbarr made a necessary switch at half time, making her mark Mary Joyce now instead of the ineffective girl that had previously been in her shadow. Whatever about body contact, Caitlín didn't want to make any eye contact with her if at all possible. That strategy didn't even get off the blue print.

As soon as they got back out on the pitch Mary gave her a dig in the back, accompanied by a hollered "*Pig!*". She knew exactly who she was.

This aggression continued.

"*Oi! Ref – off the ball!*" shouted Nate, trying to draw the attention of the referee to the constant jostling Mary was inflicting on Caitlín.

"*Come on, Ballantur!*" Babs shouted as loud as she could.

Waxy continued his commentary. "*The artery has been truly severed to St. Catherine's Mary Joyce. Caitlín Kennedy is capitalising on the ball being fed into the left-hand corner and is powerfully belting it back up the field.*"

The game continued.

"*That's your ball, Caitlín!*" shouted Nate as he watched the ball being propelled in Caitlín's direction.

Caitlín leapt into the air, colliding with Mary and knocking her to the ground.

"*I flattened you before! Don't think I can't do it again!*" threatened Caitlín.

There was no doubt that Caitlín was lighter on her feet but Mary's strength made their battle on the field equally squared.

"*Go on, Caitlín!*" yelled Shelly, watching Caitlín storm up the field and score a beauty of a point just when the team needed it.

"*The points are flying over the bar here quicker than Slattery's pub,*" continued Waxy, live on air. "*We've seen a show of cracking good points coming from both sides which means the teams are now level, but the clock is ticking. This is heart-stopping stuff! The contest between Caitlín Kennedy and Mary Joyce has become as strategically important as Napoleon's battlefield. St. Catherine's are trying their best to get the ball to Mary Joyce but gatekeeper Caitlín Kennedy is earning her stripes here on her debut for Ballantur and is successfully shutting her out. Now, St. Catherine's Kathleen Walsh sends a handy puck to Josie Nyland. Nyland knows time is of the essence and swiftly drives it over to Julia Crosby, who has outrun her opponent ensuring safe passage to Maggie Sweeney. Oh, this is poetry in motion by the St. Catherine girls! Like an egg-and-spoon race she continues to sprint up the field with the ball and is able to push off Delia Hennelly with her free arm. St. Catherine's are determined to maintain their good record and are not going down without a fight here. She finds space and drives the ball down to Mary Joyce, but no! Caitlín Kennedy has got there first and crushed the last-ditch attempt by St. Catherine's. Oooooh! That's got to hurt! Kennedy is on the ground due to a late challenge by Mary Joyce. The game is halted. The referee is running over. He's been intercepted by an irate supporter – I think it's Nate Wheatley! Kennedy has picked herself up but is cradling her hand. She's being helped off the field. The referee is showing Mary Joyce a straight red card now and even though it is the eleventh hour, it is so deserved. The infliction occurred after contact was made with the ball. It was a deliberate hit. This is unbelievable stuff. Ballantur have been awarded a penalty and rightly so. Sheila Noone steps up to take it. The pressure on her is paramount but she looks reasonably composed, which is more than I can say for the rest of us. You could hear a pin drop. Here we go. She scoops up the ball, drives it hard. But, nooo! It's wide. She's on her knees. The reference has blown his whistle. She can't believe it, we can't believe it! The light has quenched for Ballantur. They fought so bravely to keep it alight, but they head away with a draw and that's more than was expected of them."*

Shelly was now at Caitlín's side and insisted taking her up to the doctor's house so he could examine her hand.

"Can you move your fingers?" she asked.

"Yes, I can. My hand isn't broken. I'll be fine." Caitlín grimaced.

"Yeah, but you're clearly in a lot of pain."

"Not as much as that imbecile will be by time I finish with her," said Caitlín, brushing past Shelly when she spotted Mary Joyce walking across the pitch. "*Hey! You!*"

Nate, anticipating a showdown, grabbed Caitlín and turned her towards him.

"She's not worth it. You rearing up on her now won't make you any better than she is. Ballanur have a good clean reputation. Think of your teammates – and your job. It will be in the paper. You leave her to me."

Coming to her senses thanks to Nate, Caitlín turned and walked the other way.

Nate followed Mary into the dressing room and wasn't afraid to call her out in front of her teammates.

"What the hell were you doing out there? You spent the whole time trying to sabotage Caitlín Kennedy. I was watching you."

"It's a physical game, mister. It gets rough. If it's too hard for you to watch, why don't you join the other ladies making the tea and sandwiches?" she replied sarcastically.

"*You listen here to me, miss.* There's a fine line between poor sportsmanship and plain thuggery and it's very clear to me what side you're on. You pull a malicious stunt like that again and I will report you the County Board and get you banned from playing altogether. You should be ashamed of yourself. You have let your team down – you're nothing but a liability to them."

"Me? My sending off gave ye a huge favour and ye still sent it wide!" She laughed hard. "Ye are pathetic. Ye couldn't kick your way out of wet paper bag."

St. Catherine's Coach butted in. "That's enough now, Mary. Both teams deserved the draw so we'll leave it at that."

Doctor Quinlan examined Caitlín's left hand. It wasn't broken but she had extensive bruising on the left side of it, especially along the small finger which took the brunt of the stick. He gave her a tube of ointment and painkillers, and told her to put some ice on it to keep the swelling to a minimum. Finally, he wrote her a sick note for work and advised that she stay at home for the next couple days. Which Caitlín refused point blank to do.

"We're in the middle of a murder investigation," she protested. "There's no way I can take time off now!"

Doctor Quinlan had to talk louder over Caitlín to make his point. "If you hurt that hand further it will take it even longer to heal. Why don't patients ever listen to me? Now go home and rest it!"

Predictably, Caitlín turned up for work the following morning. She wasn't a bit surprised that Sergeant Lamb had already heard about her injury. News travelled faster than a greyhound around this town.

Tully arrived into the station just as the two of them were right in the thick of it.

"I said go home, Kennedy!"

"But honestly, it's fine! Look! The swelling has gone down. As long as I'm not lifting anything heavy, I'll be fine."

"I am not allowing you to come into the workplace contrary to the medical advice of your General Practitioner."

"But we're in the middle of the inquiry and, if you don't mind me saying so, sir, we've hit a bit of a brick wall so we really need all hands on deck."

"In other words – you don't think we'll manage without you."

"No, that's not what I'm saying at all," said Caitlín defensively.

Both held their fire momentarily, before loading up again.

"Maybe you should consider a different extra curriculum activity, Kennedy. High impact sports like that should be left to the men. We can take the hits."

Caitlín was fit to explode at that remark and was ready to hit him where it really hurt. She stormed out of the station instead.

Nate Wheatley screeched his truck to a halt and swerved into the footpath when he saw Caitlín pounding down the main street. After a brief catch-up between them, Caitlín continued to complain about the conduct of Mary Joyce.

"But thanks for persuading me to back down with Mary after the match," she said.

"In your state of anger? If I hadn't we'd be sending her home in a flask!" he said, laughing. "You need to control your temper on the pitch – it could have consequences for a job like yours."

Caitlín didn't care much for him patronising her but knew he only meant well. Unfortunately, she got another unwanted opinion when she walked into Cassie Quirke's shop as the talkative proprietor had also unsurprisingly heard about what happened.

"Honestly, Garda Kennedy, it's no sport for a woman," she said with a tut of disproval.

"It was nothing to do with sport. This is the woman I arrested for stealing your jewellery and she was just maliciously trying to get back at me as a bangharda."

"That's no job for a woman either. There are certain things that women should steer clear of if you ask me."

"I'm not asking you! So if it's not too much trouble, can you please give me my change or maybe you think women shouldn't be allowed to have money either!"

When she arrived back at her house, she met Wesley Pollard pulling out of her driveway. He slowed down on her approach and stopped his car. His plaster of Paris had been removed and he was able to drive again.

"Hello, Caitlín, I've just been to the station. Your sergeant filled me in on what happened to you. You poor thing, are you all right?"

"I'm grand. I keep telling everyone it's not as bad as it looks," she replied, holding up her bandaged hand. "I'm more than able to go to work but they won't let me. Oh, and don't worry, I'll be right as rain for the rally."

"That's good," he said, "but unfortunately I have a bit of bad news on that front. My mechanic is really busy at the moment and isn't able to go and get the car in England as soon as we had hoped."

"But I need it as soon as possible for practice!" said Caitlín.

Wesley picked up on her anxiety but couldn't offer her any words of comfort other than telling her he would be in touch again as soon as he could.

Caitlín went into her house and walked around restlessly. Pulling her runners out from underneath the couch, she put them on and laced them up. By the time she opened the front door it was raining. Sod it, she thought, can this day get any worse? She banged the door shut after her and took off jogging down the road.

Running in the rain on her own brought calmness to her racing mind which is just what she needed.

An hour later she arrived back at her house in a more pacified state. Shelly was in the kitchen making lunch.

"Hi, Shells, what are you doing home?"

"I came back to check on you. I knew well your sergeant would send you home."

"Present company excused but I wish people weren't making such a fuss," said Caitlín.

"Like it or not, you have another well-wisher now," said Shelly, nodding towards the window. "Wesley Pollard is here."

"Again? He was already here this morning to tell me they can't collect the car in England yet," Caitlín said over her shoulder as she walked to the front door to welcome him in.

"Hello, ladies. I'm terribly sorry to be making a nuisance of myself but I know how worried you are about getting the car and I agree with you – getting as much practice in before the rally is imperative if we are to have any kind of success. I don't know why I didn't think of this before but I was discussing the matter again with my mechanic since and he suggested that you should go and collect the car yourself. Only if you feel you're up to driving, of course?"

"Me?" replied Caitlín in disbelief.

"Why not?" encouraged Wesley. You said you're on leave at the moment so if you think your injured hand wouldn't prohibit you from driving, then maybe you should."

"Where is the car exactly?"

"As I told you, it's in Cornwall in the southwest of England. You could get the boat from Rosslare to Pembroke and then a ferry crossing from there to Port Isaac in Cornwall. Believe you me, by the time you drive back to Ballantur, you and the car would be very well acquainted. What do you think?"

"I don't know, Wesley. It's a big journey, sounds daunting."

"I'd go with you myself but all that sitting down wouldn't be good for the circulation," said Wesley, tapping the shinbone of his recovering leg with his walking stick.

Caitlín felt under pressure. While Wesley had been very reasonable with her this far, she couldn't help feeling he was telling her to do this rather than asking.

"I take your point, Wesley. It would be a great opportunity to get familiar with the car and more importantly get it over here as soon as possible but, I don't know, I don't think I'd like to go on my own."

"I'll go with you!" butted in Shelly.

"But how will you get off work if you don't give Doctor Quinlan enough notice?" asked Caitlín.

"He's the one on to me about taking my annual leave. I haven't taken any because I didn't want to waste it hanging around here. Go on, Caitlín, do us both a favour."

"It's up to you, Caitlín, I won't pressure you if you are not comfortable with it – or if it would interfere with your recovery," said Wesley, looking away.

"Oh alright. In for a penny, in for a pound. Cornwall, here we come!" agreed Caitlín.

"*Woo-hoo!*" squealed Shelly in delight.

"Brilliant, that's my girl. I was hoping you'd say yes. This solves all our problems. Leave the organising to me," said a satisfied Wesley.

Chapter 21

A bridge too far

The scenery travelling around the bendy roads of Cornwall was beautiful. A bounty of wild flowers were vying for space in the hedgerows, exploding like fireworks. Green and rural, just like the West of Ireland, thought Caitlín, except for the large fields that were cultivated and groomed to within an inch of their hedges. The beaches by the coast were the showstoppers. A plethora of little coves, each one prettier than the last and all adorned with the turquoise sea that was playfully running in and out on the sand. "A charm bracelet of beaches" as Shelly aptly described them.

However, their new admiration was brought to an abrupt halt when they were dropped at the homestead of the vendor of the car.

"Is it a junk yard or a scrap yard?" asked Shelly sarcastically.

"Is there a difference?" replied Caitlín as they tried to take in the museum of rust in front of them.

Old cars, tractors and other unidentifiable partial machinery lay strewn at the frontage of the house. Suddenly, an angry dog made a vicious run towards them only to be yanked back when his chain ran out.

"Let's get out of here, this can't be the right place," said Shelly, clutching her beating heart.

"Hang on a minute," replied Caitlín, scanning the yard. And then she saw it. *Love at first sight*. Her Ford Capri which was shining among the debris of metal like a phoenix rising out of the ashes.

A creaking noise came from the front door and a rotund man wearing greasy navy overalls stepped out.

"All right, Flower, settle, will ya?" he said to the barking dog.

The dog shut up and retreated.

"*Eh* up, what we got 'ere then?" he asked in his distinct Cornish accent before looking the two girls up and down."I say! Two right Diablos!"

"What's a Diablo?" Caitlín whispered to Shelly.

"I think it's a state-of-the-art butter churn," she replied, unimpressed.

"Ladies, what can I do for ye? Ye look petrified," he said, chuckling.

"We were told to ask for Ronnie, at this address," said Caitlín. "We're here on behalf of Wesley Pollard. We're collecting the Ford Capri."

The man sat down slowly on a discarded lorry axel with no rush on him."You've come to the right place. I'm Ronnie. How's Wesley? I know him for years. Top bloke."

"He's very well. Is that our car over there?" said Caitlín.

"Aye, 'tis too. Which of you two dolls is driving it for the rally?"

"I am," said Caitlín.

"Wesley always had an eye for a good-looking woman," he said, smirking.

Becoming uncomfortable in Ronnie's lecherous presence, Caitlín tried to move things on. "Can we get the keys from you, please? We're eager to get on the road. We have such a long journey ahead of us."

"You can." Ronnie leaned back and folded his arms, deliberately trying to delay them either out of loneliness or devilment. "But you'll have to come into the 'ouse first. You'll be needing your paperwork, won't ya?"

Reluctantly the two girls followed Ronnie inside. Caitlín attended to the papers while Shelly looked around, failing to make sense of the chaos. The room they were standing in was half sitting room, half workshop. A roughly sawn loaf of white bread and several cups of half-drunk black tea littered one side of the dining table while a motorbike engine placed on newspapers to soak its leaking oil sat on the other.

"And, more importantly, how is Tom?" Ronnie enquired of Caitlín.

"Tom? Tom who?" she replied.

"Tom, Wesley's mechanic. He was the one who was supposed to be picking up the car, but once he heard you were available, he decided to let you do it instead."

"Oh yes, I must thank him. I need all the practice I can get."

"So you don't know him?" Ronnie asked, with a peculiar look on his face.

"Haven't had the pleasure yet. Now, if you don't mind, Ronnie, we'd better get going," Caitlín said, trying to close down the convoluted conversation.

VROOM, VROOM!

"Do you hear that? squealed Caitlín as she revved the engine of the Ford Capri. "Now, let's the hell out of here!"

"Mind the dog!" shouted Shelly, as the two racy ladies sped out of Ronnie's labyrinth of metal.

A short time later, they pulled into a lay-by in the small town of Port Isaac. This was a popular vantage point for tourists to look out over the sea below and take in the majestic cliffs and surrounding area. They got a few impressed looks of approval from fellow car enthusiasts admiring their stylish set of wheels. Caitlín couldn't resist taking a look of pride back over her shoulder when she walked away from it. But getting something to eat was Shelly's priority and they were happy to try out the local cuisine at a traditional stone-clad pub called The Queen's Oar where Wesley Pollard had also arranged for them to stay for the night. An overfriendly barmaid talked them into trying the Cornish Pasties and two pints of their best bitter called 'Cornish Gold'. They discovered the beer was palatable but the pasties they could take or leave. Shelly didn't have any grá for the lamb-and-vegetable filling in a fold of shortcrust pastry. Caitlín tried to give it the benefit of the doubt but didn't finish hers either. With both of them agreeing they were still hungry, Caitlín suggested dessert but Shelly said adamantly, "Not here".

Shelly went on the hunt for ice cream while Caitlín took their handbags and jackets and headed to the beach which was accessed via a small road down a steep hill but not before looking up to check again on her new pride and joy. She laid the jackets on the sand and sat down, taking in the panoramic seascape. Oh, this is the life, she thought and leaned back to soak up the sun. The horseshoe shape of the cove provided a natural windbreaker. To Caitlín's right, she could see people on the top of the cliff taking photographs with the radiant blue sea as their backdrop. To her left she noticed that Mother Nature had taken quite a bite into the cliffs, leaving a gap between one part and another. Amazingly, someone with high optimism and great nerves had built a house on the top of it. A precarious rope-bridge connected this cliff to the next one if one wanted to avoid the long walk around. Wow, what a place to live, Caitlín thought as she breathed in the sea air and dug her bare feet into the warm sand.

A walk down a small cobblestone narrow street brought Shelly to a quaint ice-cream parlour. Its pastel-coloured exterior walls were as tantalising as the rainbow colours of the ice cream on display inside. The jolly man behind the counter took the order of this giddy girl who ordered a large strawberry cone for herself and a caramel one for Caitlín.

"Watch out for the seagulls," he teased. "They love ice cream, especially strawberry!"

On reaching the beach, Shelly handed Caitlín her cone and sat down beside her. "This is the life!" she said.

"That's just what I was thinking!" said Caitlín. "Well, apart from Ronnie. He was a bit of a weirdo, wasn't he?"

"You're never happy," teased Shelly. "But I know you like Tully."

"I know you like Tully too."

"Look, you saw him first so I'll bow out if you're interested."

"I don't know. I thought I was until Detective Cullen came along but he shot me down like a pheasant when I suggested he'd come over for dinner. I thought the way to a man's heart was through his stomach."

"He's not looking for dinner, he just wants dessert. You should forget both of them if you ask me. Neither of them are right for you."

"Oh, please don't tell me *'there's plenty more fish in the sea'.*"

"I won't," said Shelly. "But there is more than one pebble on the beach!"

Then suddenly and without warning a shadow loomed overhead and the menace swooped in and plucked Shelly's ice cream right out of her hand.

"*Argh!*" She jumped up and starting running down the beach after the offending seagull.

Caitlín followed her for the sheer hilarity of it all, laughing out loud. The delicate ice cream quickly fell out of the grasp of the seagull's claws.

It landed right in the middle of a precious sandcastle under construction, causing the five-year-old builder to cry hysterically and run to the arms of his oblivious mother. This made Caitlín laugh even more. She was bent over with her hands on her knees.

"*Thief!*" shouted Shelly who had stopped too.

"I know, from right under your nose," said Caitlín, who was still belly-laughing and trying to catch her breath.

"*No! Thief! Thief at our bags! Look! He's got your car keys!*"

"*Jesus Christ! Run!*"

The smile wiped off their faces, they ran as fast as they could after the male perpetrator. Without looking back, he ran to the bottom of the cliff and up a steep stony zigzag path that ascended to the top. Eventually he became aware he was being pursued by Caitlín, with Shelly not far behind.

Once he had reached the summit he turned right and ran along the edge of the cliff. Trying to test the nerve of the girls on his tail, he made straight for the rope bridge. Its swaying suspension disorientated Caitlín at first but she soon found her footing and kept going.

Unfortunately, the same could not be said for Shelly.

"*Caitlín!*" she cried out.

Caitlín looked back over her shoulder. She saw Shelly lying down on the bridge. "*Get up! Come on! We nearly have him!*" she yelled, presuming Shelly had just tripped over.

"*Caitlín, help me!*" Shelly cried out again.

Realising now there was something wrong, Caitlín ran back to Shelly.

"What's wrong with you? Did you fall?" she asked.

"No. I can't move. I don't know what's wrong with me," replied Shelly who was shaking, sweating and breathing raggedly.

Caitlín read the situation immediately. "You're having a panic attack. Are you afraid of heights?"

Shelly didn't need to answer. She had her eyes tightly closed. She couldn't bear to look down through the gaps in the timber boards beneath her. The sandy beach below appeared to be a very long way down.

"You'll be grand," said Caitlín. She caught Shelly under the oxters and dragged her back to the grass verge of the cliff. "Look, Shell, you're safe now, back on land."

Shelly opened her eyes and exhaled loudly.

"Stay here!" ordered Caitlín and she took off like a hare again.

Fortunately, she was met across the bridge by the thief who was now being held by the scruff of the neck by the extended arm of a man who had witnessed the commotion from the top of the cliff.

"I believe these are yours?" he said to Caitlín, handing her keys back to her. "Do you want me to call the police?"

"No, thanks," she replied. "But I don't which is worse here, the seagulls or the pickpockets!"

Ordinarily, she would have thrown the book at this juvenile thug but she'd got her keys back so she was satisfied to leave it at that and go back and check on Shelly. Besides, she had more serious things to deal with back in Ireland.

Chapter 22

A sporting chance

"Did you lock the back door?" Babs Wheatley asked Nate as they were about to get into her car outside their house.

"I did. Did you lock the front door?" asked Nate, opening the door of the passenger side. "Ah here, what's this?" he asked, referring to an obstacle lying across the seat.

"Oh, sorry, Nate, it's a curtain rail for the bathroom. I forgot to take it out of the car."

"I suppose you'll want me to hang it up?"

"No, I'll get someone right to do it."

"*What?* Michelangelo would envy my handyman skills."

"Oh come on, Nate, we both know you're not able to crack an egg," teased Babs.

"Give it to me, I'll drop it behind the wall," said Nate.

"No, it might get wet."

"It's not going to rain today. It's roasting."

"It might be showery though – will you put it in the house, please?"

"Oh, alright," complied Nate. "But I don't want us to be late, the team will already be there."

This frivolous display of domestic normality was becoming more commonplace between them, indicating that they were back on track.

Annually, Sports Day in Ballantur was a big occasion. It truly offered something for everyone: races for the giddy children aged between six and sixteen comprising of two-legged races, sack races, egg-and-spoon races, and an embarrassing father's race and mother's race. If one wasn't into competing, the spectacle of watching all the activities was always immensely enjoyable. Parents and friends alike lined up by the nylon rope barrier and shouted words of encouragement at their loved ones, amid fits of laughter at the follies of their efforts. It was the Leonards first day out as a family since Grace's funeral. Tadgh Leonard won a medal for coming third in the Under-14's race. His grandparents were delighted that something had put a smile on his face again. Cassie Quirke and Dennis Slattery competed against one another in an economic sense, trying to poach customers to their stalls with an array of essentials such as minerals, sweets and chocolate – the Breakfast of Champions for some of these young participants. These vendors were pipped at the post though as the ice-cream man had an enviable queue of all ages at his van, lining up for their 99's.

Of course there was a more serious side to it too, mostly brought by the out-of-towners, or the proper athletes who came to claim the big cash prizes for winning the 100 metre sprint or the 10,000 metre run.

Another event that took pride of place was the men's Tug O' War. Ballantur had a good run competing in it over the last few years on their own turf and at other Inter-County Sports Days. The only team that had found their Achilles heel was Swinford. They stripped Ballantur of the County title last year and now Ballantur were determined to win it back, especially if Nate Wheatley had anything to do with it. Nate was the anchor man and the patriarch of the team which consisted of eight members.

"Right, lads, this is our first test this year and it's against Swinford," rallied Nate, wiping his sweaty hands on his trousers. "They only beat us last year by a shadow. If we are going to start this like we mean to go on, we need to beat them today."

Nate picked up the long thick rope which had a white handkerchief tied at its centre. Thirteen feet on either side of that, white insulating tape was bound tightly around it to signify a marker for each team. A red flag pierced the ground and when one of the white markers was pulled beyond the flag, the victory went to the team that pulled it over. The winners would be the best of three rounds.

"No, you two spread out," continued Nate who was giving direction to his teammates. "We need to even out the weight so we have a better grip on the rope. For feck sake, Benny, who'd you borrow the slippers from? Cinderella? How are you going to dig your heels in wearing those? Babs, come here, see if you can get a pair of boots somewhere for Benny."

"I don't think anyone will be wearing boots today, it's too warm," she said.

Nate wasn't listening; he was too busy wrapping the big rope around him like a python ready to squeeze its prey. The whistle blew for the first time. Ballantur took up their stance while staring at the eight burly men in opposition doing likewise.

"Remember, lads, dig those heels in, straight legs and lean back," ordered Nate before the whistle blew again.

This time the adjudicator dropped his hand to signal the start.

"*Pull!*" shouted Nate.

Immediately, they were dragged forward, grazing close to the red flag.

"Hold firm, lads, keep your position!" shouted Nate from the back.

Under great strain they admirably gained their ground back until Benny slipped and they were hurtled forward, awarding the first round to Swinford. Meanwhile, Babs found a pair of boots attached to Pa Leonard's feet. He was more than happy to oblige in this emergency, despite Elsie's embarrassment at his holey socks.

With Benny now strapped into sturdier footwear, round two went to Ballantur. A big crowd gathered around them for the final pull and the parochial spectators were very vocal shouting and whooping to drive on Ballantur.

The third round was the most lengthy and stagnant with neither side losing an inch of ground. Suddenly, Nate slipped at the back and the rope came within a cat's whisker of the flag. Nate shuffled himself back up and pulled even harder to make up the ground. With a Herculean effort, he roared out from the strain. Then Swinford suffered a faller which Ballantur capitalized on. They pulled for all they were worth and watched the handkerchief edge slower and slower towards their side of the flag. The whistle blew and the adjudicator raised his arm, pointing to the left indicating Ballantur were the winners. A huge cheer rang out. Hearty handshakes and claps on the back were plentiful.

Nate was delighted as he was handed a small silver cup.

"Come on lads, the pints are on me!" he said, rejoicing.

"I think you owe me one too," said Pa Leonard, who was standing in the grass in his socks. My lucky boots did the trick. You'll have to put them up on the mantelpiece beside your trophy."

"Well, at least you'll see them, which is more than I can say for this!" said Nate, nodding humorously at the small silver cup received for such a big effort. But at least they had the title back and that meant the world to Nate.

Meanwhile, Caitlín's and Shelly's spirits had greatly improved on their way home. With their precious car safely parked in the hold of the ferry, they set sail for Ireland. The evening sun was making the sea sparkle like a carpet of diamonds. The two passengers sat outside on the deck enjoying a drink. They even contemplated going on another holiday together, but a cityscape this time, not by the sea, and they certainly didn't want to carry out any obligations while they were at it. They suggested loads of places, hotels and dream villas and continued their brainstorming while driving the car off the ferry and through customs at Rosslare Port.

When the barrier in front of them wasn't being lifted Caitlín stared at the custom officers in their little hut who were staring back at them and talking intently among themselves.

"Something is wrong," she said to Shelly.

"No, there isn't, they just want to look at two hot babes in a hot car."

Four officers came out of the hut and walked around the car with one of them indicating to Caitlín to wind down the window.

"Turn off your engine please, miss. Where are you travelling from, ladies?"

"Cornwall!" shouted Shelly with a little too much enthusiasm.

"Here's my identification," said Caitlín. "I'm Garda Caitlín Kennedy. Is there a problem?"

"Do you own this vehicle?"

"Yes, I do." The affirmation made Caitlín smile. "I mean, no, a friend of mine just bought it from a vendor in Cornwall and I am driving it back to Mayo on his behalf."

"How convenient," replied the officer smugly. "Show me your paperwork, please."

"Here's my driver's licence and the logbook. I know it has to be registered and taxed here yet but I am insured to drive it." Caitlín was trying to be as co-operative as she could.

The officer said nothing and took her papers away to consult with his colleagues.

"What's going on, Caitlín?" asked Shelly.

"I don't know. I don't think I overlooked any of the administration."

"Can you both please step out of the vehicle and leave the keys in the ignition," ordered the officer on his return. "Come with me, please."

The two confused ladies followed him into the main building. Caitlín looked back and saw another officer drive her car into their yard.

Caitlín and Shelly were split up and both detained for vigorous questioning detailing the timeline of their trip, including from where and whom they collected the car and who exactly they were collecting it for and what they did after collecting it.

Shelly was truthfully generous and left nothing out, including the seagull attack and the panic attack. Caitlín too co-operated, explaining that she was driving this particular car in an upcoming rally in a few days and that is why it made sense for her to collect it, so she could get used to driving it in advance.

Eventually she put a halt to the interrogation, demanding to know why they were being detained.

"While you and your friend were enjoying your refreshments on the top deck, Poppy our sniffer dog was looking for treats of her own below deck," said the leading officer. "After a routine check of all the stationary vehicles, Poppy drew our attention to your fancy car and in particular to the two-pound bag of cannabis that was found inside it."

"What, that can't be right!" Caitlín protested. "All that was in our car was our bags, jackets and spare tyre in the boot. I checked that myself. Where exactly did you find this drug?"

"In a compartment under the backseat," said the expressionless officer, who had seen this scenario so many times before.

Fuck, thought Caitlín to herself, putting her head in her hands. "I don't believe this," she said, looking up. "I can assure you, as a dedicated member of the Garda, I know nothing about this and I can vouch one-hundred percent for my friend Shelly too. Neither of us partakes in any way, shape or form with drugs of any description. We've been set up!"

The next couple of hours were spent going over everything again. Caitlín campaigned for Wesley's innocence too. She hadn't known him very long but, going on her own judgement of character, dealing with drugs was a world well removed from Wesley's lifestyle. He was an older, well-to-do gentleman with a passion for cars and racing. Besides, he was married to a woman that the devil himself would hide from, but of course she didn't say that. However, she explained that she found 'Ronnie', the man who sold them the car, a dubious character. Then wheels in her head starting turning. She went on to explain that she recalled Ronnie referring to Tom who was Wesley's mechanic. She pointed out that it was this 'Tom' who recommended her specifically to collect the car, despite the fact that they had never even met.

"So you think this man framed you? Did he know you were a member of An Garda Síochána?" asked the officer.

"I presume so. Wesley would have told him all about me."

"And you still believe he was brazen enough to implicate you in this?" asked the officer, looking at his colleague.

"With all due respect, from my experience, to some men when a uniform includes a skirt it doesn't earn the same dues. Although, on second thoughts, maybe he thought with the presentation of my professional ID it would be shoo-in without any sort of suspicion whatsoever. Oh, I don't know!" Caitlín was frustrated. "If I were ye I would start by taking Shelly and me out of the equation and focusing your investigation on Tom and Ronnie instead."

A weary Caitlín and Shelly were finally released early the next morning, pending further enquiries, but without the car. It had been impounded. Once Caitlín was beyond earshot of anyone she unleashed a barrage of colourful language while kicking the daylights out of a plastic rubbish bin to alleviate her frustrations.

"*Caitlín, calm down!*" shouted Shelly, annoyed at her outburst.

"How can I calm down? How the hell can I go back to Wesley and tell him that I have no car because it's been impounded due to me being arrested under the suspicion of smuggling narcotics into the country! I swear to God, between Mary Joyce nearly breaking my hand and now this, what else is going to go wrong on me?"

Shelly caught Caitlín by the forearm. "I know your luck has got threadbare, that's for sure. But wait and see, this mess will sort itself it out too. Give me Wesley's number. I'll ring him and tell him what happened. I'll say you're too upset to talk to him now. He seems like a nice fellow, he'll know this isn't your fault. Now come on – by hook or by crook we'll make it home to Ballantur."

It wasn't only Caitlín and Shelly who had endured a tumultuous night. Nate and Babs' idyllic sports day took a turn for the worst as they left Slattery's pub. They had indulged in the celebration of the win so Babs had decided to be good citizen and not drive.

"Bet you wouldn't be so moral if it was raining!" teased Nate.

Babs laughed. Nate held her hand. It was one of those balmy summer nights that encouraged a tapestry of fragrance from the honeysuckle and sweet-meadow to mingle in the air. A cuckoo could be heard somewhere in the distance and, even though it was nearly 11 o'clock, dusk was only beginning to settle gently like a feather.

Turning into their drive, they could hear Cody barking at the back of the house.

"I'll go and see what is wrong with him – it's probably only a bird he's after," said Nate.

"That dog is for the flipping birds," said Babs to herself as she pulled the key out of her handbag and headed for the front door.

When Nate turned at the gable wall he immediately could see that their back door had been forced open.

Without any fear he walked straight in.

"*Babs!*" he called out.

"*Oh my God! Nate! Have we just been robbed?*" cried Babs, who had just walked in the front door.

They met in the hallway and tried to take in what they could see in the fading light. Suddenly, they heard a noise.

"What was that, Nate?"

"Put on the light!" ordered Nate.

Then a figure ran from one of the bedrooms and hit Nate on the back of the head with a hard object. Blackness.

———— ❈ ————

When Nate came to he was surrounded by Babs, Doctor Quinlan, Sergeant Lamb and Garda Tully.

"Can you hear me, Nate? Can you see us?" asked the doctor.

They had propped Nate up in a sitting position against the wall.

"Yeah," he replied, blinking to refocus. "What happened?"

"You were assaulted, mate, hit on the back of the head with a curtain rail," said Garda Tully. "Can you remember anything?"

"There was someone in the house, they broke in through the back door," recalled Nate, shakily getting on his feet.

"*Whoa there, big fella*," said the concerned doctor. "Take it easy. Do you feel dizzy or nauseous?"

"No. How long was I blacked out for?"

"Only a few minutes. I rang the doctor and the gardaí," said Babs.

"What about the robber? What did he take?"

"I don't know yet, Nate. I haven't even looked. I thought he had killed you." Babs was flushed in the face with all the commotion.

The doctor got a chair for Nate and told him to sit down for a while. He also encouraged him to drink as much water as he could, noticing the alcohol on his breath. Finally, he told him if at any point he was feeling unwell during the night to ring him immediately.

Babs walked around the house and into their bedroom with the two gardaí in tow. She held her hand to her mouth – she couldn't believe the state it was in. Everything was pulled asunder. She had to choose her steps carefully to avoid standing on their personal items that were scattered everywhere on the floor. No room had been left unturned. She despaired about putting it all back together.

Tully despaired at how much shite people could accumulate.

"The robber was here for a while, Babs, judging by how much he rifled through," pointed out Sergeant Lamb. "I'd say he was watching the house or he could have been at the Sports Day and saw ye heading into Slattery's. It would appear that he was looking for something specific. Any ideas?"

"No. He probably thought Nate kept cash in the house from his takings but he always lodges it in the bank on his way home," replied Babs, picking a few things up off the floor.

"Don't touch anything yet! We need to take fingerprints," said Tully hastily. "Did you get a look at him?"

"*Em*, he was about the same height as me, dressed in dark clothing. He wore a black woollen hat and a black scarf wrapped around his face – all that was visible were his dark eyes. It happened so quickly – he disappeared like a shot."

"He didn't get away as clean as he thought," said Nate who frightened the life out of everyone by his sudden appearance at the bedroom door.

"Jesus, my heart, Nate! You should be sitting down," said a jumpy Babs. "What are you on about?"

"That leather bag on the floor. It must be his. I've never seen it before." Nate pointed to the brown satchel.

Babs's heart sank. Oh no, she said to herself, closing her eyes. She had forgotten all about Rosario's bag and how she had hidden it in the wardrobe the day he came to see her.

But now everyone could see it as well as its contents which were tipped out – the expired blue-mould cannoli, the bottle of olive oil and the box of lemon-scented soaps. Babs knew she would have to come clean about this – she couldn't expect her onlookers to believe anything other than the truth. The specialised gifts were unique to Sicily.

"The bag belonged to Rosario Fratelli," she admitted. "He brought me those few bits when he came to visit me the day before he died."

"And you didn't mention this when you were being questioned?" asked Sergeant Lamb.

"I don't think a packet of desserts and a box of soap were contributing factors to his murder," she replied sarcastically.

"Fair enough," nodded Tully.

Nate walked out.

It wasn't the gardaí Babs needed to convince. Just when the dust had settled between herself and Nate, the pin of a new grenade had been pulled. Noting the tension rising, Sergeant Lamb told them to stay in Slattery's for the night while he and Tully examined the crime scene. Babs grabbed a few things for her overnight bag and, not forgetting the dog, she prepared a dish of leftovers for him and brought them outside. She set the food down for Cody who was sitting patiently beside Nate.

"So another lie, this time about the bag," said Nate who watched the hungry dog eat his supper.

"It wasn't a lie. What's the big deal about a few lousy souvenirs from Italy? Our home has just been robbed and that's all you can think about?"

"Well, I don't what to think anymore," said Nate. "The minute I think the dust has settled another sandstorm blows up and it's always generated by you."

Chapter 23

One for the road

Nate and Babs anticipated a restless night in Slattery's Guesthouse – in separate rooms. While Babs lay awake recalling the awkwardness of the discovery of the bag, all of sudden she recalled Rosario's gilet. She bolted upright in the bed. She remembered shoving it into the wardrobe and putting the locket he gave her into its pocket. If Nate was upset about out-of-date pastries she couldn't imagine how he angry he would be if she revealed Rosario had also gave her a cherished piece of jewellery. She decided she would look for it tomorrow and say nothing to no one.

Sergeant Lamb and Tully had continued to examine the scene at the Wheatley household.

"So what do you think, Sarge?"

"It's hard to say," replied Sergeant Lamb, shrugging his shoulders. "It wasn't random. They were being watched by someone. But, as Babs suggested, it might have been by somebody who thought Nate kept a lot of cash in the house and they knew the pair of them would be away attending the sports day. Of course, the other scenario is ..." he lowered his voice as if someone was listening, "it could be connected to Rosario Fratelli's murder. They were looking for something in particular and they might have believed he had given it to Babs, which means the Wheatleys could have been under surveillance since the murder. They obviously hadn't found it though because they were still tearing the place apart by the time Nate and Babs came home."

"So what horse are you putting your money on?" asked Tully.

"The odds-on favourite would be a straightforward robbery looking for money. But I have a bad feeling about this, *especially* where Babs Wheatley is concerned. This culprit, whoever he is, could be the real killer and the last thing we want is the locals being petrified of this person who is still on the loose and coming back for more."

Babs returned to her house the next morning and quietly stepped inside like she was afraid to provoke any foreboding atmosphere that might still be lingering. She brought the dog in with her and had rolled the daily newspaper into a baton. Nate had commenced his rounds early either because he couldn't face returning to the house yet or he couldn't face Babs. Or both. She felt it was her.

The ordeal of returning to her homely refuge heightened her senses. Without reason she sniffed the air but there was nothing to smell. The sight of everything misplaced around her filled her with dread. She reached down and picked two photographs off the floor. The glass within their frames had been smashed. Touching the one of herself and Nate on their wedding day, she wondered if they would ever be that happy again. The other frame contained a beautiful photograph of herself and her sister sitting beside their now deceased mother while enjoying a picnic by the shores of Lough Conn in Pontoon. While the robber paid no heed to these or any of their other personal items, Babs couldn't help feeling that everything had been contaminated now, spoilt. Their innocence had been exposed and what made them special had gone. It was a violation of everything she stood for. An intrusion unnerving the heart and peace of the mind. Cassie Quirke had told her earlier that morning that she had felt like that too after she had been burgled and how Babs would feel like that for a while, but once everything was put back in its rightful place she would feel like she was "home" again.

Babs dealt with what she could remedy easily first before steeling herself to face what she had been putting off: Rosario's locket. With her fingers crossed in her mind, she reached into the wardrobe and pulled out her coat or *funeral coat* as her late mother labelled any winter coat. Whatever name it went by, Babs was relieved to see that it still concealed Rosario's gilet underneath. While pulling the locket out of the right-hand side pocket something else came with it. She untangled two small keys which were attached to a key-ring labelled *Banca Libertà, Taormina, Sicily*. But her attention was equally drawn to the inside pocket – the weight of something was dragging it down. A brown envelope revealed a surprising wad of Italian liras. She sat down on the bed. While Babs was not familiar with the currency, she could tell its denominations were mindboggling compared to the Irish punt. She checked the currency exchange rates in the paper and estimated it was equivalent to three thousand punts. She was surprised he had left it behind him in his gilet. Could it be the money he was going to use for the deposit to buy the property in Westport, she wondered, and was it this money the robber was looking for? In any event, if it was an indication of Rosario's financial viability, opening a restaurant here in Ireland was something he was very capable of.

———— ❈ ————

Caitlín couldn't wait to sort out the drugs bust as soon as she could when she returned to work. Sergeant Lamb greeted her from his office when she arrived.

"Garda Kennedy! How nice to see you," he said with a false grin. "I heard that you had taken a trip. Did you bring us back any nice souvenirs?"

She knew he knew.

"I'll save you the trouble of trying to justify your misdemeanours, shall I? I already received a call from the Customs Officer at the port in Rosslare, asking me to verify my knowledge of a certain Garda Caitlín Kennedy, stationed at Ballantur, which I confirmed without hesitation. Well, you could have knocked me down with a feather with what he said next. How you had been arrested on suspicion of smuggling drugs into the country! I have to hand it to you, I didn't see that coming."

"I was framed! Obviously. Someone put those drugs in the car under the back seat. I would never be involved in anything of the sort – you know that!" said Caitlín, irritated at the sergeant's sarcasm.

"I vouched for your good character, Kennedy, but other than that it's out of my hands – there is nothing else I can do. As you know the matter is being investigated."

Caitlín was surprised and very disappointed that he wasn't going make more of an effort to help her, but she wouldn't give him the satisfaction of pleading with him, so she dropped it. "Did anything else turn up in the murder enquiry?" she asked.

"Yes! There has been a significant development," Sergeant Lamb announced briskly. "Nate and Babs Wheatley's house was broken into and robbed. Nate came upon the robber and unfortunately was assaulted by this individual but he's okay. We have a suspicion that they were searching for something connected to the murder of Rosario Fratelli."

"God!" said Caitlín, genuinely shocked. "Right, so where do you want me to start?"

"At home with your feet up apparently," replied Sergeant Lamb. He pursed his lips. "When I said it was out of my hands, I meant it. You're suspended until further notice until your *drug smuggling* is resolved."

"Oh, come on, sir! We need all hands on deck. The killer could be in our midst!" she pleaded.

"*Do you think I don't know that!*" he shouted in anger. "First of all you hijack a car belonging to this Mr. *Pollack* or whatever he's called, which had the potential to initiate all sorts of catastrophic legal proceedings against the Department, then you injure your hand leaving me with no choice but to take you out of the equation for a few days, but now, now you go off and come back up to your neck in a drugs heist with an indefinite suspension when we never needed as much help as we do now! I never told you this, Kennedy, but when I was permitted to recruit another member of the force I had the option of employing a man or one of these new 'banghardas', so I went with the latter thinking how harmless you would be, but do you know what? You have my heart scalded since you got here. Now, get the hell out of my sight!"

Caitlín fled the station, fighting back the tears. She ran down the main street, nearly creaming Babs Wheatley who was walking into the square with a suitcase.

"*Whoa!* What's wrong? Where are you going in such a hurry?" Babs asked.

"As far away from here as is possible. Where are *you* going?" asked Caitlín, noticing Bab's luggage.

"Only Slattery's Guesthouse, I'm afraid. I'm staying there for the moment. Where have you been? I've been looking for you."

"Long story. Let me buy you a drink. You look like you need it," said Caitlín.

"I could say the same about you, mate," said Babs.

Over gin and tonics, Caitlín went first and unloaded all the bad incidents that befell herself and Shelly in Cornwall, finishing with the drugs arrest showstopper and her suspension.

"Geez, never a dull moment! I'd love to go on holiday with you! No, seriously, you poor thing. Obviously they know you had nothing to do with it, right?"

"They're investigating it but if they don't find any evidence to incriminate the real culprit I could be in trouble, as in goodbye to my job," Caitlín replied, lighting a cigarette and flinging the box on the table.

"It won't come to that. They have no evidence to link you to the crime. Surely Sergeant Lamb will stand by you?"

"Not at the moment, he won't. He's on a very short wire and it's definitely a red one – and my on-going disappointments are just about to cut it. He's livid that I am suspended, especially with this new development about the robbery which you have to tell me about."

"Hang on, you'll need another drink for that," said Babs, turning towards the bar to order another round.

By the time Babs had got to the end of her story, including the bit about Nate giving her the cold shoulder which she referred to as the "New Cold War", she felt overwhelmed and became tearful.

"I'm so sorry, Babs. A break-in of any kind is a horrible experience. Your home is your sanctuary, the place where you feel safe. The thought of some stranger going through what is so precious to you, while they treat it like rubbish, must be unbearable."

Caitlín's understanding didn't seem to alleviate Babs's emotions and she was becoming even more upset.

"It'll be okay, Babs," said Caitlín, rubbing her shoulder. "I'll help you clear up the house. We'll have it looking as good as new in no time."

"It's not just that," sobbed Babs, then opened her clenched hand and showed Caitlín the heart locket with a small red garnet stone in its left corner. "Rosario gave it to me the day before he died. Garda Tully told me this morning he is being buried in Sicily this week. I never got to say goodbye to him properly."

"I can tell he was very dear to you. And the way you spent your last moments with him was an awful experience. No wonder you're upset. Here, let me get you another drink," offered Caitlín.

Sitting down again beside Babs, Caitlín was itching to ask the million-dollar question.

"So, do you think this was a random break-in or is it connected to Rosario's murder?" she asked, trying to sound casual.

"I'm blue in the face going over it with Sergeant Lamb and that detective fellow. The sergeant is always suspicious of me. He even had the nerve to ask me if I had a passport, like I was a flight risk or something!"

"Never mind that," said Caitlín. "But do *you* think the robber was looking for something connected to Rosario?"

This made Babs pause. She held back about the money she found. "If I'm honest – then, yes, I do."

"Babs, I am going to share with you some privileged information but only because I believe it's for your own safety." Caitlín paused. "I'm beginning to think that trouble might have followed Rosario from Italy. His killer may be Italian."

"But what about the two Irish suspects, Finn and Madge Costigan?"

"Both of those suspects have strong motivations, that's for sure, and we are still pursuing those lines of enquiries but I have to admit we have hit a bit of a brick wall. I think there could be more answers in Sicily than there are here."

"What about the Italian police?" asked Babs. "Are they any help?"

"Not much, to be honest – they're relying on us for answers. The Irish Embassy in Rome has also put us in touch with a contact in Sicily but he's only a civil servant so we're very limited in getting any resources there."

The two ladies sat in silence, feeling defeated.

"I have an idea!" Babs announced in a suddenly upbeat manner.

"Well, they're bit thin on the ground so let's hear it," said Caitlín.

"Let's to Italy!"

Caitlín laughed out loud. "I think you've got Dutch courage – Italian style."

"I'm serious."

"Give me one good reason."

"I'll give you three," replied a resolute Babs. "One, I want to say goodbye to Rosario properly. Two, you just said there might be more clues to his murder there than there are here. Three, I want whoever killed him to be brought to justice. I feel like this is my entire fault. If he hadn't come here to Ballantur to see me, he might still be alive and I don't want that hanging over me for the rest of my life."

"I understand that, Babs, but I don't think you and I going there now is the right time."

"It's the perfect time! You're suspended from work, you have no car to practise in for the rally and you also need to rest your injured hand. If anyone needed a break right now, it's you!"

"It's a good pitch, Babs, but no, I don't think so," said Caitlín.

"Why, what's stopping you?" demanded Babs.

"Ah, money for a start," said Caitlín with a laugh.

"I'll pay for you," offered Babs easily, thinking of her new windfall.

"What? No way. Don't be daft!" Caitlín was having none of it.

"You can pay me back then when you have it."

"That's very generous of you, Babs, but no, I can't accept that."

Babs stared at Caitlín, getting annoyed. "Look, I'm not ready to go back to my house yet, not just because of the heap it's in but I'm not ready to face Nate. I keep letting him down. But, at the same time, Rosario meant so much to me too and if I can't get justice for what happened to him or least say goodbye to him, well then, I feel like I'm letting him down also."

"Oh, so it's turning into a *guilt* trip as well as everything else?" challenged Caitlín. "It sounds like going to a lot of trouble that might amount to nothing, Babs."

"A small ripple can make a big ring. It could provide you with a breakthrough you will never find here. There's only one catch. I have a feeling your lovely boss might ask me to surrender my passport so we need to go tomorrow."

"Why would he?"

"As I told you already, he asked me if I have a passport. I'm still accused of murder, the robbery might have something to do with me and he knows Nate and I are on the warpath so maybe he thinks I'm going to buckle and bolt out of here."

Caitlín stared at Babs in disbelief. Was she always this crazy, she wondered.

"So what's it going to be?" pressed Babs. "Are you in or out?"

"*I'm in!*" said Caitlín, bowing to the pressure.

"Good woman! One for the road?"

"And two for the ditch!" responded Caitlín, clinking her glass with Babs and toasting to their adventure ahead.

Chapter 24

White feathers

Planes, trains and a boat ride later, the two tired prima donnas stepped onto the Sicilian pier. If Babs and Caitlín thought it warm at home they weren't at all prepared for the waft of heat that stifled them when they arrived onto the island, situated off the mainland at the southern toe of Italy. The two Sweaty Bettys walked through the meandering streets of the picturesque town of Taormina. Babs was very taken with its charms, leaving Caitlín to figure out where the civic office was. Seeing they had no plan at all, Caitlín thought it would be a good place to start. It was there Lorenzo, their contact in Sicily, worked. He had been appointed by the Irish Embassy in Rome and had been much more amenable than any assistance they had got so far from the Italian Carabinieri.

"Caitlín?" Lorenzo rose to his feet to greet the two visitors in his office.

Truth be told, they were delighted to get out of the sun.

"You must be Lorenzo? This is my acquaintance, Babs Wheatley."

"I'm Lorenzo McMahon."

"McMahon?" said Babs and burst out laughing.

"Yes, my mother is Italian and my father is Irish – from Kinsale in County Cork."

"Well, your mother obviously wielded the stronger gene," said Babs, referring to his black wavy hair, chocolate-brown eyes and sallow skin. But she could nearly detect a Cork lilt in his accent. She estimated he was around thirty years of age.

As well as Lorenzo being amusing, his Irish heritage certainly made the two women relax before they went on to discuss Rosario Fratelli and his murder in Ireland. Despite it being thirty degrees outside, Babs was a true Irishwoman and graciously accepted a cup of tea from Lorenzo but was flummoxed when it served with hot milk, that being the Italian custom.

"*Dio riposi l'anima sua!* May God rest his soul," said Lorenzo when they were up to speed with their respective reports. "I presume you don't know he was laid to rest yesterday?"

Babs didn't know. She squeezed her hands around her china cup to compose herself but could still feel a lump rising in her throat.

Caitlín noticed her sadness. "Perhaps we could go and visit his grave?" she suggested softly, in the hope it might give Babs some comfort.

Babs stared ahead. "I don't want to remember where he's dead. I want to remember where he was alive." She looked at Lorenzo. "Can you take me to his farm?"

Lorenzo looked at Caitlín in alarm, not knowing what to say.

I knew this trip would be a bad idea, Caitlín thought. "I don't know how appropriate that is, Babs – the family are grieving. Maybe there is something else we could do?"

"I didn't come all this way to buy postcards. I want to see where he spent his life living and working. Don't you want to talk to his family for your investigations?"

"Yes, I do," answered Caitlín feebly, "but we didn't know the poor man was only buried yesterday."

"We're only here for a few days. If we say it's police business then they'll have to talk to us," persisted Babs.

"Okay, why don't I contact the family and ask them if it would be suitable for you to visit them tomorrow," interjected Lorenzo, sensing the tension. "Regardless of the outcome, we have plenty else to be getting on with, so I will meet you in the morning at my house – say eleven o'clock? Here are directions to a boarding house which is only a few streets away from where I live. Now go, relax after your long trip, enjoy the evening exploring our beautiful town and all it has to offer." Then he finished with real Italian finesse, "Have some dinner al fresco, drink some wine, dance a little and embrace our dolce vita!"

The two took Lorenzo's advice and after a well-deserved rest at their basic but clean guesthouse, they found their second wind. They wandered down the streets which were buzzing with activity and awash with tourists who came to savour this popular town. Many came to see the historic Greco Roman Amphitheatre or to enjoy the popular walk out to the idyllic island known as the Isola Bella. Shops and street traders within the town sold many desired foodstuffs and souvenirs such as olive oil, lemoncello, almonds and trays of tantalising cannoli. The source of all this opulent food was the rich volcanic soils from their beloved fearsome mountain – St. Etna. Not only did she provide a rich diet from the earth, her black volcanic rock was crushed into small pieces and impressively crafted into beautiful pieces of jewellery such as bracelets, necklaces and key rings. This, in particular, caught Caitlín's eye and she bought a few pieces to take home. But the true gift to remember was free for all in the square known as Piazza IX Aprile where the tourists were captivated by the stunning view that could be seen from the terrace on the cliff edge of the square. It was a vista to remain in the mind forever – the tall elegant cypress trees and winding roads that sauntered down to the water to form a breath-taking panoramic view of the Ionian Sea. Artists ignored the bustling crowd and concentrated solely on permanently capturing the view with their brushworks to sell to some lucky tourists who could take it home. The piazza was adorned on one side by the Church of Sant' Agostino with the beautiful church of San Giuseppe at the back.

Street performers took up precious space on the marble-chequered paving, playing their accordions or mandolins, serenading the visitors and persuading them to part with a few lira. Eventually, Babs and Caitlín's sense of sight was overpowered by their sense of smell and they realised how hungry they were.

"What was the name of that restaurant Lorenzo recommended again, Al Fresh?" asked Caitlín.

"*Al fresco!* It means dining out in the fresh air."

They were both delighted to get a table at the outdoor café at the edge of the square.

"*Focaccia,*" said the waiter, leaving a basket of bread on their table.

"Excuse me?" asked Caitlín, in disbelief at what she thought he had just said to her.

"It's just the name of the bread, I think," Babs rushed in before Caitlín returned the compliment.

"I don't think I'm very culturally aware of Italy," Caitlín sighed.

The waiter returned and left a jug of Chianti wine and two glasses on the table.

"So you won't be wanting any of this then?" teased Babs, as she filled their two glasses.

After a delicious meal of exotic spaghetti bolognese, there was still a little bit of room for the highly recommended tiramisu, which the two diners couldn't resist. Besides, they didn't want to leave this prime location now because a band had set up at one end of the square. Coloured bulbs that hung diagonally across the square were turned on, so some outdoor dancing could commence and how could one resist on this perfectly warm summer's night? An ambience of romance and merriment was in the air. Babs and Caitlín were fixated, watching all the stylish people around them, and got caught up in the intoxicating atmosphere. Soon they, too, were singing along to the songs they surprisingly knew already – like '*Quando, Quando, Quando*', '*O Sole Mio*' and '*Tu Vuo Fa l'Americano*'. Their invigorating beat filled the dance floor and one man asked Babs for a dance, which she bashfully accepted.

"Here, mind my things," she said, winking at Caitlín and smiling like a horse who had just won the Galway Plate.

Caitlín felt rejected that no-one had asked her and coolly lit a cigarette to take the vulnerable look off herself. Three songs later, Babs returned to the table, all out of breath and nodding in gratitude to the Italian man who favoured her.

"Oh my god, I'm roasting after that," gloated Babs, flopping down on her chair. "Here, pass me back my gilet!"

"Why are you carrying that flipping thing around all day? It's boiling here – you don't even need it," retorted Caitlín, throwing the garment over at her.

"And you don't need to be smoking either, young lady. It's bad for you!" Babs snapped back, annoyed at Caitlin for having so little regard for Rosario's gilet. "Sorry, I think the heat is getting to me," she added, smoothing down the garment.

"I'm sorry too. If we need this trip to be a success we'll have to pull together."

This remark resonated with Babs. She knew she would have to be honest with Caitlín about the talk she'd had with Rosario so Caitlín would have a chance to investigate his death properly.

"Caitlín, for the purposes of clarity I need to tell you a few things and I'm sorry I didn't tell you sooner, but I hope when you hear them you'll understand why."

Caitlín looked at her with caution, wondering what Babs was going to come out with.

"This all began when Rosario sent a postcard out of blue a few weeks ago with a short message suggesting he wanted me back in his life. Seeing it was thirty years since I had heard from him, I didn't know what to make of that. But then he turned up at my door and asked me to run away with him to open a restaurant somewhere in Ireland." Babs looked away from Caitlín but, without giving her a chance to react, she continued. "The gilet isn't mine, it's Rosario's. He left it behind him in the house the day he came to see me. And he couldn't call back for it that evening because he knew Nate would be home. I didn't want Nate to see it so I hid it in the wardrobe. It might have been what the robber was looking for because there were Italian liras, in notes, in the inside pocket. Caitlín, I counted the equivalent of three thousand Irish punts and there were also these."

Babs took out the small keys and placed them on the table.

"Jesus, Babs!" said Caitlín, very annoyed. She stood up. Then she sat down again. "Are you having a laugh? How the *hell* did you not mention all this before?"

"Because of Sergeant Lamb."

"Why would he stop you?"

"It's hard to share intimate feelings with a Venus flytrap. Ah, Caitlín, I hate the way he judges me, like I'm some sort of scarlet woman who brings trouble on herself."

"Then why didn't you tell me? Or Tully?"

"Honestly, I forgot all about the gilet, I got such a shock from the murder. I swear. I didn't even know what day of the week it was, never mind anything else. I only remembered it when our house was broken into and Nate spotted a bag with a few souvenirs Rosario had given me."

Caitlín picked up the keys to examine them. "I'd say they are for a safety deposit box in the bank and, if he was carrying around that amount of money on him so loosely, there might be a lot more where that came from."

"That's what I was thinking," said Babs.

"Pity you didn't do a lot more sharing and a lot less thinking!" snapped Caitlín.

"Don't be like that with me. I'm sorry. Like you said, we have to pull together now. We won't go forward if we keep looking backwards."

"Babs, I need to know that I can trust you. It's a criminal offence to withhold information like that! You could get into serious trouble. You could jeopardise the whole investigation."

"Oh please, Caitlín, I need you to be a friend to me now, not a garda."

"I'll be whatever you need me to be, but *no more secrets*. Agreed?"

"Agreed. But one more thing. Remember I *did* tell ye that Rosario was under duress from the Mafia but he had found a way out. Well, what if that new avenue wasn't any more moral that the one he was already engaged in? Maybe when we talk to his family tomorrow we can find out more."

"Okay, calm down, Miss Marple. I'd sleep on a washing line right now I'm so tired. Let's get a good night's kip and see what tomorrow brings."

The following morning, they set out for Lorenzo's house. He had drawn a little map for them with all the landmarks of Taormina on it, most of which they were hoping to see later that day.

"How warm is it out there?"asked Caitlín as they headed out the door.

"Hotter than a two-dollar pistol!" replied Babs in a Southern drawl, giddy at getting a chance to explore some of the island.

Lorenzo showed them to his car and they giggled at how cute his little red convertible Fiat 500 was. They drove in the direction of the city of Catania. Lorenzo was full of knowledge about the island and generously shared it with them. They passed the volcanic Mount Etna which was quiet apart from a small manifestation of smoke circulating around the summit which Babs swore was just a cloud. Lorenzo, like all Sicilians was very proud of this mountain. 'She', as he referred to the mountain, was full of character and created a love-hate relationship with the island's inhabitants who ironically attached their houses to her base like limpet shells on a sea rock. The lava that flowed down her skirt of land over the centuries enriched the soil with nutrients like gold dust. The produce that grew there so abundantly and magnificently earned the island another name internationally: 'God's Kitchen'. The ladies were surprised at how hilly the landscape was and every few minutes they appeared to be driving over a very high viaduct connecting one hill to the next. Before long Lorenzo had pulled over for a compulsory expresso at a small café. Caitlín was glad to get some reprieve from the cramped back seat of the car, thinking it wasn't so cute after all. Yawning, she loosened the belt on her dress for more comfort and stretched her arms in the air.

"Hurry up, slowcoach!" Babs called. "Do you need to go back to your tomb, oh sorry, I mean your room? You look awful. Are you alright?"

"I didn't sleep that well – your *new* information kept me awake. I kept trying to figure out how it could be connected to Rosario's murder."

"Here you are," said Lorenzo, setting down their espressos on the outdoor table in three of the smallest white cups Babs and Caitlín had ever seen.

Despite the size, its effect wasn't long kicking in and Caitlín felt all the better for it.

Lorenzo continued to promote Sicily and further informed them that there was going to be a big procession for Our Lady in Taormina later that evening when the heat of the sun bowed out. He described it as an enchantment to behold and how all the streets would be lined with people who would then follow the very ornate statue of Our Lady down the Corso Umberto and onwards towards the pier. The statue would be carried on a beautiful platform adorned with candles and wreaths of flowers. The weight of it all demanded a team of interchanging burly men with good stamina to guarantee its safe passage down to the sea. At this stage it would be dark and the wreaths containing a lit candle within them would be placed on the water to float away, in memory of all the souls lost at sea. Babs and Caitlín remarked at how touching that sounded and looked forward to attending it when they returned.

They then endured a barrage of questions from Lorenzo about Ireland and its characteristics. He had been on holidays there once when he was very small, so he didn't remember much but was hopeful he would return sometime to visit his aunts, uncles and cousins in Kinsale.

When the car pulled to a halt outside the homestead of the Fratellis, Babs took a deep breath. Suddenly, she feared that she might not really know the man she thought she knew so well.

After a few unanswered knocks on the front door, the disappointed investigating party turned to leave. Then a ginger cat ran through a gate and two women appeared in the driveway. They were Rosario's daughters – Sofia and Bianca.

Condolences and introductions were exchanged and the siblings welcomed them eagerly as they were anxious to find out what they knew regarding their father's murder. They explained that very little had been done to date here in Sicily and seemingly the Italian police were relying on the Irish authorities for information.

"We are very grateful that the Irish police have sent an official over here to investigate," said Sofia in the perfect English she had learnt from her father.

Caitlín smiled sarcastically at Babs, both of them wondering how grateful Sergeant Lamb would be when he found out where they had gone.

Caitlín then said she wanted to go over the murder with them, the brutality of which Bianca said she didn't want to hear. Babs didn't want to hear it again either so she suggested to Bianca that she take her for a walk around their lovely farm.

After an awkward obligatory start about the weather, Ireland, Italy and so forth, Bianca got the courage to ask Babs exactly who she was and how she knew her father. Babs truthfully told her that they had a relationship years ago when they were young and how out of the blue Rosario had come to visit her recently and told her his plans to open up a restaurant in Ireland. Bianca told Babs she did recall that her mother once remarked that her father had left his heart in Ireland.

The end of their walk through the weathering olive groves brought them right down to the edge of the sea. Two swans bobbed idly on the surface, scrutinising their spectators. Before too long they cheekily waddled ashore in the hope that the visitors would have some food for them.

"Papa had them spoilt – he was always throwing them bits and pieces. You'd be surprised at what they would eat."

Bianca told her that this was her father's favourite spot. She gestured to Babs to sit on the rocks beside her and both of them silently gazed out for a while at the shimmering blue water.

"Your mother was right though," said Babs. "Your father *did* leave his heart in Ireland." Then she pulled the heart locket Rosario had given her. She smiled at Bianca. "Now it's time to give it back." And she threw it far out into the sea.

Meanwhile, Caitlín and Lorenzo were up at the house, having a more factual talk with Sofia. Caitlín told her that Rosario was carrying a significant sum of cash on him and how he had been talking about setting up a business in Ireland before he was killed. Caitlín didn't know how appropriate it was to be asking about the source of his funds but she had to consider that it might be significant to the case. Sofia was obviously not comfortable discussing the topic. Caitlín had to get more authoritative and point out how the money might have been a motivating factor in his death and, if there was a grey area about where it came from they would have to disclose this, as otherwise the murderer might never be found. She told her that this was a burden they should not have to bear for the rest of their lives.

"There was nothing immoral about the way my father made his money. In fact, he should be acknowledged for it," Sofia replied defensively. "He spent far too long reaping rewards for the benefit of others but at last he found a way to profit exclusively for himself while still helping so many along the way. There are bad people on this island who are known for extorting money from people, and my family and neighbours suffered the same fate. For years he had to give them a cut out of his revenue from the shop and the farm and, even when the olives failed, they still put him under pressure to pay them. It was by pure chance a noble opportunity presented itself and one that he managed to carry out in secret for a long time. It all began one day when he went down to the cove to feed the swans ...”

Rosario's precious pets were on the beach, looking like they were pestering somebody but he couldn't see anyone. He walked up to his two feathered friends and followed their gaze which was focused on the rocks. He still couldn't see anything so he climbed up the rocks and then got the shock of his life. Blinking up at him from an oasis inside the crags were about fifty human eyes. They cowered so tightly together when they saw him that he could sense untold fear in their hearts.

He raised his hands in the air in a surrendering motion, to indicate that he was no threat, and said: "Okay, it's okay. I'm not going to hurt you."

He instinctively knew they were migrants trying to land illegally on the mainland of Italy. He recalled the boat wreckage he had seen not so long ago but at least this time there were survivors. Every now and again he had heard of them arriving further up the east coast of the island, so could only presume they were off course arriving here.

"Can you take us to the mainland? Please?" said a man in English. We are exhausted and hungry with little energy left. Please help us."

"I'm sorry. I am not the right person to ask, I don't have the resources you need. Where are you from?

"We are from all over central Africa. Our countries are ravaged by poverty and starvation. We had to leave. We already have endured incredible walking distances for weeks. We walked up through central Libya and set sail from Misrata."

"You know the streets of Italy are not paved in gold either, especially down here in the south," said Rosario. "Do you not have a contact or an aid, or someone arranging a transfer for you?"

"We had," said the man. "But those who have gone before us have been treated terribly by our organisers. Word reached us back home not to trust them anymore. We didn't know for a long time but their money was being taken by the people who are supposed to be helping them. They promised them jobs and nice places to live, but when they got here they were tricked into slavery and prostitution, ending up in situations no better than where they left. That is why we decided to land here and try and make it on our own. Please help us!"

The man held his hands together, as if in prayer, before climbing up on the rock beside Rosario.

"What is your name?"

"Jabari," replied the humble man, bowing to Rosario.

"Jabari, I am sorry for your troubles but, like I said, I don't have any means to help you," said Rosario, turning away.

"No! Please, we will pay you!" beseeched Jabari and grabbed Rosario by the arm.

Rosario glanced back at this group of desperate people who, at a word from Jabari, began pulling money, coins and jewellery out of their few belongings.

Rosario walked away, along the water's edge. He came upon their abandoned makeshift boat. Then, peering inside, he was shocked to see the body of a woman and two children who sadly hadn't survived this exhausting journey with no food, fresh water or shelter from the sun. Rosario didn't want them to have died in vain. This was the second time he had come across this kind of tragedy. Spurred on by the injustice of it, he walked back to the group of people and told them to lie low until he returned again at the hour of darkness.

True to his word, Rosario and his family came back to the beach after dark when the moonlight reflected on the gentle waves. With a horse and cart they brought buckets of drinking water, bread, cheese and fruit to the weary migrants. Flour sacks were handed around as blankets to provide modest warmth in the cool summer night. Rosario informed Jabari that he himself would take them through the hills on foot because the local informers would be monitoring the roads. By light, if he could, he would try and organise a bus to take them along the coast further north and then a boat to Reggio Calabria on the mainland. He stressed that he could not promise them anything but he would do his best. Jabari told him that a good intention was always better than an empty promise.

This operation proved successful and the partnership between Rosario and Jabari grew from strength to strength with Jabari himself becoming the contact for similar beleaguered people who made hazardous sailings across the sea and were prepared to pay for safe passage. Rosario would be waiting to continue taking them on their journey to a better life. But it was a perilous relationship for all involved, including Rosario. If the Mafia ever found out he had taken over and monopolised one of their lucrative sources of revenue then he would pay the highest price of them all.

Caitlín was enthralled by Rosario's tenacity and courage. "Did anyone know about them?"

"The neighbours knew, and had mixed feelings about it. Some thought he was crazy. They said he was signing his own death warrant with the risk of the Mafia finding out. Others said he was virtuous and brave and then there were those who were jealous. They hated that he had found a new venture, following the failure of the olives, and was making a living without being subjected to extortion."

"Did anyone rat on him?" asked Lorenzo.

"Yes, he was found out, but not by a neighbour," confirmed Sofia. "It was Saverio Filosa or 'The Fox' as Papa called him. He was now the boss of his own illegal organisation. 'Savi', as he was known, spent nearly a lifetime working on our farm and shop with us, under the instruction of the Mafia, and despite all the attempts by my granduncle and my father to steer him in the right path, he reneged. I remember my father said to me one time that feral is a freedom that cannot be tamed. I know now he was referring to Savi. It was a huge betrayal to Papa who knew his life was in danger so that is why he made new plans to leave Sicily and move back to Ireland."

Sofia stopped talking, hearing Babs and Bianca returning to the house.

"The farm is so beautiful – it goes right down to the sea," said Babs.

"She met '121' and '122'," said Bianca, smiling at Sofia.

"That's the two swans," said Sofia. "We could never tell the difference between them except for the tags on their feet. Typically, Papa was one of the first to get involved in a programme to track their migration every year. They usually fly inland during winter for shelter and food and come back here for the summer."

Besides the locket, Babs wanted to leave everything else she had belonging to Rosario with their rightful owners. She handed them Rosario's gilet and more importantly the wad of liras that was in its pocket.

Finally she placed the two small keys on the table.

Caitlín said she thought they could be used for a safety deposit box in a financial institution. The two daughters confirmed that their father had an account and a safety deposit box in the Banca Libertà in town.

"So what could be in them?" asked Bianca.

"Could be anything," replied Caitlín. "Jewellery, bonds, shares, cash."

"But why wouldn't he just put the money into his bank account?" asked Lorenzo.

"Maybe he doubted their confidentiality," said Caitlín. "Was wary of doing it over the counter and through the books. At least if he was putting money directly into the deposit boxes he could keep it a secret."

"Let's go and find out!" said an eager Sofia.

"Hang on, Sofia," said Bianca. "Let's wait a few days at least before we go sorting out his business and financial affairs. We only buried Papa *two days* ago!"

"Don't you want to know? Whatever is in those boxes could hold the key to his murder. And, these people from Ireland are only here for a couple of days. We need to help them as much as we can. Come on, we can get a ride back into town with them now."

"You can go on your own. I have to go to work," Bianca said, leaving the room, clearly not happy with the situation.

Sofia paused before getting into the car and gazed ahead. A big black car passed slowly down the road. "It's *them*," she said in quiet disgust. "They have been watching our house since the funeral."

On their way back into town, Lorenzo was intrigued to see an faded old tin sign hanging sideways at the side of the road. He braked and came to a halt.

"That sign was for the Mirabella Olive Grove Farm," he said. "I heard about it all my life. Sofia, is she still there? Mirabella?"

"Yes, I believe she is. She was affected by the disease but Marco Carbone, the owner, wouldn't let them tear her down in the end. But I think she's dead now," replied Sofia sadly.

"That is the olive tree that is said to be one thousand years old," Lorenzo explained to Babs and Caitlín. "A terrible disease affected the olive trees in 1961 and the government had to destroy a lot of olive groves to contain it."

"How terrible!" said Caitlín. "Were Rosario's olive trees affected?"

"Yes, they were," said Sofia, "but they were spared in the end as they were not as tainted as many others."

"Can we see it?" asked Lorenzo and, without waiting for an answer, he released the brake and swerved into the laneway to the farm.

"But what about the bank?" protested Sofia.

"We won't be long," he said, chancing his arm.

Chapter 25

Flight or fight

A young woman came out of the house to greet the arrival of the Fiat 500. Sofia introduced her as Marco's daughter, Fiorella, who was particularly friendly with Sofia. Fiorella kindly invited everyone to join the family for refreshments on the veranda. The zesty homemade lemonade with a sprig of mint was relished by all on this hot summer's afternoon. Politely, Lorenzo allowed Fiorella and Sofia to discuss Rosario's funeral. Fiorella's knowledge of it indicated that she had been in attendance.

When appropriate, Lorenzo enquired as to the present status of the farm and more importantly the welfare of Mirabella. Conscious of the fact that Babs and Catilín did not speak Italian, Fiorella, who worked as a tour guide part-time, conversed in English.

"Ah, yes, 'Mirabella the Wonderful'!" sighed Fiorella. "You know, when this farm was at the height of its success, Mirabella was one of the biggest draws around here for miles. People came from far and wide to see her. 'The Old Lady' some called her. Others believed she had magic and healing powers. They rubbed the bark or snapped off a leaf in the hope it would bring the same long life to them as she had sustained. The tree is still there but the disease did untold damage to her. She is nothing more than a relic now, but my father still wouldn't let her be felled. He stopped them even as they were poised to fell her. The whole thing broke his heart."

"Forgive me, Fiorella," interrupted Sofia. "I meant to ask you, how is he?"

"Good. He is making a lot of progress. We were ringing him every week with the all the news from around here but now he's in a transgression stage so he isn't allowed any phone calls from the family. The retreat leaders said they want him to deal with various issues without any emotional triggers. I am going to Reggio di Calabria next weekend so I'll visit him then."

"Did they ever find out what caused the olive tree disease?" asked Babs, recalling how Rosario had mentioned to her about the trees failing.

"They did somewhat, eventually," said Fiorella, looking sympathetically at Sofia. "All they said was that it was a bacteria probably carried by an insect, other than our common olive fly, that had inadvertently been imported here. The bacteria would enter the leaves of the trees through the bite of infected insects then quickly multiply, preventing the tree the ability to absorb water and nutrients which would eventually cause it to die. Naturally the insect travelled from tree to tree and it didn't take long for the island to have an epidemic on their hands."

"The diagnosis was such a relief," said Sofia strongly. "Nearly all of the farmers blamed my father for following his advanced programmes, as directed by the Department of Agriculture I might add, when in fact it had nothing to do with him at all."

"Would it possible to see Mirabella? If it's not too much trouble?" asked Lorenzo.

"Can I come?" asked Sofia. "I haven't see her in years. I know where she is."

"Me too," Babs said. "Caitlín?"

"No, you're alright. I'm quite happy to sit here in the shade." She smiled at the three groupies who then headed down the lane to the olive farm.

Fiorella topped up Caitlín's lemonade before offering her a cigarette.

"No, thanks, I'm trying not to," said Caitlín.

"I shouldn't be either. These belong to Papa," said Fiorella with a guilty laugh. She threw the box on the wicker table between them and Caitlín noticed the brand.

After the two women began to relax with each other, Caitlín began to quiz Fiorella, to see what her impression of Rosario was.

"People always had mixed emotions about him. At the beginning they were very taken with him, impressed by his knowledge of the olives and all these new innovative ways he was showing them to make a success of their farms. Unfortunately, when the crops failed everyone blamed him for meddling with nature too much. But luckily my friendship with Sofia and Bianca survived. We all grew up together and went to the same schools. We never let their conflict affect us."

"Did you know about Rosario's plans to move back to Ireland?" Caitlín was hoping she wasn't disclosing something that was a private family matter.

"Yes, we heard that Rosario had been running a secret migrant operation, but was found out. We knew it was in his best interests to leave and bravo to him for finding a way to free himself from the noose that is still hanging around everyone else's neck here, if you know what I mean."

Eventually chatter in the yard signalled the return of the others. Caitlín joined them outside and they said their goodbyes to Fiorella.

"Okay, we really need to get to the bank now before it closes," said Sofia, making for the car.

Caitlín turned to Babs and Lorenzo and quickly asked them, "Right, did ye find out anything useful?"

This was the first time the three of them got a chance to be on their own since morning. Babs and Lorenzo shook their heads.

"Well, something is not sitting right with me about Marco Carbone," said Caitlín. "Rosario was seen talking to an unidentified Italian man before he died in Ireland. At Rosario's murder scene I collected all the fresh cigarette butts on the ground outside. I remember thinking one of them was 'foreign' looking –a white-tipped one. Fiorella smokes and offered me one too but she said they belonged to her father. They're called 'Corona', all white in length, including the tip. But it was the emblem on them that I recognised, a gold crown, just like the one we have retained in evidence has. And another thing, I found an unusual broken bead at the murder scene which I'd never seen before but now I see it all over the place here in Sicily. It's that black lava stone, kind of plain and porous. What if Marco dropped it at the scene like the cigarette butt?"

"But that bead could have belonged to Rosario," said Lorenzo. "It's very circumstantial evidence, Caitlín. Marco is unwell, he isn't even here. He's at a retreat on the mainland."

"But, what if this so-called 'retreat' is just a code for, well, you know, for a –"

"A cuckoo farm!" snapped Babs, cutting Caitlín off.

"A *psychiatric hospital*," Caitlín said, with a disapproving look at Babs. "Maybe the poor man had a breakdown. It sounds like he took the collapse of his business very badly and blamed Rosario for it."

"Oh come on, he hardly followed Rosario all the way to Ireland and killed him!" said Lorenzo.

"This farm has been in Marco's family for generations," said Caitlín. "It must have been devastating for him to lose it through no fault of his own and, who knows, maybe he owes a lot of money to the Mafia too. That kind of pressure can drive a man to do things he never thought he was capable of."

"I guess," conceded Lorenzo, "but before we get carried away the only way to find out is to see if Marco really is at that retreat."

"Agreed. Ring and ask them," ordered Babs.

"They won't give out that kind of information to a stranger, silly!" said Caitlín.

"Ask Fiorella to do it so," suggested Babs.

"We can't do that either! What are we going to say, eh? 'Oh by the way, Fiorella, can you ring that place where your father is meant to be and ask them if he left it to go over to Ireland to murder someone!'"

"I'll ring them," said Lorenzo.

"But they won't tell you either!" said Caitlín, getting agitated.

"They will if I pretend I'm ringing from the Council about a grant, or a fund, or something of the likes that he may be entitled to, like a subsidy towards his medical treatment."

"It's worth a shot," said Babs.

The three investigators had a giddy nervousness about them, or relief in disguise, that they might be finally getting somewhere.

A tailback of cars, horse-drawn carts and bicycles delayed them greatly returning to the town of Taormina that evening because the procession of Our Lady was well underway. Luckily, because of the midday siesta, the bank had late opening hours. Caitlín and Sofia gingerly climbed up the steps to its entrance while Babs and Lorenzo were happy to sit outside in the sun and watch the procession.

Sofia was shown to a vault by a bank official. A few minutes later, looking distressed, she returned to Caitlín who had been waiting for her in the lobby.

"It's no use," she said. "These stupid keys only open the lockers. There's a deposit box inside each one but they have a combination lock of numbers. I tried our birthdays, the date of their wedding, membership numbers, his date of birth, but nothing worked. How will we ever find out what he used?"

"Okay, let's think for a minute," said Caitlín. "How many digits do you need?"

"Four. Can you have a look, please, Caitlín," said Sofia, sounding desperate.

Caitlín accompanied her to the vault.

"See what I mean?" said Sofia, showing the boxes to Caitlín. "Maybe the bank official will open them for us, seeing that Papa is ... you know."

"Hang on. Before we get the official, why don't we have another go?"

"And try what?"

"It's only an idea, but try 0121 and 0122."

"Oh my god! I never thought of those!"

She tried the numbers.

"*Bingo!*" she squealed, clapping her hands together when the two steel boxes clicked open.

"*Shh, shh,*" whispered Caitlín, trying to encourage Sofia to be discreet, especially now that a well-dressed couple had joined them in the vault to open their own deposit boxes.

"Look, Caitlín!" Sofia whispered back, very excited at the contents. There was a significant amount of cash in each box. "How much do you think there is?"

"I'm not sure, but enough to buy a chipper I would think," said Caitlín.

Their fixation on this treasury prevented them from noticing that the gentleman who had come into the vault with the woman was now standing behind Sofia. Eventually, Caitlin felt a presence and turned to see he was pointing a gun at them.

"*Fare la valigie!*" said his female accomplice who shoved two black leather bags at them.

"You heard the woman – get packing!" the man said quietly. "Just taking back what you took from us."

Despite his calm demeanour, Caitlín knew he was not messing.

Moments later, just as she was about to transfer the last wad of notes into the second bag, the vault door opened and the official showed another customer to their safety-deposit box. Their mysterious gunman had to conceal his firearm in the pocket of his coat.

It was flight or fight, so Caitlín shoved a bag of money at Sofia, grabbed the other, and they made a run for the exit. Caitlín slammed the vault door shut behind her and they both ran to the security guard. Sofia told him as quickly as she could how they were just held at gunpoint in the vault. The guard seemed hesitant to do anything.

"We have to get out of here," whispered Sofia. "I'm not sure what side that guy is on."

They ran out of the bank and down the steps to Babs and Lorenzo.

"We were followed here," said Sophia, out of breath. "A man held us at gunpoint in there and told us to hand over the money we found in the vault. He must be Mafia. We locked him in there and ran!"

"But why didn't you just give it to him?" asked Babs, staring at the bags nervously.

"Because if they get their hands on it, the Fratellis will never see it again," said Caitlín.

"Look, two more of them are getting out of that car and coming for us," pointed out Lorenzo.

"Well, let's just confront them – there are only two of them and four of us," suggested Babs, plucky all of a sudden.

"They are not here for negotiations. They're armed!" said Caitlín. "Who the hell is keeping their hands in their coat pockets in this weather?"

"Let's split up," said Lorenzo. "Give me one of those bags. Sofia, come with me. You two, make your way back to my house, and be careful. *Run!*"

The procession was now entering the Corso Umberto. The decorated and elaborate statue was adorned with wreaths of flowers and candles. It was proudly held high by the pallbearers underneath. Decades of the rosary were being murmured by the large crowd that followed the clergy and the cortege down the street.

It was into this flow of people that Caitlín and Babs dispersed themselves. But now, in Caitlín's mind's eye every man she saw in a suit appeared to be watching them. It was like a bad dream. She hoped safety in numbers would deter them from trying to do anything harmful to them in public. Another arrow to their bow was the fact that it was getting dark, so their foreign appearance would not be as noticeable. The procession was scheduled to coincide with dusk falling. Each wreath contained a candle. These would be lit down at the pier and left to float on the water.

They safely made it to the water's edge but then didn't have much cover. They stood in front of the now lowered statue where the wreaths were being unloaded onto trays, ready to be taken out on the boats.

Caitlín dropped the bag of money into a box of wreaths behind her as she saw a man in a suit approaching them.

"*Money!*" he snarled at them.

He hadn't seen her hide it. "We don't have it. Your colleague already took it off us," said Caitlín, chancing her arm.

The man looked at her in confusion. Caitlín realised he probably had very little English.

"No money!" she gestured to him, waving her empty hands in the air. "Your *amigo* has it!" She pointed to another suited man she saw out of the corner of her eye some distance away, standing by a pillar. Not seeing the money on them, their suit walked off.

"Do you think that worked, Babs?"

"I don't know. I think *amigo* is Spanish," replied Babs, who looked like she was on another planet.

"Quick, let's the grab the money and get the hell out of here," said Caitlín.

But, when they turned around all the wreaths were gone. They had been put onto the boats bobbing in the sea.

"*Shit!* What are we going to do now?" asked Babs.

"We need to get that money back. It might be the only way to get out of here alive. Can you row?"

"Row? I used to, but haven't for years."

"We have no choice. Come on!" ordered Caitlín.

The two of them jumped into a small rowing boat.

"Grab that oar," said Caitlin.

They set off and found themselves circling, with Caitlín rowing splashily and ineffectually while Babs quickly got into her stride.

"Relax, Caitlín, we're completely out of sync!"

"Ya think?" said Caitlín, continuing to splash her oar into the water.

"Pull with your arms and push with your legs," directed Babs.

Caitlín was struggling. She couldn't get a feel for the oars and nearly hit a man with one of them as they narrowly missed his boat.

They made some progress and aimlessly circled around the other boats while the wreaths were being dispatched into the water.

The organisers started to shout at them for disrupting the procession. Caitlín was glad their yells were in Italian because she guessed they were not very appropriate for such a pious occasion. The bag's black colour made it hard to see but eventually Bab's beady eye spotted an unsuspecting man moving it out of his way quickly so he could reach his wreath at bottom of his boat.

"I see it!" said Babs. "Just stop rowing altogether, Caitlín! You're making things worse. I'll try and veer us over."

After some ruthless clattering into some other boats, Babs by sheer luck rather than grace aligned her boat beside the one she wanted.

"*My handbag, it's here!*" she shouted as she scooped it up.

More unsavoury heckling ensued from the men in the other boats with some angrily gesturing to them to get out of the water.

"*It's a miracle! Praise be Our Lady!*" Babs cried out.

"Will you *shut up*, Babs! You're only drawing more attention to us. Now try and row this fucking thing back to the pier!"

After a succession of hapless attempts they made it to the steps.

"We'll have to go to the police for help, Caitlín!" said Babs.

"No time, Babs. To your left, there's another suit coming for us. *Run!*"

"Jesus, they're like a rash that won't go away. Caitlín, I can't keep this up!"

They ran back towards the centre of the town and down a side street where both of them had to stop to catch their breath.

"I'm not fit like you. I can't outrun these people and, for God's sake, neither can you," said Babs, flopping down on the ground.

A shot rang out in the air.

"Oh my God, they're shooting at us," shrieked Babs, scrambling again to her feet.

"No, they're not. It's fireworks for the procession," said Caitlín, pointing up to the sky which was now an explosion of radiant colour. "Show me the map so we can see where Lorenzo's house is."

The fireworks gave them enough light to make out that they were only two streets away.

"*Buona sera, ladies!* What a beautiful night, no?" announced a man, walking out of the shadows beside them.

They knew immediately he wasn't out for a midnight stroll.

"*Hand over the money,*" he said, pointing a gun at them.

"It's not your money, said Caitlín defiantly.

"It is *our* money. Rosario Fratelli already tricked us out of it once, and we will not be fooled a second time. You look like a pretty girl, not a stupid one."

Another firework was propelled into the air. Its spent debris fell in a burnt shoal around them. This startled the gunman who began brushing it off his clothes for fear it might burn him.

"*Go!*" yelled Caitlín, pushing Babs into a run.

The gunman took a shot at them but missed, the sound disguised by more exploding fireworks.

They ran around the corner and through the first open door they saw, which was the entrance to a church. With seconds to spare they hid around the back of the door but the gunman was hot on their heels and arrived in immediately after them. Letting him take a few steps up the aisle, they swung around the door and ran out again. Caitlín began to pull the door shut behind them, hoping she could lock it, but the gunman turned and lunged towards them, catching the door with his left hand. Caitlín continued to bang it closed, ignoring the man's cry of pain as his hand was caught between the jamb and door. There was no key in the lock. She got Babs to hold the door while she pulled the belt of her dress off and tied the handle of the door to a lamp mounted on the wall, trapping their pursuer inside. It bought them enough time to get away.

Once they were inside Lorenzo's house and out of danger, Babs squeezed the life out of Caitlín.

"I'm so sorry! This is all my fault! I should never have suggested coming here," she cried.

Caitlín assured her she was fine and she was not to blame for any of this.

"But we have definitely poked the hornet's nest," she said. "We need to leave." A reality that they were both very aware of.

"I agree," said Lorenzo. "I've already collected your bags from the boarding house."

Lorenzo and Sofia had managed to successfully outrun their pursuer too. Sofia had already telephoned her sister Bianca and both of them planned to leave Sicily during the night with their money and head for the mainland to stay with family there.

"But what about the police? We need to tell them what's happened!" insisted Babs.

Lorenzo and Sofia cast a considered look at one another.

"I don't think that might be the best idea, Babs," said Lorenzo. "Things work a bit different around here sometimes. The police might not provide the protection you need. It only takes one corrupt policeman to tell these guys where you are. I will help you leave for Ireland in the morning and I'm coming with you."

"What? Why?" asked Babs. "No disrespect, but Caitlín is a trained police officer, you are a – a civil servant. What protection could you give us from those armed men?"

"He could give them a paper cut," said Caitlín.

They all laughed with a sense of relief, especially Caitlín and Babs after the near-death experience that they had literally escaped by a spark.

The following morning at the train station, Lorenzo went about making his creative phone call to the rehab centre to check on Marco Carbone.

"Lorenzo is alright, he's a decent fellow," Caitlín remarked to Babs.

"Oh, he's a bit of *alright*, alright!" said Babs with a laugh, winking at Caitlín.

"Behave yourself. Now I know why you get into trouble."

"It's not my fault men find me irresistible."

"Pity it didn't work last night when your man was pointing his gun at us. *Shh*, Lorenzo's coming back."

"Okay, I couldn't talk to Marco Carbone – because he's not there. The secretary said he discharged himself from the centre over two weeks ago."

"We closing in on him!" said Babs, rubbing her hands together.

"Yeah, but where is he now? His daughters still think he's in the rehab place," said Catilin.

"What will we do now?" asked Lorenzo.

"What can we do? We'll continue our investigations at home," said Caitlín, picking up her suitcase and walking up the platform.

Chapter 26

There for the taking

To Babs' pleasant surprise, Nate was happy to see her when she returned. He thought she had had left him and gone to live in Italy, due to his overreaction to the robbery and blaming her for it. When she told him what had happened to them over there, Nate was in awe of his tenacious wife and admired her determination to get to the truth and so grateful that she was not hurt.

———

Caitlín was already waiting for Sergeant Lamb and Tully when they arrived into work the next morning. She didn't know what reaction she would receive from the sergeant as a result of her absconding to Sicily under the pretext of carrying out the investigation even though she was suspended, so she decided to fight fire with fire. She launched into what happened before he even opened his mouth. She rattled off the whole account of meeting Rosario's family and how they told her about him orchestrating lucrative covert migrant operations under his enemy's nose, meeting the Carbone family, being held at gunpoint in a bank and chased through the streets of Taormina under a hail of fireworks and bullets.

Sergeant Lamb and Tully were rendered utterly speechless.

"So what you are saying is that you didn't bring me back a T-shirt?" said Tully,

Sergeant Lamb shook his head at Tully. "So now you think it was the Mafia or a similar illegal organisation that killed Rosario?" he said, taking off his cap and scratching his head.

"No, they just want his money which they believe he owes them," said Caitlín.

"*What?*" Sergeant Lamb and Tully exclaimed in unison.

"I think it was a neighbour of his in Sicily. His name is Marco Carbone."

"I'm lost, Kennedy," said the sergeant.

"A lot of neighbours blamed Rosario for the loss of their olive groves through projects pioneered by him under the instructions of the Department for Agriculture. It turned out that it was not his fault at all, it was a bacterial thing but anyway, the thing is, one neighbour in particular didn't drop his grudge against Rosario because his loss was greater than everyone else, having a bigger farm that went back for generations."

"So hang on, you think he came all the way over here – *to Ballantur, to kill him?*" asked Sergeant Lamb incredulously.

"It can't be ruled out, sir! I have circumstantial evidence to link him to the murder. The unusual white-tipped cigarette butt I found outside Slattery's is the same brand as Marco Carbone smoked in Italy. Here, I bought a box of them to show ye." She handed the box to Tully. "Look at the emblem of the crown on the tip. And look at these," she continued, producing the various pieces of jewellery she bought in Sicily. "These are the same type of beads as the one I found on the floor in Rosario's room. It's volcanic rock from Mount Etna. They are unique to Sicily. I know it might have belonged to Rosario but can we just keep an open mind on it? Finally, wait till you hear this: Mr. Carbone's daughter told us that he was mentally unwell and had been sent away to a retreat centre somewhere on mainland Italy about six weeks ago. Our contact in Sicily, Lorenzo McMahon –" she could tell his surname was jarring in their heads, "telephoned that place yesterday morning and was informed that Mr. Carbone checked himself out over two weeks ago! Without his family knowing. Giving him loads of time to plan his revenge and follow Rosario here."

"And Rosario was seen by that woman on the train who said she saw him talking to another Italian man, who as of yet remains unidentified," added in Tully who was now coming around to Caitlín's way of thinking.

"So have you completely exonerated Babs Wheatley after your cosy little trip together?" asked Sergeant Lamb. "And what about the strong lines of enquiry we are conducting on the other very possible suspects – Donnacha Finnerty and Madge Costigan? Have we completely been wasting our time?"

"I have no doubt that Babs Wheatley is innocent but, with regard to the others, they are definitely still in the mix – they both have strong motivations," said Caitlín.

"But how would Marco Carbone have known Rosario's plans for coming here?" asked Tully.

"Despite the competitive tension between the two farms, Rosario's daughters and Mr. Carbone's daughter, Fiorella, are friendly," said Caitlín. "Fiorella knew all about Rosario's new start in Ireland when we interviewed her and we can presume she innocently told her father about it."

"So where is this guy now?" asked Tully.

"We don't know," replied Caitlín.

"He's probably long gone back to Italy – if he was ever here," said Sergeant Lamb. "So we might be able to volley this bloody investigation back to the Italians. What did the Carabinieri say about all of this?"

"I didn't report it yet," said Caitlín, apprehensively knowing this was going to poke the bear.

The sergeant looked at her in astonishment. "You mean to tell me that you, as a police officer who was held at gunpoint, shot at and chased by members of an illegal organisation didn't report it? What the hell is the matter with you?"

"Back pockets, sir," Caitlín replied. She knew it was going to be hard to convince the sergeant. "Back pockets," she repeated. "We don't know who's in them. Some police officers over there are on the wrong side of law when it comes to their pay packet. Without knowing who I was speaking to, exchanging information like that could have put us in danger. And they could close our investigation down altogether and we'd never get justice for Rosario's murder. Not to mention the danger we could put his family in and we have a responsibility there."

"The danger you put them in! You just couldn't leave well enough alone!" said the sergeant, getting angry.

"All I'm asking is for us to take a step back for a minute and analyse exactly what we are dealing with, then use what we know for the benefit of the investigation before drawing any attention upon us that we don't want."

"You have twenty-four hours," announced Sergeant Lamb, looking her straight in the eye. "I am obliged to report an incident wherein a member of our Force is compromised, whether that be in Taormina or Termonfeckin!"

"Where do you want us to start?" asked Tully.

"Get on to the transport authorities and see if we can establish when or where this Scarlet Pimpernel entered the country," directed Sergeant Lamb.

"What about my suspension? Is there any update?" asked Caitlín.

"Well, if you'd let me get a word in, Kennedy, I might get the chance to tell you that it was lifted yesterday with no consequences to bear."

"No way!"

"The police in Cornwall searched the premises of the guy that sold you the car and found more of the same drugs there. He admitted to planting them in your car. Seemingly, he and the mechanic that works for your Mr. Wesley Pollard here had a little smuggling operation going on. This wasn't the first time they had organised the distribution of illegal narcotics into this country."

Caitlín's thoughts immediately went to the car. Sergeant Lamb read her mind.

"And before you ask, the car has been returned to Mr. Pollard who was delighted to hear that you'll be burning rubber tomorrow in the rally after all. But you can put the brakes on that distraction for now – get back to work!"

Caitlín skipped out of the station at lunchtime. She couldn't wait to tell Babs her good news about being back on the job. She collected Lorenzo who was staying at her cottage and both of them headed into Castlebar. Lorenzo went for a walk-about while Caitlín ran into the Humbert Hotel and was surprised to see Babs behind the reception.

"Look at you! Back in your uniform!" Babs said. "They cleared your name then, I take it?" Babs was delighted for her.

"Yep. Out of the dog house and back on the beat. But, never mind me, look at you! What are you doing behind the reception desk?"

"Mary, our usual receptionist, rang in sick today. I know I wanted to do this, but I'm completely thrown into the deep end. I don't know what I'm meant to be doing." Babs was sounding anxious.

The shrill ring of the telephone made her jump. She looked at it as if it would bite her. Then she picked it up.

"*Good afternoon. The Humbert Hotel. How can I help you?*" she said in a posh voice that made Caitlín pull a funny face at her.

Babs started to frantically scribble down as much details as she could from the prospective guest on the phone.

She put down the phone at last. "Oh God, did I make a balls of that? Did I get all the necessary details?" she said.

"Don't ask me!" said Caitlín. "Why don't you look in the reservations book to see how Mary records the bookings."

The two of them peered at the previous reservations and together called out the relevant columns: name, address, phone number, check-in date, check-out date, breakfast, dinner, special requests.

"Yes! I got all of that," confirmed Babs, now delighted with herself for successfully securing her first guest. "Caitlín? Caitlín, what's wrong?"

Caitlín had become fixated on something in the book.

"*Oh my God, Babs, look!* See that reservation there. It's Marco Carbone! Right under our noses all this time."

"He's *here*? Staying in the Humbert?" asked Babs in disbelief. "No! But why is he still hanging around?"

"He obviously has unfinished business," said Caitlín.

"What will we do? Are you going to arrest him?"

"You're damn right I am. Quick, get your manager."

Babs returned with Mr. Sweeney, the general manager, who was huffing and puffing.

"You're not the only one looking for that shyster!" he cried. "He's after doing a runner without paying for his room! Mary told me before she went home yesterday that two foreign men came in and requested to see him. She rang his room and he asked her to send them up. The housemaid who went in to clean his room this morning said he must have left in a hurry. There was a half-eaten sandwich and a slobbered glass of milk tipped over on the bedside locker and our room key just left thrown on the bed. We gathered up his belongings and put them in a box."

"I need to see them immediately," said Caitlín.

On their way to their lost-and-found section Mr. Sweeney asked Caitlín what she thought.

"He didn't leave. He was taken," she said with a sense of dread. "It's unusual to leave half-eaten food and especially his key if he was going out. We'll have to interview all the staff to see if they saw the two strange men hanging around the hotel or if he received any messages or telephone calls. I'll ring the station and let them know. Babs, can you start rounding up your colleagues, please?"

Caitlín went through his personal affects and found nothing of interest until she unfolded a pair of trousers and noticed a key ring attached to a belt loop. It was similar to the ones she had seen in Sicily except the bead attached to this one was broken.

The round of interviews with the hotel staff proved futile. They remarked on not seeing much of Marco since he arrived. He only dined in the restaurant the evening he arrived and didn't come across as very sociable. However, Caitlín's hunch was getting stronger so she examined the cutlery used in the hotel, in particular the steak knives. She discovered they were the same make and type of the one used to stab Rosario. The team of gardaí and Detective Cullen now accepted that Marco Carbone was their No.1 suspect for Rosario's murder, as backed up by Caitlín's observational fact-finding mission in Sicily. His lengthy stay in Ireland also led them to believe the robbery at the Wheatleys' house was connected to him. But, for now, all they could do was to issue a circulatory request to all other Garda Stations and transport authorities that they were looking for him as a definite person of interest, who may have been abducted. Caitlín was allowed to take leave for the rest of the evening as the rally was the next day and she and Mr. Pollard had a lot to discuss, never mind their racing strategy. But she had one more thing to do first. She dashed back to the station with Marco's broken key ring. Her hands were shaking when she opened the evidence box and took out the broken bead she had already retained from the murder scene. She merged the two pieces together and they fit so seamlessly you couldn't even see the fracture. She knew she had him now.

There was already a whir of excitement in the town in anticipation of the rally. Several classes of racing cars were already parked up in the square such Mini Minors, Hillman Imps, Hillman Hunters, Volkswagen Beetles and Austins. The town's Committee had welcomed the event with open arms, knowing that it would bring visitors to it, which was good for the local businesses not to mention a great endorsement. The main street and the square were covered in bunting and two huge banners hung at the entrance and exit of town advertising *"Ballantur Car Rally 1963"*.

Nate Wheatley came across Caitlín and Wesley who were standing at their car with a map of the route spread across the bonnet.

"She's a little beauty," declared Nate, who without invitation sat into the driver's seat and fiddled with the gear stick and rear-view mirror before opening the glove compartment for a nosy look. He placed his hands on the steering wheel and across the leather upholstery. But, despite all its bells and whistles, no better man than Nate to notice what was missing.

"Do you know what, Caitlín?" he said, sticking his head out the window. "It's meant to be fierce hot tomorrow – you'll need a bottle of water or you'll be parched with the thirst."

"He's right," agreed Wesley. "It's important to stay hydrated, especially when you'll be under so much pressure."

"Okay, I'll just bring a few bottles with me," said Caitlín, shrugging her shoulders.

"No. You need to do what I do," said Nate smugly. "I have an enamel bottle attached to the dashboard with a straw sticking out of it. It means I don't have to take my eyes or hands off the road, I just lean over and sip."

"That's a good idea," agreed Caitlín. "Wesley, can you make up something like that this evening?"

"I don't think so. I fired the mechanic over the drugs bust and I'm ashamed to say that I am not that handy myself."

"Don't you worry, Caitlín! I'll concoct something for you and we'll fit it in the morning," beamed Nate, delighted to help.

"Thanks, Nate. That settles everything now, apart from my nerves! Have you any cure for them?" said Caitlín, laughing.

"Brandy ... which you won't be having seeing that you are getting behind the wheel of a car." Nate squirmed, suddenly remembering he was talking to a garda.

Chapter 27

A Race in Time

The following morning in Ballantur was a busy one. All the cars competing in the rally had now arrived to take part and they were parked up on the green at the top of the town. Hordes of young men and boys fluttered around the cars like bees. They all had a zealous interest in these racing cars and now had an opportunity to see them in the flesh, or metal, as in this case. Tadgh Leonard was one such fervent fan and ran from car to car peering in the windows to see what they looked like on the inside. All the boys had their favourites and would watch eagerly from the many designated vantage points along the route. Drivers, owners and mechanics huddled around, going over their racing strategies. A timber platform was erected at the top of the town for all the local dignitaries and race officials to watch the race commence.

Then a big black car pulled alongside.

Nate was on a mission and met Caitlín and Wesley at their car where he set about fitting a makeshift bracket to the heater to hold the water bottle. Him foostering with it for longer than was expected made Caitlín anxious. She just wanted to get into the car and get settled.

"That's great, Nate," she encouraged, trying to hurry him up.

"Still looks a bit lopsided to me."

"It's grand, don't worry about it how it looks, as long as it keeps me hydrated that's all that matters. Now why don't you head off and find yourself a good spot to watch the race," she said, practically pulling him out of the car.

"I have that covered. Babs and Lorenzo are already gone off to find us a prime view. Good luck, Caitlín. Give her wellie!"

Caitlín drove her car up to the starting point among the other competitors. All the drivers were impatiently revving their engines, fraying the nerves of those watching them.

Nate walked up the main street and down again the other side, stopping to see what Pa Leonard, Sergeant Lamb and Garda Tully were talking about.

"Did any of you see Babs?" he asked, pretending to have a purpose to stop. Immediately he sensed that all was not well. "Has something happened, Pa?"

"My shotgun has gone missing," he replied.

"A missing wife and a missing shotgun –wouldn't that would put the fear of God into any man!" joked Nate.

Sergeant Lamb and Tully looked at one another, joining together a less humorous set of dots.

"Where did you leave it?" asked Nate.

"Across the back seat of the car. I was shooting crows. They're playing hell with the seed in the long field. Then I ran into Quirke's for a message for Elsie. When I came back out, it was gone."

"Was it loaded, Pa?" asked Tully.

"No, but I had a box of cartridges beside it and they're gone too."

"Why the hell didn't you cover it with a coat or a blanket or something? It was careless to leave a firearm exposed like that," scolded

Sergeant Lamb, annoyed at such lack of responsibility. "Any youngster could have got their hands on it."

"The race has brought a lot of strangers into the town. You wouldn't know what kind of a latchico took it," said Nate.

Back at the start line, all the participating cars were rearing to go like thoroughbreds out of their stalls. While the loud noise and the smoke were uncomfortable for many, no one was immune to the excitement it was causing.

The chequered flag was raised. Then, with what seemed like forever, it spliced through the air like a sword.

"*And, the first is off!*" reported Waxy Carolan, who was broadcasting live, watching it all unfold from the bird's eye view of his watch tower with the aid of a pair of binoculars. "*Now they're not all out the gap like Brown's cows at the same time. They all have timed individual starts because the roads are not wide enough for overtaking.*"

Caitlín's slow start was unremarkable but she knew the real gains would be made on the road. The route itself was a myriad of byroads that criss-crossed through the surrounds of Ballantur, all of which were strictly closed to other road users for the duration of the rally. There was little room to overtake, so if a car did catch up the courtesy fell on the driver in front to let his competitor pass him out as soon as he could. The world beyond Caitlín's cabin was out of her focus. She didn't notice all the people sitting on gates or standing on stone walls to watch the cars whiz by at high speeds and taking the corners as tight as possible. She mightn't have had the killer instinct like some of other more experienced veterans, but she was happy with how she was doing and hoped to move up the field with a steady but progressive approach. However, her plan was soon scuppered when she arrived at Friar's Hill. One of the cars had stalled towards the top of it and there was a queue of three cars behind it, all of them honking their horns and shouting in anger at the delay. All Caitlín could do was look on with frustration too. The driver descended from the stationary car and with the help of two spectators they pushed the car towards the driveway of the nearest house.

In the meantime, Caitlín observed that the next black car behind it was not competing in the race and it vexed her that they chose to ignore the official advice and stay off the road for the rally. It had no race number and the biggest giveaway of all was that there were four people sitting in it. Two in front and two the back. Suddenly, one of the passengers in the back seat glanced back.

It was Babs Wheatley. Immediately, her head seemed to be pushed around again by a man sitting beside her. A white bandage was visible on his left hand. It was the man from Sicily who had chased them. He had followed them home! But who was sitting in the front? Marco Carbone? She knew Babs was in danger but didn't know what to do. The broken-down car was now moved off the road and all the cars were moving again. Caitlín followed but, by the time she had got to the top of the hill, the road went into a bend with two other roads leading off it. The other cars had disappeared and she didn't know what road the black car had taken. Would they have gone with the official route so they could speed their way out of Ballantur? Or would they have chosen the quieter road to go unseen? Caitlín's gut told her to stay with the race route. Forced to slow right down coming into another tight bend she spotted someone sitting on a flat-roofed shed from the corner of her eye. Pulling over, she was grateful to see it was young Tadgh Leonard.

"*Tadgh!*" She bellowed and beckoned him over while she wound down the window. "I need you to do two very important things, immediately. Is Waxy broadcasting the race?"

"Yeah, he's been at it all morning."

"Good, run across the field there behind you as fast as you can and up to the old mill. That's where he's doing it from – top floor. Tell him to report on the whereabouts of a dangerous stray car, it's a black Rover. If he gives you any lip, tell him it's a Garda matter and besides that he owes me one. Then find Sergeant Lamb or Tully and tell them that Babs Wheatley is in danger and that she has been taken away in that black car, the one I want Waxy to follow. Do you understand, Tadgh? This is really important. *Now, go!* As fast as you can."

Caitlín sped off in one direction and Tadgh in another. She put on the radio and tuned into Calico Jack FM who had just indicated that some of the drivers had completed a loop already. She drove up to the crossroads, ready to give chase as soon as she could. Listening intently, she finally got the information she needed.

"Now, we have an unusual set of circumstances. We appear to have a rogue car participating in the race. It is a black Rover, obviously with no race number on it. The stewards are trying to direct it out of the race. Maybe it's a car that's got lost and has ended up in the middle of this unintentionally, but it's travelling nearly as fast as the others so I'm not sure what's going on, to be honest. It's just turned onto the Shangort Road!"

Caitlín sped off, grateful that Waxy was deliberately keeping her informed of the car's whereabouts.

"The rogue car is now on the Creeva road," reported Waxy.

Caitlín put her foot down. Bab's life depended on it. After another bout of commentating on the actual race, Waxy dropped another reference to the black car.

"... and if anyone is still worried about the loose horse, well, that car is now travelling north on the Bunnafada Road in the opposite direction to the race and out of harm's way."

Caitlín felt like she was losing them and knew she would have to do something drastic to catch up. She was travelling parallel to the River Silt and remembered the day she chased the robber into it. Although he didn't actually make it to the other side that day, it didn't deter her, so on her approach down to its brink at the same spot as before she slowed down her car, unlike the robber who had plunged straight into it. The recent dry spell meant the water level was now even lower than before but she knew she would only be successful by using the right amount of acceleration, just enough bite to keep moving but not too much to stall on the rocky riverbed. The sweat was coming out through her but she concentrated as hard as she could and progressively made it across to the slipway on the other side. It was the longest minute of her life. She bombed up the field, then slowed down again to manoeuvre out the narrow gate. The black car whizzed by. Caitlín was on its tail. She flashed her lights and blew her horn. Babs looked back and saw Caitlín behind them. Her abductor said something to the driver and their car sped up. So did Caitlín. Then, suddenly, the car turned left with Caitlín in pursuit. It drove straight on and, when Caitlín realised exactly which way they were going, her blood ran backwards. They were back on the race route but this time travelling in the wrong direction which did not go unbeknownst to Waxy.

"What the hell? I can see that rogue car back on the circuit but going the wrong way! It's being followed by another car, a race car, No. 16 – hang on, that's our local girl, Caitlín Kennedy! Surely she knows the right way to go but both cars are going hell for leather – this is suicide stuff. They are going to meet the other oncoming rally cars and the roads are too narrow for them to pass! This is so dangerous. The stewards are going to have to put a halt to this. The race is going completely out of control. Oh! Hold on a minute – the black car has met No. 28 and both cars have slammed on

the brakes to avoid colliding. They have met outside Corleys' house so there is a bit of a clearing there. This is crazy. The black car is reversing now – old style like myself – the driver has the door open with his head out to see where he is going. But now I can see Caitlín Kennedy coming around the corner – oh God, she won't see the car reversing. Ooh Jesus! The door of the black car has just been swiped right off its hinges! Caitlín Kennedy has just clipped it straight off as she served to avoid him! The other race driver is still trying to get through. Like a stunt man he is nearly driving sideways up on the embankment. He's done it! He's gone! The black car is off again too, minus a door. How the driver is maintaining his nerve I do not know. There is something very sinister going on here. I'm glued to my binoculars here and I think ... yes, it is, a Garda car is now in full flight too, flashers on and heading towards this hysteria. For those of you who don't know, Caitlín Kennedy is a bangharda herself which is making me think she is in pursuit of this strange car for criminal activity and has been forced to abandon her performance in the race. This is outrageous stuff. They are driving against the current here on very narrow twisty roads – it's lunacy. And at the speed they're both going, they'll soon be back in Ballantur town which of course the spectators will not be expecting, so anyone listening to this needs to warn the stewards these two renegades are heading for them!"

The sweat and adrenalin were still pumping out of Caitlín and she knew she was a catalyst to a very perilous situation but if she let this car out of her sight, she might never see Babs alive again.

Meanwhile, Waxy had everyone listening on the edge of their seats.

"Yeah, I was right, they're back on the main road now heading directly for the town. The Garda car has now caught up to them and has joined in the chase. Unbelievable! The black car has just torn up the main street with No. 16 and the squad car after it. The crowd are clearly confused, they don't know what is going on. The stewards are running around – they

don't know what is going on either. This is out of control. The black car has now turned onto Rossavard Road. Oh God, it's crashed! It's crashed! It took the corner too tight and collided with John Malone's trailer of hay which he had refused to move. The car tried to avoid it but crashed into the telegraph pole instead. The electricity cable has snapped with the jolt and I can see it's a live wire, there are sparks coming out it which are igniting with the hay and the trailer is now on fire! The occupants of the car are now getting out. I'm not sure if they are alright. There appears to be four of them. No.16 and the Garda car have arrived on the scene. Hang on to your seats, folks, this is cracking stuff!"

But there certainly was no sense of swashbuckling adventure on the ground. Caitlín jumped out of her car and ran towards Babs to see if she was okay.

"*Not so fast!*" shouted the man with the bandaged hand – better known as Saverio Filosa or 'Savi' to his friends and Rosario. He pulled out Pa Leonard's shotgun and pointed it Caitlín. "*Stay back!*"

"Okay, steady now there, mister," said Sergeant Lamb calmly. "You've just had a very serious car crash and we just want to make sure everyone is alright. Lorenzo, you better translate where necessary so everyone calms down a bit."

Lorenzo had raised the alarm when he saw Babs being bundled into the black car earlier and persuaded Sergeant Lamb and Tully to take him with them.

Savi said nothing. He and his accomplice flanked a third man, so he couldn't get away. The gardaí could only presume this was Marco Carbone.

"They think Rosario gave me money," blurted out Babs. "I've told them over and over – he didn't!"

"Why do you think Rosario Fratelli gave this lady money?" Caitlín asked of Savi.

Babs interjected, "Because that man there, Marco Carbone, told that guy – Savi." She pointed at them in turn so the gardaí knew who was who.

"Isn't that what brought you to Sicily, to get more of it?" Savi asked Babs.

"No, no, we went there to investigate Rosario's murder. The money that was in the safe in the bank we gave back to his family," said Babs as quick as she could to convince him.

"It's okay," said Caitlín, nodding at Babs, trying to relieve her anxiety. "She's telling the truth, I was with her."

"Ah, yes, you caught my hand in the door," commented Savi, suddenly recognising Caitlín from their encounter.

"And you have a lousy aim," retorted Caitlín.

"Let's sort this out among us," interjected Sergeant Lamb, angry with Caitlín for riling Savi, the man who was still pointing a shotgun at her.

Savi ignored this remark, not taking his eyes off Caitlín. "And did you find the murderer?"

"Yes, I believe we did and we have the evidence to prove it," replied Caitlín, "Isn't that right, Mr. Carbone?"

"You know I did it?" asked Marco, breaking his silence and stepping forward.

Savi caught him by the collar and pulled him back.

"I killed him," confessed Marco. "I didn't mean to but I had lost everything because of Rosario and his crazy ideas yet he went on to prosper, while I went on to watch everything I worked for, everything my father and his father worked for perish before my eyes. I knew Rosario was coming here to buy a restaurant and start a new life. That wasn't fair.

I followed him here and I saw him going into that woman's house." He pointed at Babs. "He was carrying a brown leather bag and left without it, so I assumed he left the money with her. I watched him booking into the local guesthouse. The next morning I went to his room and begged him for some money, in compensation for the livelihood that he ruined on me. But he just laughed at me," said Marco, becoming emotional. "I got so angry. I just pulled out the knife and stabbed him."

Savi laughed. "And now *we* are all laughing at you. You are pathetic. When I heard back home that Rosario had been murdered, I knew you had messed it up, and when you didn't come back I thought you had run away with the money which you said you would give to me to pay your debts."

"I stayed here because I still thought I could get it from this woman."

"So, you are admitting to the murder of Rosario Fratelli?" asked Sergeant Lamb.

"Yes!" replied Marco, again stepping away from Savi. "Please, arrest me. A life in prison is a sentence far more bearable than that a life of indebtedness to these cruel men."

"You better start showing some respect," hissed Savi to Marco, pointing the shotgun at him, "or I'll spare you serving any sentence!"

"See what I mean," said Marco to the gardaí.

"Grab her!" ordered Savi to his comrade, nodding at Babs.

"Leave her alone!" shouted Caitlín. "She told you – she doesn't have any money belonging to Rosario!"

"She provides a currency of another kind," smirked Savi. "Insurance that we get away from here or else she and Carbone each get a bullet in the head. Get back! Stand away from your cars."

Waxy Carolan was still broadcasting this turn of events live on air, describing it as a hostage situation involving the gardaí, Babs Wheatley and four other men that he could not identify and how two of these men were now pushing Babs and Marco into the back seat of Caitlín's rally car, before they themselves hopped into the front and drove off.

"But the gardaí are not giving up," reported Waxy. *"Garda Kennedy and Garda Tully have jumped into the Garda car and are gone after them. Sergeant Lamb and another man are still at the scene of the crashed car. Other Garda cars are arriving, presumably dispatched from Castlebar. No.16 which is being driven by the strangers is speeding on again, and what is to become of Babs Wheatley remains to be seen. This has become a sensational day, I cannot believe what is unfolding before my eyes. The Garda car is now hot on the heels of the abductors who are flying down the steep Black Hill Road with sheer abandonment. They'd want to slow down because it ends in a sharp turn to the right. Oh no! They couldn't take it! It doesn't look like they tried to slow down at all. The black Capri has smashed straight through the posts and wire fence and is heading for the stone wall at the end of the field. They don't look like they have control. I don't understand why they're not trying to slow down. The car has hit the wall and conked out! Maybe so have the passengers. It looks very serious. It'll be a miracle if no one is hurt. Garda Kennedy and Garda Tully are on the scene now, both of them running to the crashed vehicle."*

Caitlín pulled a dazed Babs out first and left her lying on the grass. Tully went to the aid of the men in the front. Both of them appeared conscious but very disorientated. Marco Carbone let himself out and staggered over to where Babs was and slumped down beside her. The two abductors knew the game was up and were unable to resist arrest.

Eventually all victims of the crash were taken away by ambulance to hospital. All three men were then arrested and charged with various criminal acts from murder to theft, abduction and possession of illegal firearm with intent to kill.

Nate was waiting for Babs at the hospital after she was treated for some minor bruising but mainly shock.

"Oh, thank God you're alright!" he squealed when he saw her. "I'm so sorry, Babs, that I wasn't there to save you!"

"But you did save me, Nate," she said with a smile. "It was your DIY skills, or lack of, that saved the day."

Nate was at a loss to understand.

"Here, ask Caitlín, she can explain it better than me."

Caitlín was at the reception desk at A&E with Lorenzo who was on the phone to the authorities in Italy.

She was happy to update Nate on the situation. "After a preliminary examination of the crashed car it looks like the enamel water bottle you had attached onto the grid of the heater broke out of its bracket. It fell under the feet of the driver and we suspect during a gear change it rolled under the brake pedal. When he tried to slow down going down the hill, the lodged bottle prevented him. The dents on the bottle are consistent with the shape of the brake pedal. This is why we believe they couldn't take the corner and crashed through the fence."

Nate would have been chuffed if he wasn't so mortified by his faulty invention.

Everybody's mood lifted greatly when they got together in Slattery's pub that evening. The race had recommenced after the stewards and emergency services deemed it safe to do so. A veteran driver from County

Roscommon had won the race with plenty of daylight between him and his closest competitor.

Caitlín was dreading meeting Wesley Pollard and felt aghast that his beautiful car had been involved in such an abhorrent debacle and ended up in a stone wall. However, Wesley was of the opinion that the publicity of the incident would raise his profile as a motor-racing philanthropist much faster than any of his conventional means to date. He knew that Caitlín being a garda and racing driver of one his cars in pursuit of these criminals would make every media outlet in the country and beyond, and he was pleased about that.

Nate had seen the lighter side by his third pint and he was now telling everyone that it was his contribution that saved the day. Babs was still trying to make sense of what had happened but mostly she was satisfied that Rosario's killer had been captured and the others arrested for her terrifying abduction. She felt that she had got the justice and vindication that both she and Rosario deserved.

Caitlín further updated Babs after Marco Carbone's interrogation. He had persuaded himself that he could prevail on Rosario to pay him compensation for the loss of his livelihood. So he promised to give this money to Savi Filosa, to whom he was in debt and who was threatening to kill him. Then he heard from his daughters about Rosario's plans to buy property in Westport and start a new life here. Almost immediately after, a friend in the port's ticket office, who was privy to Marco's plan, alerted him to the fact that Rosario had left the island on a one-way ticket. Marco realised that his one hope of resolving his situation had flown the coop. He had no option but to follow him. Savi also had his own agenda, reckoning that Rosario owed him because he had infiltrated his migrant operations.

Babs shook her head in amazement at this tangled web. "But how did Marco get in and out of Slattery's that morning without anyone seeing him?" she asked then.

"Pure uncalculated luck," replied Caitlín. "Just like you, he walked in the open door and up the stairs without anybody seeing him. He met Rosario coming out of the guest bathroom up the hall and they both went into his bedroom to talk – for the second time. He admitted it was him who was seen talking to Rosario on the train from Dublin to Westport. When the conversation in Slattery's didn't go to plan, Marco lost his temper and stabbed Rosario. He said he had only brought the knife to threaten him. Rosario tried to defend himself and it was during this brief scuffle that a key ring attached to Marco's trousers got caught on Rosario's belt and broke. It had a one of those lava stones on it from Sicily. I had already picked up a broken piece from the murder scene. Then when I saw the broken key ring in Marco's belongings yesterday I knew they had to be a match. The two pieces fitted back together perfectly. This undoubtedly placed Marco at the scene of the crime. When Marco heard the vacuum cleaner starting in the room next door he panicked and fled without the knife, which he admitted he took from the dining room in the Humbert hotel."

Babs couldn't believe it. "I set the tables in the hotel with those knives every day. I didn't even notice they were the same."

Caitlín said if they had never gone away they would never have been able to solve this case at home.

Sergeant Lamb had to hand it Caitlín. He told her he was proud of her tenacity and diligence during the investigation and conceded that her strong instincts were turning her into a unique investigator. Tully, too, praised her for her hunch about Marco Carbone and her driving ambition which she had in more ways than one!

"Let me buy you a drink," Tully offered, handing her a vodka and coke.

"You just did!" smiled Caitlín, taking it from him.

"No, I mean, let me buy you a drink, just you and me on our own. How about Friday night? Before the Sergeant splits up our rosters again."

"I'm sorry, Tully, I can't," she replied awkwardly. "I'm taking a few days off – properly this time. I've told Lorenzo I would drive him to Cork to visit his relatives there."

"Oh, that's alright," replied Tully, disappointment evident on his face.

"I'm sure Shelly wouldn't mind taking my place," she suggested, winking at Tully who gave her a cheeky grin in return.

Things returned to normal in Ballantur quickly because the community wanted to move on from the dark association their second murder had drawn over their town.

That September Molly and Tadgh stood in their bedroom in their Aunt Claire's house in Dublin. It was their first day at their new school and Claire was fussing about, fixing their uniforms before flittering out of the room to get something else. Molly was so scared of this big day ahead that she was on the verge of crying. Tadgh resolutely hated the thought of it and wanted to run away.

"*Ta Da!*" said Claire gleefully when she returned with two spanking new duffel coats their grandmother, Elsie, had made for them.

Molly's coat was grey and Tadgh's coat was navy, both complete with leather cord fastenings and wooden toggle buttons. This cheered them up immediately and when they put their hands into the pockets each of them pulled out a pebble wrapped in a note which read: *"Just because I'm not here doesn't mean I'm not with you. Mam."* The children recognised the pebbles as being similar to the ones on their mother's grave. Molly and Tadgh smiled at one another, allowing a sense of comfort and hope into their weakened souls.

And that following spring in an olive grove in Sicily, Mirabella stretched and yawned and suddenly out of the tips of her branches green shoots flickered open in the sunlight. She wasn't ready to give up either.

THE END